Middle Spoon

ALSO BY ALEJANDRO VARELA

The Town of Babylon

The People Who Report More Stress

Middle Spoon

Alejandro Varela

VIKING

VIKING

An imprint of Penguin Random House LLC
1745 Broadway, New York, NY 10019
penguinrandomhouse.com

Copyright © 2025 by Alejandro Varela

Penguin Random House values and supports copyright.
Copyright fuels creativity, encourages diverse voices, promotes free speech,
and creates a vibrant culture. Thank you for buying an authorized edition
of this book and for complying with copyright laws by not reproducing,
scanning, or distributing any part of it in any form without permission. You
are supporting writers and allowing Penguin Random House to continue
to publish books for every reader. Please note that no part of this book
may be used or reproduced in any manner for the purpose of
training artificial intelligence technologies or systems.

VIKING is a registered trademark of Penguin Random House LLC.

Grateful acknowledgment is made for permission to reprint lyrics from
"What Have I Done to Deserve This?" Words and music by Chris Lowe, Neil Tennant,
and Allee Willis. Copyright © 1987 Cage Music Limited, Songs Of Universal, Inc.,
and Streamline Moderne Music. All rights for Cage Music Limited administered
worldwide by Kobalt Songs Music Publishing. All rights for Streamline Moderne
Music administered by Songs Of Universal, Inc. All rights reserved.
Used by permission. Reprinted by permission of Hal Leonard LLC.

Designed by Alexis Sulaimani

LIBRARY OF CONGRESS CATALOGING-IN-PUBLICATION DATA
Names: Varela, Alejandro, 1979– author.
Title: Middle spoon / Alejandro Varela.
Description: New York : Viking, 2025.
Identifiers: LCCN 2024053393 (print) | LCCN 2024053394 (ebook) |
ISBN 9780593835173 (hardcover) | ISBN 9780593835180 (ebook)
Subjects: LCSH: Non-monogamous relationships—Fiction. |
LCGFT: Gay fiction. | Novels.
Classification: LCC PS3622.A7413 M53 2025 (print) |
LCC PS3622.A7413 (ebook) | DDC 813/.6—dc23/eng/20250221
LC record available at https://lccn.loc.gov/2024053393
LC ebook record available at https://lccn.loc.gov/2024053394

Printed in the United States of America
1st Printing

The authorized representative in the EU for product safety and
compliance is Penguin Random House Ireland, Morrison Chambers,
32 Nassau Street, Dublin D02 YH68, Ireland, https://eu-contact.penguin.ie.

For everyone who, given the opportunity, chooses not to sneeze or cough into their hands. And for Aidan, whose adventures are only just beginning.

Middle Spoon

Dear Ben,

I'm sipping amaro, the one you liked to drink before bed, the bottle with the cap made of melted wax. It's an extravagant pour. I'm lucid but intoxicated—before the digestif, there were two glasses of sake; before that, two martinis. There was a plate of food, too, mostly protein. I'm not telling you this for the sake of telling you. I guess, in a way, I'm preparing you.

Wait a second . . . Before this very moment, it had never occurred to me that *sake* (the Japanese drink made of fermented rice) and *sake* (noun; meaning, for the purpose of) are heteronyms. Odd to have missed this connection.

That was a stupid way to begin an email. Honest, but stupid.

Let me try again.

Dear Ben,

I wouldn't have thought it possible for me at this age and at this otherwise fruitful moment in my life to plumb a new low. Having been socialized in a less-than-ideal environment, one disproportionately characterized by financial stress and all of its insalubrious consequences, I thought I knew what it meant to be a damaged animal, to be psychologically contorted by the acute pains that accompany a chronic state of survival. In a word: anxiety. In two: anxiety and disappointment. This isn't to say my damage was particularly terrible or that good doesn't come from bad or that making a dollar out of fifteen cents isn't an undervalued life skill, but my experiences were just terrible enough for me to develop a permanent reference point, one of lower elevation, from where I could still see in all directions, the better as well as the worse places.

In adolescence, this seeing became an obsessive, even if low-stakes, vigilance, not only of my immediate surroundings, but of things possible, irrespective of time or reality's limitations. I could imagine it; therefore, it was real. Worse yet, if I thought it was happening, it probably was.

For as long as the ignorance of youth remained intact, my vigilance proved to be a manageable, albeit vague and incremental, state of declivity. A humorous quirk without human consequences. But then angst and self-awareness entered the arena, with their penchants for swarming and stabbing, for piercing the patina of pretense, effectively dismantling the fire wall between truth and truth, which is to say my truth and *the* truth. I was trapped inside of something cyclical, something that rockets, something that plummets. Up, then down. Up and down. Up. Down.

But even bad has its benefits.

MIDDLE SPOON

The unsung attribute of formative stress, of the kind brought about by hierarchies—race, class, sex, proximity to immigration—is that, despite its accompanying destabilization, the stress becomes something of a crutch and, depending on the circumstances, a friend—or the drug a friend slips into your hand at the club. And before you know it, you're unrecognizable without it.

To the unsuspecting audience, the differences between a person who expertly contains their chaos and one who lives chaos-free are imperceptible, an illusion that only compounds the dreaded experience because we, which is to say, people like me, are left weathering the neurological lawlessness alone, more concerned with obfuscation than repair, and often uncertain of our opponent. Is it Them? Us? The system that contains all?

Yes.

Also, no.

The war isn't against ourselves, per se, but against the past and its material conditions, which is effectively a long-term battle with society, but yes, practically speaking, also a battle with ourselves. All roads lead back to early days: our gaits, the tenor of our voices, our wardrobe palettes, how we perceive others, how we perceive others perceiving us, how we handle rejection, how much we grind our teeth at night. All of it determined by factors not predetermined but instead molded onto us. Not a gilding so much as an unnecessary fondant.

Oh, please, you must be thinking. No one is spared the ritual of conditioning. Yes, but when the conditioning is unpleasant, life unspools in a less-than-pleasant way, with little regard for the future environments in which the unspooling takes place.

Do you understand what I mean, Ben? Everything sucks when the beginning sucks.

But I believed, until now, my general dissatisfaction was sufficient preparation for whatever might come my way. I couldn't be disappointed because disappointment wasn't an event but a state of being.

I was wrong. And I can confirm, here, now, in this hazy land replete with perspectives, that liberation doesn't accompany every awakening. I am free's obverse, nothing grander than an illusion.

I've finished the amaro, and everyone's asleep. I'm in a bad place. It's a realm previously unknown to me. Somewhere nether. Somewhere suffocating and all-consuming. A new low, Ben, for which you might not be the cause or the effect but the catalyst. And, as with most of life's calamities and indignities, I can't help but feel that this one, too, intersects with the immutable things, those insouciantly destructive, socially fabricated political categories that, in a society without hierarchies, would simply be beautiful attributes but are instead used to create distances, to isolate the protagonist from their less-than-ideal context—come to think of it, not an altogether negative conundrum, to be kept from the unpleasantness by the very thing that triggered the unpleasantness.

It's not a competition, but I guess what I'm really saying is I'm in a worse place than the bad place you're in because I started in a worse place.

You see, animals are social above all else, no matter the ilk. Even when the club is shitty, we want to be allowed inside. Certainly, we don't want to be excluded because of a thing we can't change, a thing we don't want to change. And woe is the person defined by multiple immutable things because those things often combine, creating a new, unnameable thing, still immutable but even more damaging insofar as the reactions it elicits, insofar as the walls. Woe is me.

And so here I sit, overwhelmed by a situation I might be handling better if I were less damaged. And less drunk.

—Me

Ben,

This is excruciating. What are you doing? Come back. I love you.

—Me

Dear Ben,

Despite the cold rain, I'd bike over—I could take the G train to the L, but the G is running in two sections, and I'd be reduced to pacing the platform at Bedford-Nostrand for twenty minutes. Better to bike. Better to wade through potholes than pace a platform during an economic recession. I'll sit on your stairs and wait for you to come home from work or drinks or whatever it is you're doing to forget me. No! I'd stand because your slumlord has never cleaned the stairwell. No! I'd sit because that would be a less threatening way to find me. And I'd bring flowers—the cheap, industrially farmed ones from the supermarket on the corner— and a couple of steaks—the overpriced grass-fed ones from the butcher by the bridge. I'd tell you about my heartbreak and ask for your advice. I'd hold your hand and the rest—not minutes; hours. I'd also find my way inside of you, my favorite place, one of many places where I felt, until a couple of days ago, I might always be welcome.

I want, I need, I want, I need: a psychological tergiversation to accompany the visceral one. I've become the protagonist I've always detested. This isn't only genetics, epigenetics, and the socioeconomic climate of the early eighties; you bear responsibility too.

Despite all of this, I'm not going anywhere. I have to respect your wishes because I presume them to be proxies for your feelings.

"I need time to get over you," you said over the phone. "After a few weeks, we can talk again."

Weeks? A few?

This isn't the sort of connection easily erased in anything less than an indefinite period of time. I don't foresee a shortcut to forgetting you, and I don't know how to begin again without first forgetting you.

Begin again? I'm sick to my stomach.

"I want you in my life" was the penultimate declaration you made. "I'd like to be friends" was the last.

I don't accept your offer. Friendship is fifth place in a sixth-grade science fair. It's pain in drag.

But neither do I want to entertain the alternative. *Never again* is an all-too-easily manipulatable rallying cry of a people who haven't fully processed their intergenerational traumas; it can't also be our fate.

I will do my best to ignore you. Even if it feels altogether wrong and, frankly, stupid, it's the plan my friends and one of my therapists—yes, I have two—have suggested. Because I have minimal experience with this category and degree of pain, the support of others is, in the best moments, a raft on which I am able to survive the turbulence and vastness of whatever this is. But often, the advice functions as a lily pad, hardy enough for a carefree toad but ill-suited for the weight of a fully grown human leaden with grief.

If it were only sadness pulling me down, I might be more hopeful, but there is another thing, also heavy, clamped around my chest. It's an abstract notion of *appropriate*. I truly don't know what to do. I don't know what right and correct are anymore. My instincts, once keen and possibly admirable, have abandoned me. This godforsaken doubt is why I'm not sopping wet on your stairwell.

In a just world, the end of love would be mediated so that all interested parties might achieve suitable outcomes, or at the very least, be given buoys, anything inflatable to help us get back to the surface. Instead, we live inside of this mass of atoms cruelly hurtling through space, our hands tied, periodically crashing against impermeable boundaries.

Ben, I hope you've ended us for the right reasons. I hope the peace of mind you were seeking outweighs the misery I feel.

It seems silly to say the obvious thing, but I love you. Even if our relationship wasn't meant to survive, I don't regret it. Despite being a curmudgeon, I held on to hope for our future in all its splendid shapelessness. We only needed more time.

—Me

Dear Ben,

Today, after six years of living without wheat, I learned that if I toast gluten-free bread twice instead of only one time, it retains better its structural integrity and consequently so does the sandwich. In a way, I owe the mindlessness that led to this discovery to you.

Thank you,
Me

PS: Today was fucking shitty: the weather and my insides.

PPS: My calendar is full of you. Tomorrow, we had reservations at the new Korean place in the East Village that Pete Wells raved about last month. On Tuesday, we had tickets for the Adrienne Kennedy play that's been long overdue its flowers. Next week, your studio's holiday party. (Who breaks up with someone just before the goddamn holidays?) In February, we were going to take a train somewhere upstate for a long weekend. "A place with a hot tub would be great," we agreed. In May, I was your plus-one for a college friend's wedding. On the seventh of each month, we'd continue the "monthiversary" meeting at the bar beneath the BQE where we first met—I'll make a point of avoiding Williamsburg on those days.

Dear Ben,

This pain will end.

This pain will end. I've told myself this at least a dozen times today.

This pain will end.

This pain will end.

This pain is a rite of passage.

This pain will end.

This pain will end.

This pain will end.

This pain will end. It has to.

This pain will end.

This pain will end.

This pain will get smaller.

This pain will become something numbing or nagging but no longer stabbing and suffocating. "It'll transform into a faint image accompanied by abstract emotions." (I read that on a self-help site catering to the recently brokenhearted, where all the stock photos were of women: alone, in groups, crying, smiling, one of them was sailing by herself.) That, too, scares me. The fading, that is—so does sailing alone. I don't want to forget my feelings. I love you, and I was enjoying the hell out of loving you. In fact, I was so caught up, I didn't see this coming.

"For starters, your humor is bleak," you said when I pressed you for an explanation.

"Not only are you breaking up with me over the phone, you're doing it because my jokes are too dark?"

MIDDLE SPOON

"No, but you focus too much on the possibility of our end, and I can't help but feel as if you're already there."

You weren't wrong, but you had it all wrong. I only ever contemplated our demise because I'm a hopeful pessimist. It's in my nature to plan for the worst, but that doesn't mean I want the worst to happen. It's merely my way of blunting the pain of surprise, a life tactic I consider normal in addition to practical. I've seen pictures of your childhood home, and I see why pain and surprise aren't on your radar. You didn't have to develop a standard operating procedure. But pessimism is how I communicate. It's how I survive. You should see pictures of my childhood home.

For what it's worth, I was learning not to doubt you. I sensed the adventures ahead of us. Endless adventures. At the very least, we were going to get on a plane together. And at some point, I was going to meet your folks and show them I was worth the effort you were putting into us. Who knows, maybe Staten Island was in the cards too.

That was a joke. I don't care for Staten Island, even if *Working Girl* is one of my favorite movies. Even if Wu-Tang is one of my favorite clans.

I hate having to clarify my humor, but I'm no longer sure of anything, least of all how you interpret me.

It's only been two and a half days.

Yours,
Me

PS: I'm going to tell Nico about what's happening. He's old enough.

PPS: I shouldn't judge Staten Island; I've never been.

Dear Ben,

I stuck to the nuts and bolts of our breakup, albeit a censored version: we liked each other; we couldn't agree on how to spend time together; it was better if we spent less time together—it sounded like nonsense even as I was speaking it. Nico remained quiet throughout.

"Do you have any questions?" I asked after a silence. The top of his little head shook from side to side near the height of my shoulder.

"I need time to formulate questions," he responded after another silence.

Formulate? I didn't use that word freely until I was in college. Nico's ten.

"Do you want me to stop telling you about this *stuff*?" I asked while he devoured his after-school doughnut from the hipster spot on Driggs that also specializes in fried chicken. That singular, overpriced pastry gives him such immense pleasure, it makes me feel like a good parent just to watch him inhale it. Five dollars for fried dough—middle-class living is truly something.

"Absolutely not, Dad," he responded. It was cold and drizzling, and we were waiting beneath a narrow awning for the cursedly infrequent B62 bus. "I want to know everything."

A short time later, as we climbed our stoop home, Nico had formulated a question: "Dad, is Ben going to be okay?"

This kid! What a thoughtful one we've raised. My husband and I must be doing something right amid all the mistakes. In that moment, pride supplanted grief and my life had depth again.

"He's going to be fine. We all are," I responded. Nico nodded and lumbered up the stairs, unperturbed by the pendulous movement of his oversize backpack or by the clangor of its decorative key chains.

As for Jules, I'm not sure what to tell them about you. I don't think they're mature enough to understand what you and I were and what we are no longer. If they ask what's become of you, I'll take full advantage of their easily distractible age.

Speaking of sharing, I almost told my mom. There she was on the other end of the line, asking me all the usual things: *What's wrong? Was that a sneeze or a cough? Something troubling you? Will you ever visit us again? Is everything okay?* But it happened that I was feeling particularly vulnerable this morning, and her innocuous concerns pierced me. I nearly chose truth: *I don't want to hear your prejudices, but I fell in love with someone deeply, and he left me, and I'm hurt, and all I need is your support, not judgment.* But I chickened out. Instead, I asked if she'd seen the announcement of the Grammy nominations.

"I didn't recognize many of them," my mother said.

"The voters are old-fashioned. They prefer awarding the mediocre output of musicians they slighted in the past or work derived from the deserving musicians they slighted in the past."

"I like la Beyoncé," she responded.

La Beyoncé has a ring to it.

Ben, I just thought of another positive outcome of our breakup: you'll be free to indulge in all the gluten and dairy you want now that I'm no longer around. Ha.

Nothing is funny anymore.

Respectfully,

Me

Dear Ben,

Fred agreed to meet me again this week, a tremendous relief considering Sandy, my other therapist, is on vacation. I wake up sad, spend the day sad, go to sleep sad. This morning, I took Nico to his bus stop, cried on the walk home, took Jules to school, cried on the walk back, jerked my husband off with coconut oil in the kitchen, ate a banana, and went to the Village to meet Fred, all in the same haze. The fluctuations between postapocalyptic zombie and award-winning Sally Field performance have become unpredictable.

"Give him time. It's only been a few days," Fred offered.

"You think he'll come around?"

"Listen, I don't think your story is completely done, but this chapter certainly is. He needs more than the life you're offering."

"That's what he said."

"He also made clear he wanted space," Fred said rather pointedly. "Try this: whenever you feel inclined to contact him, write it down instead. Same as you do with your general anxiety."

A year ago, which was about three years after I first saw Fred—he's also a couples counselor who helped my husband and me work through a period of strife—he asked if I was the sort of person who checked the stove multiple times before he left his home.

"Yes."

"Are you the sort who walks back home to check the stove after he's already checked it multiple times before leaving his home?"

"Yes."

"Hmmm," he said. "Try this: When intrusive or repetitive thoughts emerge, imagine tagging them, like fish you've thrown back into the sea. Every time they reappear, envision the tag. Say to yourself, *I've already thrown this one back*, and move on."

"What if I start overthinking about fish?"

"Just try it. And if that doesn't work, write it down. Do you carry around pen and paper?"

"I have a notes app on my phone."

And that's how this all began. Instead of carrying around my doubts, frustrations, and fears, for nearly a year, I've put them into emails that almost never reach their intended audience.

"Do the same with Ben," he said a few days ago, during an emergency video session with me. "Every single thing you want to say to him or about him, just write it down."

"Can't I just meet you more often until this passes?"

"That wouldn't be healthy for you."

"Should I send you the emails?"

"I don't think it's necessary," Fred said, without taking a moment to consider my offer.

"It'd make me feel better to send them to someone. They could inform our sessions."

"Listen, in the past, you've tended to be very prolific, and I'm not looking for homework."

I'm not looking for homework. Fred says that from time to time. It's meant to be a joke, but there's truth to it, because when I asked him this morning what he thought of the last three days' worth of emails, which I had in fact sent to him, all he said was "Wow."

"Probably wise I didn't send them to Ben?" I asked Fred this morning.

"Don't get me wrong. This is definitely the medium for you to be vulnerable."

"But . . . ?"

Fred gripped his lips gently with his thumb and index finger before giving them a gentle twist, screwlike. He does this whenever he's about to be direct in a way that he fears might hurt me. While I waited for his words, I scanned the wall of books behind him, hundreds, mostly psychology textbooks, a few philosophy ones too.

"You're not throwing the fish back. Keep writing, and not just about Ben. Work on yourself. And keep the emails in the draft folder."

I wasn't sure if he meant I shouldn't continue sending them to him, and I was too embarrassed to ask.

"Can we have two sessions again next week?"

"Yes, but only next week. We have to build your coping mechanisms."

As I rose from the couch and oriented myself toward the door, I began to cry, an irrepressible blubbering. Fred got up too.

"I'm scared," I said.

His eyes filled with tears. "I know."

"I'm afraid to be alone, Fred. What if I'm trapped in this headspace forever?"

"You won't be. I promise you." Fred grabbed my elbow. "Some things I cannot guarantee, but this I will." He handed me a tissue.

"Have you ever had your heart broken?" I asked.

"We'd need more than one session to list the number of lovers who've left me in tears, and I'm not looking for homework," he replied. A weak grin and a furrowed brow appeared on his face like a palimpsest of grief.

Suddenly, we were both members of yet another club.

I'd selected Fred from a list of therapists on a website. My husband and I agreed our counselor should be queer. I argued he should also be a person of color: "I'll feel outnumbered if it's two white men and me." There were no pictures on the health insurance web page, but I was fairly certain from his name—Alfredo Gonzalez—that he was Latino. A cursory internet search revealed he was Black, buff, and stylish—dark brown, enormous biceps, and gold chain drop earrings.

The irony and inconsistency of wanting a non-white person as a therapist, so as to not feel like the odd one out, yet having two white partners isn't lost on me. "The heart wants what it wants," Fred said when you and I first started dating. "On the other hand, the media is influential, and power is seductive," he also said.

I chose to receive his assessment as solidarity and not admonishment.

—Me

Dear Ben,

It's just before noon, day four. This is maddening. Call me. Please. Stop letting time slip away. I love you.

—Me

Dear Ben,

I caved.

Our phone conversation last night should be sufficient proof that cold turkey is our only way forward. Hearing you cry, hearing your voice as soft and as fragile as mine, confirmed the suffering was mutual. It was a terrible torture not to have the permission to comfort you, to no longer know my rights as it concerned your being.

And yet, our conversation seeded hope in me. After we'd recounted how difficult the previous days had been, after you told me about how the *Times* had bought one of your illustrations for the health section, after I told you I'd canceled a presentation at work because I couldn't imagine myself standing in front of twenty biostatisticians extolling the virtues of the Gini coefficient for measuring wealth inequalities, after all that, I whispered, "I'm in pain."

"Me too," you responded.

"I love you."

"So do I."

"Maybe we can talk again?" I proposed, still whispering, fearing my family might hear me from the other room.

"I, uh—" you began.

"Not tomorrow or the day after, but maybe in a few days?" I explained.

"Maybe," you said.

The moment I hung up, I began entertaining a way back to you. I felt certain neither of us was going to allow this relationship to dissolve. I told myself there was a clear symmetry of emotions—both of us standing in our respective forests, like diseased trees, hollowing at the same rate.

I was elated, the way I'd been during our best moments together. I felt hungry too. Not a figurative appetite. I could, for the first time in days, eat with the sort of desire and desperation of someone who'd eaten well for most of his life but who had been recently subjected to an involuntary fast.

Our call ended, and I waited seventeen minutes to text you. I'd wanted to do so sooner, but I feared invalidating our milestone. Instead, I took a hit of pot, a few spoonfuls of tom yum, and a couple of gluten enzymes because I wasn't certain of the broth's nutritional makeup. Only then did I allow myself to type one simple message: "Thank you for taking my call." You reciprocated with a pleasant-faced emoji, nothing more. But at least it was instant, which I took as an invitation to reiterate my desire to talk again in the coming days. Even if we weren't getting back together, it was healthy to grieve together, I argued. "It's possible," you replied. On we went for a few rounds of messages, despite my husband's eyebrows and Nico's and Jules's recriminations: "No screens at the table, Dad!" I tucked my phone between the tablecloth and my thigh and continued checking it throughout dinner, desperate to know if you'd said more, and just as desperate to stop myself from sending more. Whenever your responses didn't adhere to our newly established cadence, I found myself back inside the undersize hamster wheel that my mind has become. The suffocating feelings that had all too briefly subsided now returned.

"Let's see" were your last words.

I responded nothing more and retreated to the barren, antiseptic land of boundaries.

I tried to distract myself with TV: first, *Derry Girls*—nah; then the new Martin McDonagh, also nah. I couldn't latch on to anything. It might have been the pot I'd smoked between dinner and the couch, but it was likely you. For days now, I haven't been able to remain focused. Your transition from great love to destabilizing obsession has been swift, equal parts earthquake, tsunami, flood, and search for human life. To be fair,

MIDDLE SPOON

my inclination toward you has from the outset bordered on deregulated adolescent yearning, but in the darkness of heartache, infatuation is no longer a bright, bountiful thing to savor; instead, a cursed beast with putrefied, balding wings.

As I dozed off on my husband's lap, wholly unconcerned with the earnest buffoonery of Colin Farrell's protagonist, my husband ran his hand against the grain of my hair.

To be clear, I didn't just share that detail—the head rubbing—to elicit jealousy. That's not my way, but I want also to be honest about the life I have with my husband. Perhaps if I'd been this transparent all along, instead of draping everything in euphemism, a more detailed picture of our lives together would have emerged, and you would have stopped wondering about our future.

"What if we reorganized our lives?" I asked after pausing Brendan Gleeson's self-mutilation.

"What do you mean?" my husband responded.

"Is there a way Ben and I could stay together that works for all of us?"

My husband remained quiet, long enough for me to rotate my head and look into his eyes, those mosaics of imperfect crystals, the kind that line the insides of great caves.

"What if I grabbed the coconut oil?" he said, pointing toward the kitchen.

"Honey, I'm being serious."

"So am I. I really enjoyed the other morning."

"We'll stain the couch."

"We could put down a towel."

"Can we finish the other conversation first? Let's meet up."

"Who?" he asked.

"The three of us."

"We have. Many times."

"Yeah, but we haven't had frank discussions about boundaries and needs and the future. Maybe if you and I both showed how willing we are to let this work, he would give this a try."

"It doesn't sound like Ben is interested in sharing you with anyone."

"I think he just needed more time to see that it would work."

"You know how I feel about this. I'm open to trying. I'd rather complicate our lives a little than see you like this."

Ben, if my husband can be so flexible, why can't you? What if you and I softened our stances a bit? We're not, after all, inventing polyamory; we're merely joining the club. The only thing standing in our way is us.

I sound like a radical self-help manual, but maybe the off-the-grid hippies have been right all along. Maybe there's something worthwhile in unorthodox relationships and atypical family structures. Maybe the world should adapt to us and not us to it.

Love,
Me

PS: I ran into David the other day. Despite wanting to go home and hide, I stopped and chatted, mostly small talk: about mutual friends who were having a baby soon; about the new Italian restaurant down the street; about Will Smith's lunacy and Chris Rock's comeuppance; about the complete failure of the Eric Adams administration. When that subsided, I told him you'd ended things, and he said it was for the best and laughed it off with the familiarity of a friend and the callousness of a rival. His reaction confirmed what I'd sensed all along: he didn't like you very much. And he's probably right about this being for the best, but he's still a dick for not being more compassionate, because self-inflicted pain hurts as much or worse than pain inflicted by someone else.

Dear Ben,

Did I ever tell you why I pursued a career in public health? It's a rather uninspired motivation, but it's sincere: I thought I'd be doing something worthy, something that might make the world better. At the very least, not make it worse. Over time, however, I came to understand that I wasn't only idealistic; I was mildly deluded and, in an unexpected bit of symmetry, falling back onto work I'd been doing since I was a kid.

Like a well-meaning octopus, public health is a social science that has its tentacles in nearly every sector of society, but much of what we, the people, experience as public health is simply health education to promote behavior change. Condoms, seat belts, tobacco cessation, vaccines, colonoscopies, mammograms, pesticide bans, speed limits: public health workers take the esoterica of science and law and communicate them accessibly to the public in an effort to reduce illness and injury. A child of immigrants is therefore a public health worker. We spend our youth interpreting and communicating not only language but ideas, concepts, and cultures to our families in order to prevent or at least attenuate the effects of isolation and marginalization, often the very precursors to illness and injury. This built-in task made me adept at recognizing confusion and identifying barriers to understanding; it made me want to synthesize and reduce life's most complicated bits into elemental and efficient sound bites.

Unfortunately, I wasn't able to put my skills to use as it concerned us. I wasn't able to read the room or skilled enough to translate my love into reassurance. Frankly, I still can't wrap my mind around what went wrong and what you needed.

I believe you left because the parameters of my life, which is to say, my husband and children, were too limiting. Our relationship's success demanded difficult conversations beyond negotiating schedules. It meant you being more involved in my family—a blended structure we'd yet to sketch. It meant compromise—possibly too much compromise. It meant adaptation to a degree none of us had ever experienced and might never have achieved. It also meant all of us seeing the value in the heterodoxy.

I research the effects of economic inequalities on health, and I teach graduate students. You're an illustrator, principally of graphics in textbooks and magazines. My husband designs semiconductor chips for data center computers. We're forty-three, thirty-four, and forty-four, respectively. My husband and I have been together since college. I met you last year. My husband and I have two children, a mortgage, and a shared sock drawer. You and I drank cocktails, sent each other scandalous pics, and browsed antiques shops in Brooklyn.

Twentysomething years of abiding love and respect cannot be subsumed by months-old love. It just can't, no matter the intensity. My husband isn't merely my husband; he's my partner, lover, and best friend. He's one of my ribs, and possibly the entire cage. Without him, there is no future, and my organs would collide into one another.

You saw my marriage and family as insurmountable barriers, but—I know this will sound wild—I think they should have been an incentive to stay.

What I offered was a future you'd never envisioned for yourself—no one, after all, imagines their life taking place several deviations from the norm. My proposal was a bit radical. Postmodern, even. Postrevolutionary, actually. (Or simply queer.) But for all its convolutions, there would have been no shortage of love and respect. Our arrangement would have been awkward at first, not just within this experimental situation, but

MIDDLE SPOON

outside too. Your parents, my parents, friends, etc. Society hasn't caught up to every permutation of love and family, but it would have. That's all history has ever shown: eventually everyone catches up.

"How do I know you're not having a midlife crisis?" you asked in your kitchen a few months ago, shirtless and holding a mason jar of water in one hand and cradling two ibuprofen tablets in the other.

"Is that what you think?" I asked.

You responded with a look that was full of both pity and anger. Pity because you'd rightfully sensed you'd stung me with your question; anger because you wanted something I wouldn't give, namely all of me. We'd just gotten home from your friend's party—a loft in Bushwick replete with bottles of rosé and bearded white millennials but not a single interesting conversation. *Drag Race* was at the center of most of these inane interactions—idiots, the lot of them. Everyone there had previously fucked everyone else there, and the carousel of gazes circled the room in a futile attempt at connecting or ensnaring someone or something new, all of it a search for validation. Admittedly, I was feeling cantankerous, a vessel for Larry Kramer's spirit: aroused, frightened, and disdainful of that batch of next-generation sybarites. I was probably also jealous of everyone's impeccable fitness and youth.

"I don't see you as a midlife distraction or as a prize or an ego boost. I'm not trying to run away from anything. I want to be with you. Nothing more or less spectacular than that," I said as you swallowed your orange pills.

"I'm doing my best to think of your needs, not only my own," I added while you chugged water. "I wouldn't be pursuing you if I didn't earnestly believe I could make you happy."

Your eyes began to tremble. I stepped toward you and caught the corner of your lips with my own as you turned your head. I kissed you again, and this time you remained still. We crawled quietly into your bed and slept fitfully, until my alarm went off at five, and I raced back to my family.

Do you remember any of that?

Love,
Me

PS: In a previous email, I suggested cold turkey was the way forward. It's certainly not the healthiest way out of this emotional quagmire, but I'm convinced it'll get us there eventually. I'm going to hunker down, use all my willpower not to contact you again. When we get through this first phase of separation, after the pain has transitioned from something acute and gnawing to dull and chronic, let's talk. Let's reevaluate. Let's consider what I've proposed. Or feel free to offer an alternative. Today, I'm hopeful. I'm open to trying. Don't underestimate me, Ben.

Please say something. I miss you.

To Whom It May Concern at the NYC Department of Sanitation,

I would like to register a complaint about your workers, in particular those assigned to my block. But first, I'd like to give context to my complaint because I wouldn't want you to think I am someone who expects perfection from the labor of others and then flies to his laptop whenever he's displeased.

From an early age, I've held the impression that garbage collectors are compensated well for their work. It's an impression I thought everyone held. Garbage collection is a crap job, but at least sanitation workers make good money and have enviable benefits, was the prevailing belief. I don't know who it was that communicated this to me, or if I heard it once or many times, or if it was direct or implied, but the idea stuck.

In retrospect, I am happy to have carried this notion throughout my formative years because it served as an example of equity in an otherwise unfair society. After all, collecting your fellow humans' scraps, in all their horrid permutations, is a thankless line of work that few of us are encouraged to pursue. And yet, it's necessary labor. Unlike, say, investment bankers, or even restaurant workers, garbage collectors are essential. Nothing luxurious about the service they provide. It makes sense that society would remunerate accordingly. And in the absence of other such examples of fairness, this one became paradigmatic of possibility.

Throughout my life, I've gleaned enough about the history of labor movements and the law to understand there is nothing generous or particularly fair about the compensation of sanitation workers. They simply organized themselves and used their power of collective bargaining to achieve whatever I'd attributed to beneficence, logic, or justice on the part of society. It's because sanitation workers managed to negotiate favorable contracts, relative to everyone else, that a narrative emerged, one that has never been to the best of my knowledge corroborated—that is, do we know for certain that they're being compensated enough to justify the wear and tear on their minds and bodies? This unsubstantiated theory is a win for capitalism because its practitioners and standard-bearers have succeeded in both making a low ceiling seem unreachable and in making the reaching of a low ceiling seem remarkable.

As unions have vanished in this country, those that remain have seen their power diminish at the negotiating table because employers no longer imagine the powerful patchwork of national and international workers who once stood metaphorically, physically, and legally behind their own workers. The decline of unions has become a feedback loop, wherein the few that remain now have more disgruntled members who question the union's effectiveness and are more likely to withhold their dues and to vote for anti-union politicians, the very politicians who championed deregulation and the shipping of jobs to more anti-labor markets, thus weakening unions, and the same charlatans who see a future in which sanitation is the purview of private companies that are beholden to exactly no one, except to the market blah blah blah and competition blah blah blah.

The consequences of the last sixty-five years must be what I've been witnessing as of late: the decay of the sanitation worker, who, if I'm being honest, has become unreliable, inconsistent, and generally bad at their job. Also, unfriendly. The proof of this phenomenon greets me every Tuesday and Friday morning, when our block resembles the aftermath of a tropical storm. Debris on the street, on the sidewalk, beneath cars, plastered to the pavement, and, of course, still inside the trash bins, which they never bother to empty fully. It appears that the sanitation workers assigned to my block can't be bothered to do much more than the mini-

MIDDLE SPOON

mum. Our bins, if they're left anywhere near our home, are full of rainwater, the aforementioned remnants of garbage and recycling, and the green dog-shit bags our horrid neighbors drop into our bins whenever they remain uncovered on the sidewalk for even ten minutes, which is every Tuesday and Friday morning because the trucks come by before we wake, just as we wake, or in order to wake us, and those little green bags accumulate at the bottom of our never-emptied bins, leaving me—my neighbors seldom reach into the bottom of anything—to pull the disgusting things out. I hate those bags so much I receive it as a blessing whenever the workers leave our bins tipped over or upside down or tucked between cars that, it should be said, don't always resist the temptation to crush the bins as they're pulling into or away from the curb. I detest, too, when the bins end up down the block in a cabal of other bins, and occasionally on the street—at times in the middle of the street!—unless they're tipped over or upside down.

Why am I bothering to email you about this? In part, because it's mind-boggling that the streets of one of the wealthiest cities in the world should be littered with trash when we have sanitation workers who come to our homes twice per week with the explicit purpose of preempting our trash from ending up on the street. I find this anomaly so jarring, I felt compelled to sit down and explain it to you.

I pray, too, that my tiny (in stature, not length) email will double as advocacy not only for me and my neighbors—in fact, not for me or my neighbors at all—but for the sanitation workers primarily and for common sense tangentially. I beseech you to revisit their contracts and to give them what they require to do their jobs appropriately. Doing so will bolster your long-held reputation, whether merited or not, as a dependable and efficient agency. Furthermore, meeting the needs of your workers will signal to the rest of us that justice isn't an illusion. If the people who do the work no one wants to do are compensated appropriately, the rest of us also have a shot. That's the message you send us. This email isn't about me or cleanliness or efficiency; it's about upholding an idea that seeds more ideas and possibilities.

I need a win. Let this be it.

Respectfully,

▄▄▄▄▄▄▄▄▄▄▄▄▄▄▄▄▄▄▄▄▄▄

▄▄▄▄▄▄▄▄▄▄▄▄▄▄

Brooklyn, NY ▄▄▄▄▄

PS: On second thought, trash collection is luxurious. After all, the vast majority of us could, to begin with, produce less refuse, and what we do produce could be taken to a nearby communal receptacle that is or is not emptied with less frequency than our current individual bins. The cleaning out of this proposed industrial container, which is certainly no longer a luxury, would still require the care of sanitation workers, but it would lessen their workload and make the entire project more efficient.

PPS: While reconsidering the labor standards for your workers, if you could also ask them to please stop slamming our trash and recycling bins against the pavement, in the process damaging them, I would be grateful.

Dear Ben,

In an effort to tamp down the catastrophic feelings that have encircled me at most moments since our breakup, I've tried to manufacture perspective. I've made earnest attempts to insert myself, psychologically speaking, into other scenarios, horrific ones, so that I might feel something else or, at the very least, to establish a reference point that allows me to weigh my pain against indisputable tragedy. I mean it. I'm not just saying this to virtue signal. I've tried, for example, to picture myself parched and without access to potable water or living in a perpetual state of violence, while nursing a broken heart. I've imagined myself beneath the weight of these excruciating emotions and simultaneously managing a terrible or chronic illness. After all, there's heartache in Jackson, Mississippi, in Flint, Michigan, in Palestine, in Yemen, in Sudan. Heartache coexists with cancer, with diabetes, with schizophrenia. People the world over are shouldering this caliber of grief while burdened with life's other calamities. Several times a day I remind myself of this, and immediately, perspective arrives—clear, irrefutable, comforting. Ephemeral too.

—Me

PS: Despite Fred's advice, I've come close to sending you these emails, but I think the medium would undercut the sentiments of the text. I don't want you to be able to delete or archive my feelings—or forward? Oh my God! I want you to sit with them. This morning, I printed them out—the emails, not my feelings. I considered bringing them to you, sliding them under your door, and then waiting until your shadow came to take my feelings away. But I didn't know if that would make things better or worse. And what if you didn't respond? What if I shared everything, and you said nothing? What if your shadow didn't even appear?

Dear Ben,

You weren't much of a socialist. To be fair, I'm not either, but I aspire to be. A good socialist, that is. Somewhere along the way, I convinced myself that of all the political ideologies available to us in this world socialism aligned neatest with my personal views. But these types of labels didn't appeal to you. "I don't know what any of those words mean: *socialist, conservative, liberal, fascist*. They're moving targets," you said after I told you I might be one—a socialist, that is. I said it fancifully, but there was an undercurrent of shame, which might be because I've been socialized to believe that socialism occupies a space somewhere between outrageous and immoral in the US context. But I'm not afraid to be one—a socialist, that is. It's simply that I'm not always comfortable identifying as one, most of all because I don't feel adept at defining socialism. You can be a capitalist Republican or a capitalist Democrat and be taken for granted, but someone outside of the dominant binary has to be prepared to defend every aspect of their beliefs, including a history through which they didn't live. I guess you were right about it being a moving target.

"So wanting to redistribute power makes you a socialist?" you asked, while we lay naked and sweaty beside each other. "You don't have to do anything to make it happen? You just have to believe in it?"

"Well, I can vote for candidates who share my beliefs," I responded, unprepared for the conversation, unsure if you were goading me or revealing your ignorance.

"Are there really that many people running for office who identify as socialist?"

"More and more, but not enough."

· *33* ·

"So once in a while you vote for someone, but you still shop at stores, and you have a bank account? Why not live off the grid somewhere?"

It was May and not warm, which was fine because I wasn't yet ready for the heat of July or the indecisive balminess of June. We'd just had sex in front of the full-length mirror next to your dresser before collapsing onto your bed. Your rhetorical questions served as red, or possibly pinko, flags. We'd been seeing each other for only a few months, but we were utilizing our flexible work schedules to great effect; at some point, I couldn't recall a day where we hadn't spent time together. Sometimes it was an entire afternoon, sometimes dinner, sometimes whatever twenty-five-minute window we could open. And although our conversation topics were broad and culturally varied—from the virtues of Lady Gaga to the irreverence of Dada to the unworthiness of *La La Land*—we managed to sidestep the political spectrum conversation, in particular the wing left of center and, more specifically, the tranche between liberal and progressive. You weren't pro-incarceration per se, but neither were you an abolitionist. You believed in a free Palestine, but you wouldn't advocate for a right of return. You weren't a fullhearted patriot, but you flinched whenever I put China's and Russia's crimes into context with those of the United States. I sensed, however, that yours were all malleable positions with which I could work or merely cohabitate. But your gut reaction to invalidate socialism because I wasn't walking the walk, as if the ground weren't lava, worried me. Would you always take contrarian, facile stances without staking positions of your own? Would I have to spend my life convincing you that focusing on a collective good was common sense?

"The cynicism is dripping out of you," I replied.

"That's not the only thing dripping out of me, babe. I have to shower."

We both smirked at your indecency. I rolled onto my side and kissed your shoulder, then your chest.

MIDDLE SPOON

"I don't really care about labels either. I just want the world to be fairer," I argued. "However we get there is fine by me."

You climbed off the bed with the precision of a long-limbed cat and made your way toward the bathroom. "I support fairness," you called out after you'd already disappeared.

As you lathered and rinsed, I stood on the other side of the shower curtain building a case for why my research on the health effects of hierarchies was a worthy contribution to societal fairness. "Just because I live in capitalism doesn't mean I'm happy about it," I added for good measure. "Starting a commune in a forest in rural Tennessee isn't going to do much to redistribute power across society. Anarchism before socialism is merely libertarianism."

You didn't respond, which made me wonder if my theorizing had crossed into arrogance.

"So what's the plan for liberation?" you said eventually. Your tone contained facetious notes, but when I peeked behind the curtain, I caught sincerity in your eyes. Or maybe it was just shampoo.

"For starters, a handful of egalitarian economic policies and some solidarity. Next week is International Workers' Day. Did you know that? Everywhere but here, everything shuts down. Everyone gets the day off."

"We have Labor Day," you responded.

"Only because Grover Cleveland was afraid of global cooperation among workers. Now we're stuck with just another shopping day in September."

The water stopped running. You slid the plastic curtain across the rusty rod.

"I love these history lessons," you said. This time your voice and your face were awash in sarcasm.

"Go ahead and laugh, but if we don't believe that we deserve more from this life, and if we aren't united, not only in this country but in every country, the guys at Davos will continue to spit in our faces and tell us it's raining."

Again you were quiet, and I didn't know if it was disdain or indecision. For my part, I chose to fill the vacuum with an anxiety that, in retrospect, might have doubled as hubris: "Well, I for one am not going to work on May Day, and I'm going to tell my students they won't be penalized for skipping class."

"May 1 is a Sunday," you said.

"Fine, well, I won't spend a dime on Sunday, and I'll skip class on Monday."

"You don't teach on Mondays or Fridays."

"What are you, my personal assistant?"

You grinned while slowly turning a cotton swab inside your ear.

"I have office hours, and I will cancel them. And I'll tell my students why."

"That'll start a revolution."

"I'm sorry, what did you say? I couldn't hear over the clanging of capitalism's chains on your wrists and ankles."

You laughed, and I was comforted by the ease of our conversation. Even if we didn't agree, even if we'd never agree, at least we'd kept talking.

When I got out of the shower, my clothes, which had been balled up on the floor in the living room, were laid out on your bed. You'd doused them with the anti-wrinkle spray that you regularly use and about which I'd been skeptical. You proved me wrong; my button-down and slacks looked as if they'd been ironed. "Wow, this is very impressive. Thank you," I said, hoping to snuff out any fires I'd lit during our ideological duel. After that day, you sprayed my clothes every time I came over—the careless urgency with which we undressed necessitated an intervention.

Thanks,
Me

PS: A week later, on Monday, May 2, my buzzer rang. When I came downstairs, you were standing on my stoop with a bag and a backpack. You must have noticed my eyes scan your belongings because you stepped toward me quickly and put your hand across my mouth. "I made the sandwiches and didn't buy any of the ingredients today," you explained. "And yes, the bread is gluten-free. And there's no mayo! And and and . . . I brought my backpack because I have my laptop with me. And no, I'm not gonna work today. I thought we could watch the season finale of *Drag Race*. I still haven't seen it."

PPS: Mayo isn't made with dairy. It's oil and egg.

PPPS: I also didn't have the heart to tell you how little I was interested in *Drag Race*, so I sat through that ridiculous spectacle of insecurity, ostentation, and empowerment, and to my surprise, I was glad I did.

Ben,

I lifted weights, twenty-pounders, one in each hand, four sets, twelve reps each, two biceps exercises and two triceps exercises, and then three sets of fifteen push-ups. I did this in front of a full-length mirror, shirtless, so that I could monitor my posture because of recent neck and shoulder pain. The by-product of lifting weights in my underwear while staring at myself is that I get turned on. I don't think this makes me a narcissist because I'm not thinking of myself so much as I am appreciating a bare chest in the midst of strenuous activity.

When I was done working out, I watched porn for twenty minutes and jerked off. I wonder if you're doing the same—

No!

I'm not going to think of you. I'm going to carry on with my day. Keep myself busy. Unfortunately, it's finals week, and I've already graded most of my students' work. The holiday break has effectively begun.

I can't stay home. The distracting chemicals that lapped up inside of me a short while ago subsided shortly after the orgasm. I'm going to the yoga studio around the corner. They have drop-in classes that I've been tempted to attend for years. I'll just keep moving. I won't allow myself a moment of idleness to think of you.

—Me

Dear Ben,

Heartbreak must be in season because the yoga class was sold out.

It was my fault in a way; I'd been much too deferential to the people who'd arrived alongside me, all of whom managed to get into the class. When it was my turn at the registration desk, the sole employee, who was also the instructor and the proprietor of the petite storefront studio, clanged a small bronze statue with an even smaller bronze mallet before bellowing in the cadence of a chanted prayer:

"Our morning class!

Is at capacity!

Sorry!

To the rest of you!"

The rest of us was simply me and a brunette in leggings with a rolled-up mat under her arm, who, for her part, said nothing and made a swift, curved-spine exit, as if she were embarrassed, as if she and I had failed in some manner, as if those failures had just been broadcast without warning to the leisure class, in the process harming our reputations. But I wasn't at all embarrassed because I didn't want to be a part of this group; I wasn't there to fit in. I was there for survival, and although I'm often riddled with the types of insecurities that both precipitate and amplify embarrassment, this yoga class rejection wasn't a major moment in my life. It didn't feel like a moment at all. Instead, it was a reminder of how many of us have no commitments on weekday mornings. Furthermore, if this low-level rejection were something powerful enough to dent the average person's confidence, I was, in that instance, exceeding expectations. To be more specific, I was the very embodiment of my father's confidence, his sense of belonging, his lack of concern. I guess you could say I was briefly him, a man who'd lived his formative years on a fine block in 1950s Bogotá, where he'd never bothered to care if anyone thought more or less of him because everyone else *was* more or less him. Yes, this morning, even if only briefly, I felt like someone who never expects the worst and whose sense of self and security are so well-founded and intact, they could be, at times, mistaken for indifference and, consequently, a lack of kindness. This, I thought, is what it must be like to be Scandinavian today. And so, I stuck my own mat beneath my arm and turned to leave, but not before I watched the instructor disappear behind a thick curtain into the dimly lit room where the breathing and stretching were about to commence. I hadn't expected him to say anything more to me, but I still found it odd, all these years later, that he didn't acknowledge me or our long-ago threesome. To be fair, I don't acknowledge him either, but I certainly would if he bothered to feign recognition whenever we crossed paths, which is often, since his children attend the same school as Jules. Before becoming a yogi, this man was an architect or lawyer who my husband and I had met online almost twelve years ago and whom we invited over for a drink as a prelude to sex, sex that, despite its low degree of difficulty—kissing, some oral—and lack of passion, managed to retain an air of friendliness, friendliness that has made his ensuing pivot toward aloofness all the more surprising.

Since that Obama-years living room dalliance, I've observed our yogi-neighbor transform from a fit, full-haired white-shirt type into a pot-bellied, balding white-shirt type with a girlfriend, and then a wife and a stroller, and then a wife, a stroller, and a scooter, and ultimately, into a very fit T-shirt guy with a perfectly shaved head and a wife, a scooter, and a balance bike. Often I thought he was living the straight version of my life—not the physical transformations but the long slide toward conformity—and how interesting it might have been if we'd kept in touch, if we'd developed a camaraderie characterized by playdates and Little League in lieu of homemade Manhattans and fellatio. On the other hand, he wasn't all that interesting, and his wife, who is currently the president of the PTA, produces similarly uninspiring feelings in me, even if she commits to eye contact and a low-wattage smile at drop-offs and pickups. None of this truly matters because Gary—his name, which I admit I'd forgotten, was on the business cards above "Instructor" and "Proprietor"—has no interest in remembering, never mind acknowledging, me. To be clear, I am neither implying nor do I suspect that Gary is closeted or leading a double or a down-low life. Nothing of the sort. I think he's settled in his sexuality and has told his wife everything she's ever wanted to know. My husband and I were probably nothing more than a pit stop on Gary's road to self-discovery. In fact, if I strain just enough, I can recall *curious* on his dating profile. If I strain a little less, I remember that he gave head as if he were applying damp sandpaper to an uneven doorframe. No, I don't believe Gary is unfriendly because he's homophobic or a liar. Gary's unfriendly because he was raised that way and because, at this point, he's forgotten who I am. And Gary's possibly not unfriendly at all but merely consumed with trying to figure himself out, which, according to my empirical data collection, has been a sexually, physically, professionally, and probably psychologically taxing journey. My best to Gary.

With nothing but time and cortisol to kill, I made my way from the yoga studio to the bookstore, whose enormity and vast color palette were matched by the size and multicultural makeup of the staff, all of them smiley and thrilled to be alive, an environment that should have seeded hope but on this day brought out my cynicism.

I made quick work of it by avoiding the humans and the shelves and instead grabbing a staff pick from the queer table (*Koolaids: The Art of War* by Rabih Alameddine), one from the Black table (*The Color Purple* by Alice Walker), and another from the (much smaller) Latinx table (Cecilia

Gentili's memoir, *Faltas: Letters to Everyone in My Hometown Who Isn't My Rapist*). On which table the happy-go-lucky booksellers would have placed the work of a Black Latinx queer author is anyone's guess. I also picked up an armful of graphic novels from the juvenile readers section, because Nico and Jules consume these glorified comic strips with a fervor typically reserved for religion or meth. Don't get me wrong, it makes me happy to have children who love to devour books, and I know you're a lifelong graphic novels connoisseur, but I fear this particular category isn't the endurance gateway to more traditional books that I was told it would be. *The important thing is they're reading!* Instead, the images-and-brief-text format seems to enable shorter attention spans, which I suspect will decrease my children's chances of getting into prestigious universities and consequently increase the difficulty quotient for securing the sorts of jobs prestigious universities afford, a plateaued mobility I expect from this generation. I don't mean Gen Alpha or Zillennials—I mean this particular node in my own lineage, the one without desperate parents or past-due utility bills or a motivational vanity. The generation that must be sold an idea by pointing to the real-time necessities of others.

En route home from the bookstore, I made my way toward the French bistro that does nothing correct except for steak frites and red wine, and just as I slid into the narrow booth of the empty restaurant, my phone rang. It was Ms. Garrison, the vice principal of Jules's elementary school.

"A fight? But they're eight years old!" I responded.

"These things happen, Mr.—"

"I have never seen Jules raise a hand to anyone. There is no more docile child."

"His—Mrs. James claims she saw Jules shove the other child."

"There has to be a reason. My kid doesn't go around picking fights."

MIDDLE SPOON

"There was an argument between Jules and the other child—"

"About what?"

"Jules claims the other child asked him—excuse me, *them*. The other child asked *them* more than a few times whether they were a boy or a girl."

"I've tried to communicate to you that this is becoming a stressful situation for Jules. They are very resilient and flexible about their gender, but everyone has their limits, which I've explained to their teachers, to other parents, to the social worker, to everyone."

"Yes, you have, but you must also appreciate that this is a new concept. Not everyone understands."

"With all due respect, Ms. Garrison, this is why I've suggested we bring in an organization to do a school-wide information session about gender expression and identity, so that everyone can get on a similar page."

"A program like that would need approval from the DOE and from the PTA, and we'd have to find time to schedule an all-day assembly."

"The DOE is on board. Our school has the latitude to arrange these sorts of trainings."

"Can we talk about this further when you come to pick up Jules?"

When I arrived at the school, the vice principal was unavailable; the school was short-staffed, and she'd been forced to monitor recess. Jules, for their part, appeared unfazed by whatever had happened. They were sitting on a bench in the main office, legs crossed, reading a graphic novel about knights and dragons, unaware of the ambient clamor or even my presence when I sat beside them.

"Oh, hi, Daddy," they said after I'd tapped them on the shoulder. Immediately, their smile turned into something more turbulent. "Am I in trouble?"

· 43 ·

"Maybe. Tell me everything on the walk home."

According to Jules, Charlie has been pestering them for weeks, and now, he was inciting other kids to also pester. Harmless by most bullying standards, but upsetting and unnecessary nonetheless.

"I didn't care," Jules continued, "because Shawna and Mila both told Charlie to shut up, but then Charlie started making fun of Mila, saying she had bad breath. And Mila started crying. So I pushed Charlie, and he tripped. And he fell. And then he started crying. That's when Mrs. James yelled."

"That's all that happened? That's why they called me?" I said to no one in particular.

Jules shrugged.

"What have I told you about keeping your hands to yourself?"

"That I should."

"Exactly."

"But you also told me to protect my friends. And you told Nico that solitarity—"

"Soli-DAR-ity."

"Soli-DAR-ity is when you do something for somebody, and they do something for you. Mila and Shawna were defending me, so I had to protect them."

"You're eight."

"I'll be nine next year."

I explained to Jules that I appreciated their motivations, but that they should first talk to an adult before resorting to physical violence.

"You told Nico not all violence is hitting."

"That's true, but—"

"Well, Charlie was doing word violence. He was hurting us with his words."

After that I wasn't sure exactly what to say because Jules wasn't entirely

MIDDLE SPOON

wrong. Instead, I doubled down on first seeking help from an adult. They claimed to have understood, but I suspect this is the tip of an iceberg or a canary in a coal mine; Jules will be facing situations like this all their life or until being nonbinary becomes the predominant gender identity, which will probably happen in Gen Beta or Delta.

—Me

Ben,

Wouldn't it be great, humane even, if couples who end at the behest of one partner, leaving the other partner spiraling, should have to appear before a tribunal of sorts, one whose task is nothing more than to ascertain clarity? A group of peers or specialists would help them both to understand why their relationship ended. Like an exit interview. Doesn't that sound great? Today, I crave clarity more than I crave you.

I haven't been able to eat with anything resembling pleasure. I eat because I know I must. I eat because I have children and responsibilities. Days of this.

For days now, I've also been trying to channel your mind, trying to convince you to message me so I can make a case for us. Have you felt me? Have you heard faint noises or sensed subtle electrical impulses? I've been reduced to DIY clairvoyance because I don't know how else to reach you. I won't call. I won't text. I won't visit. It has to be you; I don't trust myself to read this situation clearly. The map of the vulgar, the vile, and the violent has been scrubbed of distances and scale.

If on a Monday night two people have a wonderful dinner and fantastic sex, and on a Tuesday morning one of them says *I love you more than I've ever loved anyone before, but it's over*, what recourse is there? Do I have the leeway to reach out in the days after the breakup? In the weeks after? Frankly, I don't know if I have the right to ever contact you again. Every instinct is submerged beneath the dreaded fears of overstepping, of rejection, of ridicule, of anger, of public retribution, of seeing a cold look on your face that tells me the feelings are no longer mutual and possibly never were. This is a cage. An invisible cage that dangles over something

MIDDLE SPOON

unknown and murky. A few days ago, I was a respected public health researcher; now, I'm a trapped animal and a feeble poet.

Can I call you, please? We don't have to get back together. Just to talk, to better understand what's happened. I want to be a decent human. A good guy. Give you space. Respect your wishes. Allow you to get over me. I don't want to be an asshole or a hashtag. But. This situation is indecent.

What even constitutes acceptable romantic human interactions in this era, particularly between two people born in different generations and advertising target groups? You once told me that no guy had ever treated you as well as I had. What, pray tell, does that title afford me?

For the last two decades, I've been in a proverbial well. Married, that is. My human-relations arsenal consists of exactly one rudimentary tool: reading the room. But this tool is obsolete in a room full of smoke.

To further complicate matters, your youth inspirits you to be more outspoken in defense of your autonomy. This is an altogether great development for society and for future generations, but as it concerns our May–December romance—it's only nine years, for Pete's sake—I'm up a creek. It's also worth mentioning that I've noticed a penchant among younger people for using the language of oppression and liberation in rather self-aggrandizing ways that allow for the avoidance of growth and healing—eavesdropping on my students is as life-affirming as it is an exercise in eye-rolling. Please, Ben, don't shun me for being human.

Not all conflict is abuse. If we ever talk again, I'm going to lend you Sarah Schulman's book.

Love,
Me

· 47 ·

Dear Ben,

I braved the downpour this morning to get to Fred's office in the West Village. Cold rain is the worst sort of rain, but I didn't hesitate to embark on my journey because I was eager to receive Fred's counsel and because it happens that I see Susan Sarandon whenever I go to his office. I never told you this because I derive an odd swell of pride from being a New Yorker who doesn't make undo fuss about celebrities, despite having many times felt my heart rate speed up in their presence. But it's true. Sarandon's routine dovetails with mine, and I can guarantee that as I approach my therapist's stately apartment building with the old palatial doors and the gilded intercom panel, she will be plodding westward along 10th Street in my direction with a leash in her hand and a small, amber-colored dog attached to the end of the cord. She'll also be wearing loose-fitting pants and large movie-star sunglasses. In the summer, sandals; in the winter, boots. (I am as big a fan of Susan the actor as I am of Susan the outspoken activist, and I don't fully understand her surfeit of critically acclaimed film roles in the '80s and '90s and the dearth afterward. I suspect it has something to do with her political views, but it's probably ageism and misogyny too.) In any case, spotting Sarandon has become a highlight of my week that didn't happen this morning, probably because of the miserable rain that soaked my pants and made the hour of therapy a rather unpleasant experience that was then made even worse by Fred's reaction to my latest batch of emails.

"They're well written, but you're still not tagging the fish."

"I am tagging them. I recognize my recurring fears."

"But you're not throwing them back into the sea, so what's the point of tagging them?"

· 48 ·

MIDDLE SPOON

"I tried to do what you said. I wrote about more than just Ben."

"Yes, but if you sink into these forlorn explorations of your sadness, you're going to be mired in it. Climb, and focus."

"Climb out of what? Focus on what?"

"Sadness and your future. What are the things that excite you? Who makes you happy?"

"I'm trying, but this breakup is preoccupying my mind. How can I possibly think about my favorite flower or my best friends or strawberry shortcake? I'm stuck, which is why I'm here instead of doing something more productive with my life. Telling me to snap out of it is not going to work. Maybe some very secure people can do that, but not me."

Fred opted for quiet after my brief tirade. He's never been harsh with me, and I've never raised my voice before, but our exchange had just amounted to a small skirmish.

"You're right," he said while smoothing the thighs of his already taut gray pants. "I might have gotten a bit impatient. You see, I think you're a great person. You have a lot going for you. A wonderful family and career. You have your youth and your health. Yes, you've been blindsided by this breakup, but consider yourself lucky it was your first experience with heartbreak. On the other hand, you're not familiar with these extreme emotions. If you could see what I see, you'd realize that this will be a blip in your timeline, nothing more. You just need to push through."

"I hear you. I swear I do. But I still don't understand what happened. I'm not only sad; I'm confused. The emotional crash and the uncertainty of everything is disorienting. I don't want to lose him."

Fred's gaze was soft and full of pity. I knew exactly what he wasn't saying.

"Okay, let's try something. Think a bit about what wasn't working in your relationship with Ben. You've said before that you weren't perfectly

· *49* ·

compatible. Focus on some of those areas, and maybe you'll understand better what happened."

"I can do that."

"Also, you said earlier you could be doing more productive things. Like what?"

"Well, I've always wanted to write a screenplay, and I've been curious about the flying trapeze."

"I thought you were afraid of heights."

"I am, but this would be controlled fear."

"Are you familiar with the term counterphobia?"

"No. Sounds like anti-fear."

"In a way. Someone who is counterphobic runs toward the things that scare them, hoping to overcome them. Some people, however, get a high from being afraid."

"Which one am I?"

"You try to overcome your fears, but it's possible to be both. Be mindful of that."

"I will."

Fred eyed the simple watch on his wrist and then pressed his hands onto his knees to lift himself out of the chair. "See you next week," he said.

As I put my rain jacket on over my damp clothes, I searched my mind for anything urgent to say or to ask before leaving, but nothing came.

"Fred, do you want me to stop sending you the emails?"

"Yes," he said without hesitation.

After the session, I searched for a restaurant on 6th Avenue that used to be one of my favorites, some of the best Chinese food in the city, but I couldn't find it. Was it possible that the restaurant was on 7th? I meandered

MIDDLE SPOON

toward the C train and found a Cuban-Chinese spot on 8th. It was a long counter with stools that swiveled but were bolted into the floor. I ate well—too much, in fact—but I didn't take the leftovers with me because it was a meat-heavy meal, and my cholesterol hovers near a worrisome threshold—you would have been incensed at the waste. It was only after I boarded the train that it dawned on me that I was two blocks from my husband's office. At any other point in my life, I would have messaged him, and he would have come downstairs, and we would have gone for a brief walk, and we would have talked about our days and the kids and our dinner plans. Instead, I was preoccupied with transferring to the L train and taking it to Williamsburg and buzzing your apartment. It was only a brief consideration because I'd imagined that scenario countless times, and therefore I could picture the neon tag cinched around this fluke's neck, leaving me no choice but to throw it back into the sea.

—Me

PS: As it concerns leftovers, you were nearly militant about never allow-ing a bit of food to spoil. In fact, you'd take all the leftovers home from our restaurant outings—every last scrap jumbled together. I liked that about you. Your penchant for conservation reminded me of my house-hold when I was growing up. My dad didn't allow us to discard any part of our meals, often combining a week's worth of remains into Sunday's lunch.

There was, from the very beginning, something familiar and easy about our interactions, and I wonder if it was rooted in values.

Dear Ben,

I drank too much last night and ended up with heartburn at one a.m. and insomnia at three. It's now four a.m., and I'm in the living room typing, desperate for a cup of coffee but afraid grinding beans will wake the others. I've spent most of the last hour reading about entanglement, the physics theory Einstein dismissed as "spooky action at a distance." In brief, the phenomenon establishes that separated particles continue to be linked—that is, two things once together will always be together. Even when separated, whatever affects object A will affect object B. Maybe this is what has happened to us: our time together was meaningful enough to have entwined us at a subatomic level. Perhaps the suffocation I'm feeling in this moment in one corner of Brooklyn has led you, in another corner of Brooklyn, to open your kitchen window, the one behind the radiator, beside your perpetually empty refrigerator. Perhaps my lack of appetite over the last few days has led to an acidic gurgle in your own stomach. Maybe one of my jilted neutrons will entice one of your misguided ones to return.

Please say something is the current and most consistent infinitesimal missive I've sent since you left. But I've felt nothing return. Perhaps my suffering is a reaction to yours.

It's only been seven days, but I'm already fed up with my own desperation, a sensation compounded by the belief that I'll soon be alone in this godforsaken misery because you strike me as the sort of person who can grow a scab rather quickly. In a few weeks, I'll call you, full of hope, but you'll already have forgotten us—*Who's this? I don't have this number saved.* You'll tell me that whatever you once felt has vanished—*Sorry, I'm*

· 52 ·

MIDDLE SPOON

seeing someone. That it's time to move on—*I gotta go, but let's grab a drink sometime!*

Please don't let that happen. Let's meet now. In a neutral place. For coffee. We both live in Brooklyn, we both work in Manhattan, I'm from Queens, we both fear Staten Island. How about the Bronx? At an old-school Dominican spot or at a trendy new café run by a half-Dominican, half–Puerto Rican guy who went to Cornell or somewhere similarly over-priced and came back to his community, to create jobs and wealth, and will one day run for city council or Congress as a progressive who prac-tices a politics of liberation but never quite names it, someone who pushes for defunding the police and investing in schools and health care instead. We could meet at that guy's café.

We don't even have to get back together. I'll hold your hand for as long as you allow, and I'll leave when you tell me to. I wouldn't ask for more. I don't know if I could handle more.

Isn't that strange? I've thought of nothing else but time travel since the breakup, and now, given the opportunity, I don't know if I could return to where we were.

On the other hand, if you've already moved on, our relationship was probably never going to last, was it? Maybe our feelings were never mutual.

I repeat to myself some variation of that last paragraph several times a day in order to accelerate the healing. I have mantras. More mantras than units of hope. The bedrock of antianxiety therapy is a solid mantra.

You weren't worth it.

We weren't truly compatible.

You're not mature enough.

I'm not mature enough.

I'm better than this.

I have a full life without you.

It was great, but now it's over.
What if you're a Zionist?
I existed before I met you.
I exist still.
Go fuck yourself for being so goddamn selfish.

I say these exaggerated things, but I can't quite stick the landing. I miss you.

Love,
Me

PS: I'd like to address the unnecessary distinction between mind and body as it concerns my current metaphysical whiplash. This faux divide contributes to the eternal misunderstanding of mental health—its risk factors, causes, outcomes, etc. The brain is a part of the body, and its various chemicals and neurotransmitters, as well as their regulation and deregulation, are, in conjunction with our experiences, predictors of our mental health. One sprains their ankle and needs recovery time. Similarly, if one has a traumatic or high-stress experience that taxes their brain and leads to mental illness, it, too, requires a period of recovery and treatment. But since our species has faced challenges studying and understanding the brain's complexities, we've treated it as an almost mythical thing and consequently relegated mental health to something fantastical, taboo, and unscientific that deserves lesser coverage in most insurance plans. Ignorance, nothing more.

Dear Me,

Snap the fuck out of it.

Think about what it took for you to achieve what you have in this life. Think about your parents and theirs and the people who came before, about whom you know nothing, and the people who held doors open, about whom you know slightly more, and those who looked the other way and did their part for you to be alive and aware. The fractured version of yourself that stands before the mirror today is not worthy of that history. Pull yourself together. Bathe. Brush your teeth. Eat breakfast. Drink water. Go outside. Breathe. And repeat all of this for as long as it takes for you to be whole again, until you are what you and all these people and passersby and ghosts wished you to be. You have always had to be better in order to be equal. And thus, you are.

Fight. Fight until you can't. And then, fight more.

—Me

Dear Ben,

I've decided I'll suffer for a month. If I still miss you at the end of that month, I'll reach out. But I won't miss you. I don't think it's possible for a human to feel as I do for that long. I'm staking a claim on that newfound belief.

I can survive thirty days without you. One month is nothing.

In the meantime, I will find comfort in having been dumped at the end of the year, when all the "Best of . . ." lists are published. As I do every December, I will comb through BFI's *Sight and Sound*, *Film Comment*, and Richard Brody's annual roundups, as well as Manohla Dargis's "And the nominees should be . . ." I will use their litanies to create my own. But first, I'll finish McDonagh's *The Banshees of Inisherin*.

—Me

Dear Ben,

I'm in the ER. I'm fine, but the bedside manner of the staff in this hospital is atrocious, to a degree that would be comedic if not for all the suffering. The nurses and medical assistants will not look me directly in the eye because doing so would require them to answer my questions or attend to my needs. My needs are simple. I want to know when they're bringing my friend a blanket. It's not cold in the ER, but she's cold because sick, dehydrated people often are cold—or do they feel cold? (Is there a difference?) Every worker here is cold too. Their dismissive attitudes are an arsenal of fogs, daggers, laser beams. I imagine a field of war as the only worse environment for the ill.

On the other hand, I'm finding the atmosphere familiar. There's a continuity between this poor care and the way you're treating me, in particular the way you behaved the last time I saw you.

The day after we broke up, I proposed we meet in person. Our relationship simply couldn't end over the phone, I argued. You agreed. After dropping Nico off at school, I made my way to your place. Both of us were exhausted, but whereas I felt desperate and did little to hide it, you appeared resolute. You were terse, never interrupting your routine: brushing your teeth, patting your curls in the mirror, washing your breakfast dishes, tucking your shirt into your pants. It was eight thirty.

Our rushed chat did nothing to bring about closure. You and I and our words continued meandering onto the street past the many people who moved with urgency and the few who didn't. At a corner, as we waited for the light to change in our favor, we had ample time to regard each other from the distance you'd imposed, which we did, until I moved

· 57 ·

closer to you and brought my face to yours. It was primarily out of habit, but I'd be lying if I said my overture wasn't also guided by hope. It didn't yet feel as if we were over, and I was aggrieved at my lack of input in the matter. I felt then as I do now: a terrible thing was happening to me only, not to us. A grand relationship was coming to an end because of a one-sided realization: *You're never going to leave your husband.*

It's true. I am never going to leave my husband. An odd point of contention on your part and an even odder epiphany because you knew from the outset I was never going to walk away from my family. This—the balancing and near juggling of multiple loves—is the fundamental component of polyamory.

When I leaned in to kiss you, you pulled away, the way someone does when a bee swirls past. I'd become, in a short period of time, something to fear.

"C'mon, babe," I said at that nothing-special intersection that separates Williamsburg from Bushwick, across the street from one of the hundreds of bodega-cum-markets that had in recent years added *Organic* to its marquee despite offering almost no organic products. You apologized for recoiling. Then you kissed me. It was simultaneously the best (familiar) and worst (distant) kiss we'd ever shared. I wish I had known it would be our last; I might have made more of it, lingered for longer, pressed my hand on the small of your back.

You could be a nurse at this hospital, Ben. Cold, guarded, angry at the unfairness of your situation, emotionally taxed, frustrated by your inability to see your future clearly, helpless in the face of the invisible structures and inefficient systems inhibiting your happiness. It's a proper shit show in this ER. People are calling out for water, for warmth, for meds, for food. And through it all, the staff remains committed to their rudeness or, rather, their aggressive apathy.

About an hour ago—I've been here for nearly four hours—I success-

MIDDLE SPOON

fully resisted posting something on social media about what I was witnessing. I feared my few followers would assume I was the patient. I also worried I didn't understand the reasons for the ineptitude and callousness of the hospital staff and would thus be placing blame at the feet of the wrong people. I'd be guilty of one of those gotcha attacks that cause shame and condemnation but lead to no solutions.

The elderly woman on the gurney next to my friend is writhing in discomfort, full-on thrashing, the hem of her gown up to her chest, her hair a static-induced terror, her white, near-translucent skin and purple veins a lost Goya painting. She's restless and screams without compunction; she's been doing so the entire time I've been here. She, too, needs a blanket. She also wants water. (WITHOUT ICE!) She wants her sister. She wants other people too. She holds her hand to her ear as if it were a phone and shouts, "Alexa, where's my sister! Alexa, get me a blanket!" For twenty uninterrupted minutes she yells for water. At last, I get up and request water.

The nurse on duty snaps at me not to get involved in another patient's care. "You have no right."

I ask if she's *Alexa*.

"Alexa?" responds the beleaguered worker with droopy lids and a mask across the lower third of her face.

I tell her it's the name the elderly woman has been calling out repeatedly.

"Oh, she means the Amazon thing."

I'm briefly embarrassed for not having made the association. I return to my seat beside my friend's temporary bed, where I have an unobstructed view of the tortured elderly patient, whom the staff ignore with what can only be called dedication, someone they could easily appease, in the process allowing all the other patients in her vicinity to rest, including my poor friend, who already finds it impossible to sleep through

· 59 ·

the fluorescent lighting, the incessant beeping of the various monitors that snake up from her arms and chest like an eviscerated robot, and of course, the old lady's spine-tingling lamentations. One tactical move could improve the lives of at least a dozen people. (BRING HER THE WATER!) Alas.

Alas means *wings* in Spanish. I can't make the connection between the two words—*alas* in Spanish and *alas* in English—but the image of a massive bird swooping into this ER to cause chaos and rescue the patients is soothing.

Earlier, as I whittled down my indignation into a concise social media message, including tags for the hospital and my state assembly member, it occurred to me that my motivation was less about providing succor or changing a system than about posting something that might elicit your concern. I knew you'd put aside our no-contact pact to inquire about my well-being. You might have even come to the hospital. I want that still. Being an ER companion would be all the more bearable with a companion of my own. But that's not going to happen. You're out, getting drunk, trying to forget me while entertaining your friend from LA, a friend to whom you've been eager to introduce me, the actor who teaches yoga for a living, who has, with age, become a yoga instructor who longs to be an actor.

Meeting each other's friends over the last year had solidified us in a way. We'd introduced people into our shared life and consequently legitimized our relationship. It was a sweet and unexpected part of this courtship. If we're being honest, you didn't seem particularly wowed by my friends—ditto—but I wasn't worried because those interactions would have become smoother and more authentic with time. Accepting Polyamory 101 was a course no one had intended to take, and one that few people were passing. Even our dearest and most supportive friends found our arrangement suspect. *When is he going to leave his husband?* several of your

MIDDLE SPOON

friends asked, whereas mine shook their heads, widened their eyes, and worried about my husband: *How's he holding up?* It turns out you and I are surrounded by people who accept unorthodox love at a distance, but who become wary up close. They needed an example, a model—an ice sculpture!—on which they might pin their doubts and watch them melt away. We might have needed that too.

Oh, how silly of me to be dissecting the hypocrisy of our friends and the absence of polyamory's representation in the world while you're probably fucking someone you met online a few hours ago, which is how you'd dealt with our previous breakup.

"I blew my neighbor twice that same weekend," you said last summer when I asked if you'd been as sad as I'd been. We were at the dimly lit and short-lived lesbian bar near your apartment. We hadn't communicated in nearly six weeks when you emailed to ask if I wanted to grab a drink. "As friends," you said. In defiance of my instincts, I met you.

"You blew him twice? The *same* day we broke up?"

"Once on Saturday and once on Sunday," you clarified.

I did my best to remain quiet instead of allowing the judgmental thing I wanted to say to continue its brain-intestines-throat-lips trajectory, an endurance exercise that took long enough for you to add, "Everyone handles pain differently."

You're right, Ben. My friend is currently in a supine position with her knees up to deal with her pain. I'm sitting quietly beside her, crafting subliminal internet posts and drafting emails I'll never send in order to deal with mine. (Full disclosure: I posted an IG story lambasting the hospital and then quickly deleted it.)

"Honey," whispers my friend, Dee, before asking if I can inquire about her impending CT scan. An indecipherable ailment has manifested in her back, her intestines, and possibly her lungs. I'm afraid for her. She's the sort of person who procrastinates instead of seeking medical attention.

· *61* ·

Last year, she had a heart attack and didn't tell anyone, not even me, not in any of the dozens of text messages we exchanged while coordinating playdates—her daughter and my eldest son are best friends—or exchanging snarky asides about the changing demographic at our kids' school. Dee and I are often the only two non-white parents on the playground.

I approach the ICU doctor about the imaging scan. I see only his forehead because of the monumental furniture—desk? counter?—between us. I walk around the modular behemoth—podium? bridge of the USS *Enterprise*?—to face him, to see him entirely. He's in a huddle of office chairs with other men in blue scrubs, men whose muscles test the tension of their sleeves but whose faces retain the geekiness that brought them to this place. All of them appear bored, tired, or distracted. That's the thing about being in a hospital: they're dire, life-changing experiences for us visitors, but they're nothing more extraordinary than a day of work for the people in uniform. Theoretically speaking, I don't blame them. It would be unreasonable and unhealthy for them to live in a constant state of agitation or alertness. And yet, it wouldn't kill them to affect a modicum of urgency.

I remind Dee's geek-jock-doc that it's been nearly two hours since she drank the prerequisite liquid for the CT scan. He looks around, flags down the first lower-level colleague he spots, and tells her to take my friend to the imaging room. That's how this whole night has progressed, or, better yet, proceeded—nothing about this is progress: *I* inquire about a result or an impending diagnostic exam, and *they* suddenly realize there are no barriers to this task having been completed sooner.

The ER is full, primarily of poverty and racism. I've deduced this from the array of illnesses on display. It resembles a homeless shelter or hospice more than what an ER should or could be. I've yet to see a twentysomething soccer player with a broken ankle or a thirtysomething construction worker with a nail through their thumb. Black people with chronic

MIDDLE SPOON

illnesses that have been ignored to the point of becoming acute are over-represented here, as are Central American day laborers—mostly for alcohol poisoning. It's as simple as America after sixty years of deregulation and a shrinking tax base and four hundred years of unaccounted-for history. And actually, I mean the United States, not *America*. The American continent is vast, and although it includes similar problems across its landmasses and archipelagos, the interventions and outcomes are markedly different depending on where we drop a pin on the map, which is to say, worse here, particularly if you look at the ratio of wealth to suffering.

It's nearly three a.m., and Dee waves at me with a near-lifeless arm. "Go home," she mumbles. She can see I'm tired even if she doesn't suspect the cause. But I fear leaving her alone. I know two Black women who died in ERs, both under forty. My friend is close to fifty, and she has a long life ahead of her. I don't want to pour regret atop what I'm already feeling. "Go. Get some sleep," she continues.

"I'm not tired."

"Yes, you are. Don't worry. My aunt will be here in the morning."

To redirect her pleas, I tell her about you. Dee is a friend, but she's not someone I was expecting to come out to as polyamorous, least of all today.

"No wonder you've been so quiet," she responds.

"Have you ever felt this sort of sadness before?"

"Course," she says, as her eyes disappear beneath their lids.

It seems I've been one of the few to never have experienced true heartbreak. Instead of relieved, I feel naive.

The beeping of the monitors rouses her: "It's real. It's grief. Give yourself time."

Everyone suggests this. But I must be the only person who realizes that love also gets lost to time. Dee asks a few more questions, primarily about my husband. "He's okay," I respond. "You know how he is, even-keeled, not bothered by the vicissitudes." I don't know how that word,

· 63 ·

vicissitudes, sneaked into the sentence. It's apt, but it's an odd word for the moment. In fact, I don't think I've ever before said the word aloud. Dee seems unfazed by my early high school vocabulary and simply nods along before nodding off again.

I brought my laptop with me, thinking I would work while she slept, but the noises don't allow anyone to sleep for very long. If Dee cobbles together three minutes, it's a luxurious nap. *Who designed this place?* I wonder. Come to think of it, I know exactly who designed the exterior of the hospital because he's my neighbor. Good guy. I'm in awe of his encyclopedic knowledge of NYC's architectural history. He has successfully converted the hospital from an institutional early '70s eyesore into a state-of-the-art and quite inviting experience, but the interior lacks warmth, as well as nooks for patients to set down their belongings, and outlets for their friends to charge their laptops. This sort of attention to functionality is outside of my neighbor-friend's scope; I don't blame him.

If I'm going to bother to critique the viscera of this ER, I should begin with its dearth of white people. Where are they? Don't they have emergencies too? Don't they need care? I know they live in this neighborhood because I've watched them move in over the last twenty-five years. I see them at the farmers market and the new New Italian restaurant with the frigid twenty-three-dollar martini.

I'm being facetious, Ben. I know the answer to my own question. The white people of this neighborhood go to the hospitals with better reputations. They take taxis for miles instead of going to the place down the street. I don't blame them. And I don't blame my neighbor-friend for this problem either.

The boat is sinking, and I've just devoted endless paragraphs to bemoaning the deck chairs. This is what happens to brown people with means. We join the political futility chorus. Thoughts for another day.

I'm sure you're sleeping now. It's nearing four a.m., and you're an early riser. But I suspect there is someone lying beside you. I envy and hate this person. And I'm beginning to hate you.

—Me

PS: I'd like to clarify something, a common and wrongly held assumption about health and race. There's nothing intrinsically unhealthy about being Black. It's the United States that's the risk factor. In countries where Black people are the majority, they have better health outcomes than in the US. A hospital in Accra or Lagos, for example, has soccer players with broken ankles and construction workers with punctured thumbs. There's nothing genetic to account for the inequities of illness between Blacks and whites in the US. It's all structural.

Dear Ben,

Last week's farmers market was canceled because of the snow, so this morning's was the first since you left. Food shopping shouldn't be a milestone, but I can't seem to disentangle you from the places we've visited together. Our Saturday morning market outings were the sort of quotidian tasks that become significant because of their frequency and accumulation. At the end of my life, I will have spent an important chunk of it procuring my groceries from these two dozen local farmers, fish- and cheesemongers, bakers, butchers, florists, and vintners. More time than I spend with some of my dearest friends.

You got a kick out of the vendors, people I've been interacting with for nearly twenty years, seeing us together. In fact, it was on one of those Saturday mornings that you first slipped your hand into my back pocket and let it rest as we made our initial stroll through the canopied promenade—a new level of comfort unlocked. I recall another Saturday when you were particularly charmed by the upbeat sarcasm between the vegan baker and me, a conversation that toggled from the specter of Trump to the lightness of dairy-free scones and back again. The humor made you tilt your head and smile in a fuller, less guarded way I hadn't seen before, leaving me to wonder if I'd also been too reserved in your presence. Another time, you teamed up with the mushroom lady to make fun of me when I misnamed one of the varieties—*chicken of the woods* instead of *hen of the woods*—a ribbing I'd found endearing, even if simplistic.

You'd insist on carrying the heavier bags despite your back pain, which in retrospect was a way of pulling your weight, literally and figuratively, because of what had become the de facto custom of my paying for almost

MIDDLE SPOON

everything. I didn't mind because doing so fit the narrative of our relationship, the one in which I'm older, the top, the one who massages your feet, the one who eats you out. There was an almost cultural or subcultural logic and possibly an expectation that I should pick up the tab. But I often wondered if I could sustain that role (the lead), a part I performed freely, happily even, because I hadn't ever played it in my marriage. It was probably unwise for me to bear the lion's share of our costs, which isn't to discount your contributions, primarily the drinks before dinner or the nightcap afterward—no small expenditure in NYC—but I was growing curious about what would happen when we took our first big trip together. Would I be expected to pay for the flights? The hotel? Since I'm a socialist at heart—in my opinion, that's where socialism must begin—I might have suggested we each pay what we could, proportional to our means and desires. (Wouldn't that make a handy phone app: an equity calculator that redistributes wealth proportional to means, needs, and history?)

I'd like to state without ambiguity that I didn't think you were cheap or a gold digger—can you imagine me saying such a thing? You would have accused me of being anti-Semitic, while simultaneously laughing in order to let me know you were kidding, as well as to undercut a genuine insecurity brought upon by hundreds (thousands?) of years of anti-Semitic tropes. Actually—

Actually, this email isn't about that because, if I give anti-Semitism preferential treatment in this email, I'll then have to find a way to insert my unequivocal solidarity with Palestinians, after which I'd have to respond to the accusation that I find it difficult to empathize with Jewish fears and histories of oppression without immediately jumping to defend Palestine, which I do because those fears and histories of oppression are often employed quite cynically to perpetuate the oppression of Palestinians, and I would throw in for good measure something like, *Look at the health statistics, at life expectancy, at socioeconomic indicators; Palestinians need all of the defenders they can get.* There is no need to go down this rabbit hole.

No, this email is not about the geopolitical boondoggle caused by the Earl of Balfour or by British colonialism or by US interests. This email is about cost-sharing in a relationship, and I have a distinct memory of you not offering to help with the groceries during our trip upstate, that time I had to present my research at the liberal arts college with the small campus but gargantuan endowment, which isn't to say the grocery store upstate has anything to do with the Saturday farmers market in Brooklyn, where I buy food primarily for my family and, therefore, never expected you to contribute, irrespective of how many meals you enjoyed from that locally grown, often organic bounty. Upstate, however, we were on a sort of vacation together, and I had paid for the extended apartment rental, and I'd picked up the dinner tabs too. It seemed only natural you should pay for the groceries, or at least offer to, something we both know I wouldn't have allowed, but the mere offer would have been a welcome gesture, even if it amounted to the performance of politeness because we both knew what the outcome was going to be and were therefore correct— efficient? to be commended?—for skipping to the natural conclusion. Perhaps that quiet honesty is at times the best sort of honesty.

This morning, I bought apples, lettuce, eggs, potatoes, onions, carrots, milk and yogurt for the kids, bison sausages, and gluten-free bread, and when the vendor under the pink tent asked if I wanted anything more than the vegan loaf, I pointed to the brownies and said, "Are those good for dealing with heartache?" to which the man with a mustache larger than his entire mouth said nothing immediately, before laughing, before that laughter subsided and his face contracted into a befuddled look that gave his mustache even more disproportionate importance, and before he relaxed into a smile that served as a prelude to "Choco-

MIDDLE SPOON

late is good for most things." But as he was ringing up the sale, I glanced at the price tag: nine dollars. For one brownie. Ben, you would have blanched and then ridiculed me, and I would have grown self-conscious about my class-jumping—I wholeheartedly agree nine dollars for a not-large brownie is beyond the pale of social mobility—but later, you would have eaten half the brownie. Yes, you would have, and I would have enjoyed watching you.

Come to think of it, those Saturday mornings were my favorite dates with you.

"You know what," I said to the vendor this morning, "I don't want the brownie after all. He wins if I eat it." The *he* was *you*. The vendor smiled knowingly, like a fellow human, and possibly a fellow gay.

Based on the number of people—eleven—I've reached out to in search of solace this past week, I've deduced that nearly everyone in the world knows the devastation of heartache, and of the nearly eight billion humans on Earth, I wouldn't be surprised if 1.5 billion of them are experiencing acute heartache right now, today. My own grief is weightier than I could have imagined; I'm cowed by the collective weight of billions of units of sadness.

It was my portion of this global burden that precipitated my logorrheic transparency at the open-air market this morning, even with the carrot and potato vendors, from whom I've always kept a healthy distance because of the insincerity of their farm-to-table quirkiness. "Are these good for heartbreak?" I said again, this time with a tray of orange and brown vegetables in my hands and a wide smile across my face, hoping to engender amity, but the hipster couple with four arms and four fingerless knitted gloves, who probably have master's degrees in the agricultural sciences from a prestigious university and who'd probably gotten up at three a.m. in order to drive several hours from rural Pennsylvania to set up their white tent in my overpriced Brooklyn neighborhood, responded nothing and handed back to me the metal tray of roots and tubers they'd just weighed before waiting for me to tap my credit card. The reactions from the other vendors—egg, apple, meat, microgreens, cider, and butternut squash—were also muted.

I don't know why I keep burdening anyone who'll listen. I assume it's because I don't want to feel alone. I want to know that support exists if I need it. I want to know I won't feel this way for long. I want someone, anyone, but in particular a stranger, to hug me. I want nothing more than to connect with someone based solely on this experience and yet never be obliged to explain who I am and where I come from and how married I am and how many children I have. I want recognition for my loss and a sympathy that undoes the cruelty of it all.

In the previous sentence, I purposefully resisted labeling you as cruel. I gave the concept an amorphous and passive treatment, when, the truth is, you were cruel.

After the market, I walked into the park with thirty pounds of groceries hanging from my shoulders, found a quiet place far from the dog shit, and wept. I sobbed without pause and without an end in sight, until it occurred to me that crying isn't always cathartic. I was merely a body overflowing with fear. I became so afraid of my unbridled emotions, I pulled the phone from my pocket and called Jenn, the sort of friend I might call only once for a matter like this, someone who's perpetually busy—she's a high school principal in Chicago—and has little time for chronic gloom or doom but will do her damnedest to solve a problem. She was groggy because she had no reason to be awake on a Saturday at 7:45 in the morning. "Darling," she said when she realized I was crying. "I could spend hours talking about this." Then she, too, began to cry.

"You need to question heteronormativity," she offered after we'd composed ourselves. "You're allowing outdated and insufficient constructs to define your relationships. Also, I'm sorry to be the bearer of bad news,

MIDDLE SPOON

but he sounds immature, this Ben human. Doesn't he see your marriage was the picture of happiness he respected *because* of the freedom it gave you to date him? He didn't understand the process that led to him."

The part of me that wanted to speak favorably on your behalf shrank beside the part of me that wanted foremost to be consoled.

Jenn recommended, in rapid succession, no fewer than four books, one YouTube therapist, and a documentary. I scrambled to type them into my phone while she carried on about the unique nature of my marriage. "The depth between you two has bestowed an uncommon degree of liberty on you both. Ben met needs your marriage couldn't. And you could only be the person he loved because of the way you've been loved. Do you understand what I mean?" she asked.

I said yes, although I hadn't yet processed her words.

Jenn wished me well but didn't offer herself for future support, which was in a way also reassuring.

After I'd finished sniffling, I made my way home, unpacked the groceries, and fried some eggs for my family, all of whom were glued to their respective devices, enjoying the enclosure of Saturday morning. My husband, probably aware of my bloodshot eyes, offered to handle the kitchen duties, but I demurred, preferring instead to keep busy, focusing on concrete, repeatable tasks—cracking, slicing, toasting, setting, pouring—and grasping at the moment of clarity and empowerment that Jenn had gifted me. (Goddess bless you, my dear, sweet Jenn!) Because of her I was able to get through today.

—Me

PS: I'm left thinking of my use of the word *enclosure*, which I invoked because I wanted to evoke a cozy-like containment. The word's historic meaning, however, is also relevant. It once referred to private property. The Enclosure Movement, which began in the eighteenth century, in Europe, aimed to take common spaces and public lands and parcel them into private property. It succeeded. And now, here we are, hundreds of years later, living in a society held hostage by European ideas, with a smallish public park and an anemic strip of sidewalk that hosts a once-a-week farmers market. Everything else is private property. Everything. Even the streets are effectively free parking for people's private property, which I am reminded of on a weekly basis, when my car-owning neighbors voice their opposition to the ten parking spots lost to the various farmers' trucks on Saturday mornings. The Enclosure Movement has effectively relegated human interaction to the margins, leaving us very few public places where we can have a good cry.

Dear Ben,

A few years ago, my husband had sex with a friend of ours and didn't tell me about it, and to make matters worse, it was unprotected sex, and to further aggravate the situation, he proceeded to have unprotected sex with me without first divulging his indiscretion.

In the interest of time, I'll give you a brief summary of nearly a year of couples counseling:

1. Having two children is stressful.

2. I can be an emotional handful myself.

3. At the time, we weren't having much sex because we were both busy with work and said children.

4. My propensity to communicate openly and my desire for brutal honesty don't always outweigh the environment of fear that I engender, which is to say, my husband was afraid to tell me because I don't handle stress particularly well and because he was afraid I'd leave him.

Also of note, our friend was on PrEP, my husband did all the available STI rapid tests before having sex with me, and our mutual friend is not our friend anymore.

I'm no longer angry at my husband or at our ex-friend, to whom I briefly introduced you at an East Village bar last year, without making mention of our history—he was the guy with the septum piercing, suspenders, and receding hairline, all of which led to a conversation later in the night where you told me you were put off by septum piercings and suspenders but found receding hairlines sexy. No, I'm no longer angry or hurt, but the infidelity weakened the resolve I'd always felt to defend the borders of my marriage. I'd spent the better part of two decades suppressing desires, feeling guilt about those desires, anxiety-ridden whenever we fell prey to those desires, but now, I care less. I remain a committed hypochondriac and a reluctant, damaged ex-Catholic, but I've learned to cut myself slack. You, Ben, are possibly a consequence of that years-ago infidelity and the ensuing softening. Although I had my husband's consent to meet you and to have sex with you, the truth is I didn't require it because he hadn't required mine. In a way, my enlightenment was born of pettiness.

I never told you this because I was ashamed. Cheating is nothing short of a massive diss. And I didn't want to announce to anyone that I'd been insulted by my own husband.

—Me

PS: Tonight I'm going to make a gluten- and dairy-free clam chowder. I was going to make it with fresh clams, but the seafood market sold out. The recipe is quite simple, so if everyone is pleased with the dish, I'll add it to the monthly meal rotation.

PPS: My sister is coming to town next week for work. We're going to grab lunch in Manhattan, and I think I'll use the occasion to tell her about you.

Ben,

The clam chowder was a success. The kids, my husband, even Lucas and Akil, despite their previously established aversions to seafood, asked for seconds. That they even came over at all was a surprise. My husband, who's been motivated by concern these days, invited them. "The distraction will do you good," he said after the doorbell rang. I suspected the distraction would serve him well too. It was a minor intervention that I would have rejected if I'd been consulted, and about which I was grateful not to have been consulted.

We met Lucas and Akil at a sex party thirteen years ago—a loft-style apartment with an enormous freight elevator in the Financial District. Nothing of a sexual nature happened between us, but we left the bacchanal at the same time and followed each other to a bar nearby. They've since become two of our dearest, as well as our only polyamorous, friends. Sexually open from the start, their relationship evolved just before the pandemic, when they each started dating other people for extended periods of time. At a distance, I've deduced that their setup works well because they don't have children or pronounced jealousies to contend with. As far as they're concerned, love and sex are best practiced without any of the traditional encumbrances imposed upon relationships.

"Fuck the next guy you meet," Akil suggested after the kids had gone to sleep.

"Fuck two or three guys," Lucas added. "No better way to get over Ben."

"I know tons of guys who think you're hot," Akil said before taking his phone out from its small Hermès case. "I can pull up their profiles now."

I caught Lucas glancing at my husband, who nodded and briefly raised one shoulder and two eyebrows, curiosity more than consent.

"I'm not ready to move on like that. Besides, I have the best partner in the world right here," I said while caressing my husband's thigh. "Why go looking for more trouble?"

Barely had those words left my mouth before I began to cry. Akil got up from the couch and approached me. He knelt down on one knee and took both of my hands in his. "Aw, babe," he said. "I'm so sorry you're feeling this. It'll pass. But honey, he's not worth it."

"I kn—"

"No, I mean it." Akil gave me a hard stare. "Ben was not worth it. We never saw what you saw in him. He's kinda cute and funny, but he's not serious enough for you. You need to date men, not boys."

I didn't know how to respond. On the one hand, it felt good to hear you be denigrated even if the reasons took me by surprise. And yet, the urge to defend your honor was stronger and in some ways tangled up in my integrity. Instead of responding, I scanned the room for evidence. Lucas's face was twisted into something awkward that told me he agreed with Akil. My husband simply looked down at his own feet.

"Does everyone feel this way?" I asked.

"Lots of us do," Akil said.

Lucas moved to the edge of the couch, to be closer to me. "Listen," he said, "Ben grew on us, but if it's just the sex, maybe you can get that elsewhere."

"It wasn't just the sex. I loved him. I still do. Just because we're years apart and our politics and music tastes don't always align doesn't mean we didn't have something good. I saw it. I felt it. You guys barely knew him."

I felt stupid in the silence that followed my declaration. Had I been oblivious to how wrong you and I were for each other? Did your friends feel the same way?

MIDDLE SPOON

When Akil and Lucas were preparing to leave, Lucas hugged me for longer than he ever had. "I hope we weren't too harsh before," he said.

"Yes and no," I responded.

"Good," he said in return.

"I—"

"Also," he whispered, "I liked Ben more than Akil did. But we agreed tough love was the better way to go today."

I patted his ass with gratitude and said nothing.

Afterward, I encouraged my husband, who'd been nodding off during the last twenty minutes of our group conversation, to go to sleep. "Cleaning up will be a nice distraction for me," I said. But it wasn't, because as I placed each dish, each glass, each spoon in the dishwasher, as I wiped down the counters and scrubbed our wooden cutting boards, and as I soaked our pots with soapy water, I wondered about the spectrum that my feelings for you occupied and if there was a band after lust and before love. Was it infatuation? Was I addicted to how you made me feel? If so, I might be able to replicate that sensation with someone else. If, however, I was in love with you the person and not you the idea, I had no choice but to wait for this pain to pass.

—Me

Ben,

The shock and denial are wearing off, and I'm beginning to taste anger. It wasn't me but you who made false promises and declarations that amounted to real promises: *I love you. Don't doubt me. Join me on this ride.* I see now that you meant one of those amusement park teacup rides where everyone spins the wheel at the center, the ones that require strength and coordination to set the heavy container in motion, until suddenly the speed begets more speed and one no longer has to spin the wheel. I never stopped turning the damn disc, but you took your hands off without my realizing it.

At the start, I found it difficult to trust you—something intangible about your unfocused mien or the furtive manner in which you peeked at your phone when you thought I wasn't looking—but my doubts were always minor in comparison to my affections for you. If ever I thought you were being less than straightforward about your feelings, in particular the ones you had for me, or your actions, in particular those you carried out when I wasn't around, I reminded myself that our limitations and boundaries were different. It would have been a losing prospect to compare my needs and desires to yours.

None of this should surprise you since I never kept quiet about any of it—my honesty, I must admit, meets the threshold for illness. I thought if I shared my fears, you'd reassure me. If I made light of them, they'd be easier to vanquish. Alas, the very thing I was preparing for, the very thing you told me was not in our cards, the thing I had recently convinced myself was not going to happen happened. Nothing has ever dropped from

MIDDLE SPOON

the sky with less warning and more heft, despite my neck being perpetually craned upward, despite my gaze being locked on the clouds.

You had a *realization*, you said. A realization? Christ, Ben! Realizations are for people on yoga retreats and acid trips. They're selfish and don't allow for mutual growth. This is *real* life. No *-ization* necessary.

Nine days ago, it occurred to you, seemingly from nowhere, that you wanted more of me, and you would only be happy if I was yours alone—in other words, if I wasn't married and didn't have children.

It took a year for this to dawn on you? That's akin to passing out on the couch with a slice of pizza in your mouth and being surprised by the ensuing heartburn, or not understanding an uptick in crime after a recession. You knew I wasn't going to leave my husband. I was clear about that from the start: I don't have unprotected sex, and I'm not leaving my husband. I think I said as much shortly after I met you. Remember?

It was January, the start of the semester, and our department invited your studio to present illustrations for the faculty, so that we might consider more reader-friendly methods for communicating health data. I grumbled about the poor use of our time, but I was almost immediately taken with your confidence and your snug pants. Afterward, the dean suggested I ask you about how to present my research visually in my upcoming book: *A Rise in Hierarchy, Blood Pressure, Glucose, and Cholesterol: How Inequity Breeds Illness.* I sat with you in our cafeteria until the workers asked us to leave. "Want to grab a drink?" I asked.

We walked to the martini bar down the street, and when we sat, you said, "I'm not a fan. They're too harsh."

"You haven't had a good martini," I responded.

Our stares then lingered long enough to let me know that we would never be colleagues. My hands trembled ever so slightly, which forced me to sequester them under my thighs.

· 79 ·

After that day, we started texting regularly, and in one of those texts, I told you about my aversion to condom-less sex.

"Have you heard of PrEP?" you responded, and then followed up with a laughter emoji.

"The drug that protects against only one sexually transmitted infection? Yes, I have heard of it."

"Lol."

"It's condoms for me," I responded.

A few months later, when we were lying in your bed, after we'd had sex without a condom because you'd gotten tested and had intimated that I was your only sexual partner, you asked me about my intentions.

"As they pertain to . . . ?"

"I don't know. Feels like this is more than what I thought it was going to be, no?"

"Yeah," I said. "It's more."

"What about your marriage?"

"What about it?"

"Is it forever?"

"It is. There's no scenario in which I leave my husband."

You didn't respond, and I knew I'd hurt you by confirming what I'd been implying all along. But I was in no position to equivocate. If I'd been noncommittal, you might have started imagining a future I couldn't have with you, instead of the one we could have together. I never told you that I, too, had begun to daydream about the unachievable.

Your quiet that day was a far cry from what you'd told me shortly after we'd met: "I've dated married guys before. I'm into polyamory. I'm built for open relationships." You said it plainly, as if your comfort were intrinsic or generational, as if I were outdated. I distinctly remember that conversation because I was surprised at how early it was happening. It was only our second week of knowing each other, after our fourth afternoon

MIDDLE SPOON

of sex. You were walking me to the bike rental station on your street, that ugly street where you live—ugly because it's surrounded by forgotten public housing, aka public housing the city has decided doesn't exist, aka public housing in New York City. The entire time we walked, you painted yourself an expert, and I recall feeling inadequate but also intrigued. Maybe I was safe to try something exciting and taboo with an expert. But now I see how wrong I was: humans are humans, and relationships aren't guided excursions. Neither of us knew what we were getting into.

As it concerns your epiphanies, I probably shouldn't be surprised. After all, you'd ended us once before.

"We never see each other," you'd said in the parking lot of Walgreens while we waited for your PrEP refill.

"I'm trying," I responded, surprised we were having this conversation because my life had become a circus act in order for me to see you as often as I'd been seeing you.

Your face became the top of a soup dumpling, as if you were about to jump out of a plane or communicate something revolutionary or hopeful, but instead, you said, "You will never be able to give me what I want."

You didn't have to say *time* or *marriage* or *children* because they were all implied.

A shitty thing was happening, but at least it was happening on a street in NYC, I told myself, one trafficked in equal proportions by Puerto Ricans, Mexicans, white gays, and vagrants, who, together, served as a cinematic backdrop for our troubles. "Let's keep trying" was the only thing I could think to say on the hottest July day I had ever experienced in my life.

"Keep trying? And what, fall in love?"

I didn't have the guts to say that your hypothetical scenario might well have been my reality. I also didn't mention that I had two steaks, four potatoes, and one plastic box of arugula in my backpack. Instead of litigating a case for me and for us, I said nothing more and walked back to the G train. The humiliation of groveling atop rejection would have been much worse than that of rejection alone.

When we reconnected, nearly six weeks later, your tune was different, a nearly unsingable aria of tolerance and possibility:

"I realize,

I can deal with this.

With your situation.

I don't need

More than what you're offering."

In other words, you knew what you were getting into. But here we are, at the end of another carousel of epiphanies.

Ben, I'm married with children and cannot give you all of me because children require care and because husbands of twenty-plus years deserve respect, even the ones who cheat once. The irony, of course, is you had me. My children and my husband went without. You had my attraction, my love, my esteem, and most importantly, my attention. I ran around this city like a bike messenger with a swollen prostate and overdue rent just so I could be with you. For the better part of this fraught year, you have been at the center of my world. I couldn't have given you more if I were a single man with no responsibilities on this blasted Earth.

Do you know how long I would have lasted with my husband if I'd bailed whenever uncertainty entered the room? Do you have any sense of how relationships work? You're supposed to air your concerns, discuss them, address them. No wonder you've never been with anyone for more than a few months. If doubts are your threshold, I fear you'll be alone for a long time.

I'm sorry. That was out of line. I didn't mean it.

Perhaps I meant some version of it.

Can you see why I'm upset? You allowed yourself the time you needed to come to a conclusion that wasn't a conclusion. It was the plot, the pre-

MIDDLE SPOON

cursor, and possibly the problem that we had to solve: you fell in love with a married man. We were doing an unsanctioned and unexpected thing in an already strange world that wants desperately for us to be uneven but never odd. Choosing the outcome we'd both feared all along deprived us of the journey.

This is madness.

"But we're happy. Why leave now? Make it make sense," I said when you broke up with me again, nine days ago. I was standing outside of Nico's school, phone to my ear, not far from all the other parents who held phones to their ears, waiting for band practice to end.

"When the time comes, you'll choose your husband over me, and that'll destroy me."

"Who says we have to make a choice? I can love you both."

"I've never seen that before, anywhere."

"It exists, and if it doesn't, we can be the first."

"I'm sorry, I can't."

"Over the phone? You're breaking up with me at five thirty p.m.? It's eighteen degrees, babe. My hands are freezing. It's a goddamn Tuesday. Nothing more inauspicious than this."

"I'm sorry," you said again.

You asking me (without asking me) to leave my family after only a handful of fairy-tale months was wild. As well as unfair. Choose the person who has been here for me for most of my life and the children who depend on me for their own lives, OR . . .

Or.

Or the guy who keeps all his doubts to himself and periodically dumps me when he gets scared? Do you see what I mean?

I'm not a gambler.

· 83 ·

Yes, it was going to get harder. It always gets harder before it gets easier. Repeat after me: harder before easier before comfortable before secure. You didn't kill a dying thing. You killed a fledgling thing. One is noble; the other, cruel.

I'm furious. And yet, in your shoes, I might have done the same.

—Me

Ben,

Today, the prime minister of the Netherlands apologized for his country's participation in the transatlantic trade of African people, one of the few European nations to ever formally acknowledge its tainted past. The media painted the mea culpa as a win for human rights, but a representative from a Dutch culture organization that focuses on Black art and history was underwhelmed. "What about reparations?" he asked.

Ben, you know how I feel about reparations because I never shut up about the topic, how essential I believe they are for our collective future and for the immediate health and safety of Black people, how anything short of full reparations amounts to continuing the legacy of slavery and upholding anti-Black racism. And before you call me out on my holier-than-thou policy positions, give me some credit. I know what I sound like. I know how intolerable I am to most people and their eyebrows, including yours, which became adept at showing displeasure whenever I went on as I have just now. Even in this moment, when I am trying so desperately to will you back to me, when I'm trying to keep up a semblance of communication, however one-sided, I still can't help but tuck in this sort of irrelevant aside. But it's not irrelevant, is it? Besides, if we were lying in bed right now, I'd mention the article about the Dutch prime minister and his underwhelming response to slavery.

Anyway, I texted you this morning. Or was it yesterday morning? Frankly, who cares about time when it's been reduced to measuring the duration and depth of my agony? It's been ten days since we last saw each other. Ten days of fitful sleep, more booze, less food. Ten days of daydreaming, of time traveling to a moment when I could have preempted our woes and instead doubled down on my reassurances. A lifetime, ten days.

"This is goddamn crazy. I'm sorry" is what I texted.

Tickets for a Broadway show we'd both wanted to see were on sale at a discounted price. Rather than sending you the link, I spent the morning vacillating—rationalizing, composing, deleting, beginning anew—for fear you'd think I was suggesting we go together instead of receiving my misguided, too-soon message as an attempt at salvaging a friendship from our wreckage. After an hour of midlevel spiraling, I abandoned my plan and went looking for you on social media, which I hadn't clicked on for nearly a week because I didn't want to know what you were doing, and I didn't want you to know that I knew what you were doing, and to be honest, I didn't want you to think I cared. But on that morning, I succumbed to my curiosity—*obsession* by another name, ever as sweet—and perused your social media, where you'd happened to post something simple yet cryptic about how sad and angry you were. At whom? About what? Why were you choosing to be sad and angry when you could have been neither? Neither! In that moment, the healing we were trying to accomplish through distance felt like a foolish exercise in elementary psychology. That's when I sent the confounded text—"This is goddamn crazy. I'm sorry"—without the link to the cheap tickets.

If you know me, you must know regret's arrival was instantaneous. The text had started as a minor, possibly noble, act, but once it began its voyage, its potential for consequences grew. I tossed the phone onto the couch and paced the living room before circling the kitchen table on my way to the bathroom. Beneath the spray of hot water, I put all of my energy into not thinking about you or my poor decisions. There was nothing to be done. My message would result in one of three possible outcomes: good response, bad response, no response. And I could weather all of them, I told myself.

MIDDLE SPOON

While leaving the bathroom, still dripping, and nonchalantly making my way to the living room, as if there were an audience of people ready to critique my lack of willpower, I did my best not to care about my phone and what it might reveal.

The small icon that tells me I have a message was waiting for me. It was you. Or better, an avatar of you. You'd sent an emoji, the one with a tear streaming down its face. The worst emoji. The most ambiguous one. It has a partial smile, which, alone, communicates happiness or something closer to contentedness, but when accompanied by a tear, gives pity precedence over sorrow. Please, Ben, don't pity me. That would be worse than hating me, worse than loving me too much, worse than never having known each other. I don't think you were pitying me. You were probably multitasking. You were working from home, too daunted by the cold to go to your studio space, and doodling on one of your large sketch pads, something for the front page of the business section of a newspaper or the cover of a magazine that wants to obfuscate greed with primary colors and cartoonlike illustrations, and although you wanted to respond to me, you didn't have the brainpower to communicate anything more empathic or interesting or honest than that emotionally stunted emoji, which, in hindsight, accurately depicted your emotional quagmire. Or maybe you were blowing one of the dozens of men who live in your phone. The men who ding. The dingers. You were probably also adhering to our pact of silence while trying not to ignore me.

With every fiber of my being, I regret that message, not only because of how little it elicited in response but because I sense I'm only entitled to a few slipups, and that situation didn't call for a message. I should have gone for a walk instead. I should have lifted those weights in my room. I should have written this email.

—Me

• 87 •

Dear Ben,

"Are you okay?"

That's what my husband whispered into my ear this morning, after he'd run his lips along my spine and kissed my neck.

I'd been awake for an hour, but without much energy to get up.

"Yes," I responded. "Why are you asking?"

"I know you're not feeling well. I see it in your face. I feel it in your silence. Nico and Jules have both asked me if you're in a bad mood."

"It'll get easier. I have therapy again in a couple of days. I'm doing my best to talk and stay active and not spiral."

"I'm here, whatever you need. I love you."

"I know, but I don't feel comfortable talking to you about this."

"It doesn't bother me. I know what we have, and I'm not threatened. I'm just worried about you."

Despite his reassurances, I couldn't say anything. Now that I can't combine these halves of my life, I want to keep them as far apart as possible.

I tucked my hand between us and ran it up his leg, until I found his cock, which I massaged gently into something no longer soft. Then I dug around for the lube in the bedside drawer and squeezed some onto my hand before climbing onto him. We both came rather quickly because we knew the kids would be up soon and because it was the first time we'd had sex in nearly a week.

After he'd gone to work and the kids were at their respective schools, I went to the holiday market at Union Square and bought four scarves and four pairs of earrings for my aunt, mother, sister, and sister-in-law, and

MIDDLE SPOON

five handcrafted wooden boomerangs that none of my nieces and nephews would be strong enough to operate. On the way home, I stopped at the grocery store for dinner's missing pieces: chicken leg quarters and endives to dress up the lettuce I'd gotten at the farmers market over the weekend. Once I'd unpacked everything, I sat on the couch and tried to read, but I couldn't focus long enough to get through an entire page, so I scoured baking videos on YouTube. While waiting for the batter to rise for a Victorian sponge cake, I watched half of *The Banshees of Inisherin* and drank my fourth glass of water.

My husband is working late tonight, so I'll pick up both kids after school. In twenty minutes, I'm going to meet Nico at the bus stop; together, we'll make our way toward Jules.

—Me

Hi, Ben,

I've been wondering if procreation is the primary reason human animals are designed to feel so strongly for one another. After all, early and intense bonding in a human dyad predicts species success. Two people who are fiercely connected will create life and possibly care for it long enough to survive. But what about us gays? What is the evolutionary point of our bonding?

What little I know about biological explanations for same-sex attraction is that our mothers' wombs were naturally suspicious of our Y chromosomes and, with hormones as their weapons, involuntarily blunted the effects of the foreign entity. In other words, our hapless haploid gametes fused into a zygote that our mothers waterboarded with estrogen and other messenger molecules. Ben, your mom and my mom tried to make us girls. The effect has been to gift us with the evolutionary markers for successful procreative mating, ipso facto, we're into men, and we seek to bond with them as if we were going to procreate.

I didn't intend for this to be a pseudo lesson in evolutionary biology— an incomplete lesson, not least of all because of its lack of clarity on lesbians, trans people, and intersex folks. I came here to tell you I turned a corner, and that I might well be on the road to recovery.

This morning I had sex with my husband. Not a particularly monumental achievement when you consider that we had sex yesterday or when held up to your record. I have no doubt you've been with more than a couple guys since our breakup. Maybe a different person every day. Perhaps one guy before every meal.

MIDDLE SPOON

There I go. Judgmental and angry. Or judgmental because I'm angry. And now angry for being judgmental. It's my new normal. Yesterday, I caught myself rereading our old text messages, and I became enraged, threw my phone across the room, hit the wall, cracked the screen.

My inability to care for myself and to not judge others is also not what I meant to dissect here. I'm writing because I want you to know that today's sex was different. Today, my husband and I were returned to our old selves, or at least our pre-breakup selves. After you left, my libido vanished, which I'd initially attributed to the depressive state, but I think guilt might have also been at play. My body had somehow come to feel that sex with my husband was tantamount to cheating on you. Before you, sex with him was great. During you, sex with him was great. Sex after you has been a disequilibrium.

I don't know if you realized how entirely I revered your body, but I suspect you did. Whenever I walked into your apartment, you'd make your way to your couch, sit back, and plant your feet onto the cushions and butterfly your legs just wide enough for your shorts to become simultaneously revelatory and coy—your apartment's climate was hospitable to bare chests and loose mesh; although terribly inefficient, NYC heating systems do provide these moments of ecstasy. I'd approach you on all fours and begin my ritual of worship, kissing your feet, then your legs. I'd dig my teeth subtly into your knees, caress your inner thighs with the tip of my nose and my lips, one side, followed by the other—I am nothing if not fair. I'd bury my face in the spaces between your legs and your balls, I'd inhale deeply, and you'd ask, *Is that yours?* And I'd say, *All of it.* This banter, too, was an evolution. Only a few months prior, I'd be the one to ask, *Is that mine?* and you'd respond, *Yes.* After the inversion of our dialogue, I knew I'd carved a safe space in your life and that you were happy

· 91 ·

for me to be there and for me to have a certain degree of ownership over your being. I was happy too.

For over a week, happiness has been inaccessible, but I believe I have turned a corner.

It began last night. My husband and I went to three holiday parties—two queer parties and one gay one—and although you weren't going to be at any of them—our social spheres overlap only ever so slightly—I entertained the possibility that we might cross paths. New York nights, after all, shrink to just a few busy streets and train lines; queer New York nights are even smaller still, a couple of corners, a few crowded subway cars. When we exited the C at 14th Street, I scanned the horde of Brooklynites streaming from the L, hoping to see you against the backdrop of white tiles and yellow beams. Out in the night air, while I gripped my husband's arm, I continued searching. On 8th Avenue, we popped into a liquor store with wooden shelves and bright lights, full of decorative ivy and partygoers, none of whom were you, despite my dutiful inspections of their outlines, their festive attire, and their faces. We bought a bottle of expensive gin and had it wrapped in silver and festooned with gold to match the season. All the while, I wished for you to appear, to be holding your hand in the Village, headed toward Julius', to take our places among the twinks, the survivors, the leather-clad, the lascivious, the potbellied—all the types that constitute our brethren.

The first party was a classic affair thrown by a gay couple in their early sixties who live in one of the stately Village apartment buildings that had probably lost a third of its residents by the early '90s. Their home was small but expertly decorated, what I imagine an episode of *Mad Men* to be, but with flair, which is to say, oaky and gay. The crowd skewed older, fifties through seventies with a few forties and even fewer thirties in the mix; there was a chance you might be there. You're a social butterfly with an admirable appreciation for queer history and older men; it wouldn't have been shocking to learn that someone in the room was an acquaintance of yours. It was an apartment replete with history, camp, and good cheer. Heaven for you.

Only moments ago, I had to take a few minutes to collect myself. I'm in my living room watching the World Cup final: Argentina v. France—"the battle of insufferables," I heard someone say on the bus a few days ago—and as I was composing this email (in a recliner, in a corner, by the bookshelves, just out of view of my husband, my kids, an aunt, and two cousins visiting from Jersey), I was felled by a lightning strike of emotion after imagining you in your apartment with some other—NO!

No! No.

This fish has been tagged. And I'm throwing it back in the water.

The holiday party hosted by the Village gays was a detailed affair: antique bowls and bountiful platters of food placed in convenient nooks throughout the apartment; small bottles of prosecco in a bathtub full of ice; a muscly, hairy-chested bartender in a bow tie who kept a small stack of flyers promoting his drag show next to the cocktail napkins. I positioned myself at the tall, dark-wood table near the front door because it was the only station with dairy- and gluten-free hors d'oeuvres. I spent most of the night pulling grapes and skewering shrimp with my toothpick, wondering how many I would have to eat before I was in danger of iodine poisoning.

I knew a few of the people in the room, but it was an hour or so before two bona fide friends arrived: Dana, a software engineer who works with my husband, and Beatrice, her wife, a spinning instructor at an Upper West Side gym, increased the lesbian quotient by 25 percent and the

BIPOC quotient by 60. Of the thirty-five people at this party, five of us weren't white. And yet, there were somehow more non-white people at this Boomer/Gen X gathering than at the millennial holiday parties I'd attended with you earlier this month.

Beatrice and I tucked ourselves into a corner, nearer to the shrimp than the grapes. She was unfazed by my subtle, albeit continuous, crustacean dissections because once Bea focuses on something, her attention is unwavering, often making one feel as if she were looking within them, which she must have been in this instance because only moments after she began asking me the most basic of questions—How's work? How are the kids?—I was overcome with sadness—a gale more than a tornado—and recoiled from her and the shrimp. "Oh, honey," she said, "I had no idea." Beatrice, who I imagined dealt out this sort of coddling on a regular basis, although usually to rich, sweaty women in leotards who were no doubt drawn to her social-worker demeanor, squeezed my hand. Her kindness did nothing to elicit words from me, but it had the unintended effect of inducing my tears. She responded by nudging me away from the throng of holiday revelers and the soft pyramid of shrimp. Whether she knew what I was feeling or was simply supporting a friend in distress, I don't know, but something about the way she called me *honey* and the way she pressed my hand between hers confirmed for me that some things are universal, and some people have superhero levels of intuition.

The second party was in a darker, smokier, larger space—a brownstone town house in need of new floors and a paint job—than the previous party; the crowd sparser, younger, and more muted. We arrived early and sneaked out without saying goodbye after thirty minutes. The fate of the second party is not unlike the fate of the unplanned middle child: arrives

MIDDLE SPOON

too soon; leaves the parent without enough time to recover from the first; is therefore less appealing; by default making the subsequent one a relative improvement.

My husband was tired and encouraged me to go to the third party alone.

"I want to invite Ben, but I know it's a bad idea," I said as we waited for the C train. I affected a casual tone to undercut the impulsivity of inebriation and to overcompensate for the shame I felt about confiding in him about you.

"If you think it'll help," he said before grazing my hand with his.

Whether my husband's equanimity is genetic (nature) or the result of his upper-middle-class upbringing (nurture) or simply epigenetic (a confluence of the two) remains a mystery.

"Don't you feel any anger or jealousy when you think of me with Ben?" I'd asked him months earlier. He was sitting at the kitchen table behind his laptop when I'd come home from a night out with you.

"Not really, no. As long as you don't leave me and you continue caring for our kids, I'm not worried."

"Not even a little bit?"

"I just don't want people thinking I'm being taken advantage of. I want everyone in our lives to know I'm on board with this."

"I'll be mindful of that."

"Thanks," he said before his gaze returned to his laptop screen.

"I can't imagine my life without you," I said in order to reassure him, but also because it was true.

He placed one of his hands on one of my thighs, without shifting his gaze from the computer. "Me neither," he said.

If Partner A can create this space for Partner B, is Partner B then wrong for making use of it?

"So you think I should call him?"

"I don't know what to say," my husband responded as we waited for the delinquent C train last night. "I'm biased. I believe you'll get over Ben if you hold out, but I also hate to see you this way. I'm sure he'd be happy to hear from you. I bet he knows he made a mistake by ending things, but he's too embarrassed to walk it back."

I was hoping something to that effect, but I'd been afraid to say it aloud. "You think?"

"Maybe. Why don't you call Traci? She'll give better advice."

Traci is a grad school friend who spent a decade as a case manager at a health clinic before becoming a photojournalist and then a wedding photographer when her local newspaper folded. She knows my entire history, and she's called me twice a day since you and I broke up.

"I don't believe in games," she said in the moments before the C arrived. "This guy is a major part of your life. Message him."

"Really?"

"Yes, as long as you accept that eight of the ten possible responses are going to devastate you. Are you ready to feel that right now?"

"I don't know, but the train is here. Thank you for answering. Call you tomorrow."

I was tired of making mistakes, but while I walked the babysitter home, I composed this text: "Going to a friend's party in Midwood. Join me, please." I agonized over that message for five blocks, until the subway app on my phone dinged to let me know there was a Q train arriving in six minutes, followed by another in twenty-six minutes. I deleted the draft message, hopped on a bike, and sped to the station to catch the earlier Q.

As I raced to the station, all I could think was, *How can there be a twenty-minute gap between trains on a Saturday night? A city of nearly eight million people, where a handful of billionaires became super-billionaires during the pandemic, and yet, we have to wait twenty minutes to get to south-*

MIDDLE SPOON

central Brooklyn. I wonder if this sort of thing upsets you. I find it maddening. Absolutely bonkers. You've been privy to my tirade on FDR's wealth tax during World War II, no? Perhaps you haven't. And now, you never will. A real shame because disseminating this bit of trivia is one of the few things I do that has the potential to make the world better. Not to put too fine a point on it, but I'm convinced that if our country's taxation history were popular knowledge, we might demand more of our elected officials.

The final party of the night was the most casual of them all—loose, flamboyant, expressive, boozy. Everyone there had been a professional dancer at some point in their lives; most moonlighted as massage therapists of one kind or another. They were liberated, queer, and low-key pompous: descendants of the East Village art punks. I rode the elevator with a lithe, sweet-faced one who'd just returned to the US from touring an Anne Teresa De Keersmaeker show throughout Europe. Our eye contact was brief and electric; his boyfriend—shorter, septum piercing, you would have been turned off—stood beside him, distracted by his phone. For the hour that I remained at the party, his gaze floated through the room, ready to engage, but instead of reciprocating, I did my damnedest to mingle and remain distracted. I treated that warm two-bedroom, two-bathroom co-op apartment like a farmers market; I told everyone everything. Apart from the host (Miguel: former neighbor; now, friend), the other guests were strangers, but none of them were made uncomfortable by my candor. Each volunteered a story and advice. Each became briefly quiet while reliving their own moments of pain. They were an expressive lot, the kind a cynical person might find annoying, but I was grateful to be in their midst and to be so readily cared for.

"I'm sorry for dredging up ghosts," I said to the guy with thick sideburns and a gold lamé shirt who'd recently divorced his partner of ten years.

"No, no. It's okay. Let's focus on you," he responded.

I then posed the question I've asked most often since our breakup: "Will this pass?"

And he gave the most frequent response: "Yes."

"Soon?"

"Depends on the relationship, but sooner than you think. Just when you least expect it, you'll get past this."

Every day, I've wanted this, for someone to take a leaf blower to the vapor of pain that's enveloped me, for someone to extend their arm and point toward a not-so-distant place and shout, *I see land! Over there!* Last night, several people did.

I am a scientist at heart. An emotional scientist, but a scientist nonetheless. It is this disposition that tells me the irrationality of my emotions has a chemical source—dopamine, oxytocin, cortisol, epinephrine. It's been only a short time since we broke up, not enough for the deregulation of chemicals to return to stasis, but in the interim, I remain afraid because of the magnitude of my feelings and the consequent lack of self—NO!

No! Fish, tagged. Back into the ocean you go!

At least my fears trigger a reaction that leads me into communion with others. Being alone on top of feeling alone would be more than I could bear.

I left the last party without kissing the guy who might have reciprocated. I tried to muster the desire. I took a hit of pot and drank a glass of wine. I sustained eye contact a few times. But I couldn't shake you, so I left with the business cards for several Feldenkrais, Alexander Technique, and Reiki practitioners. No fewer than eight cards.

MIDDLE SPOON

This morning, I woke again to a warmth on my back. It was the way I often woke you. My husband's body moved with the confidence of expectation. "Happy birthday," I whispered. I hadn't forgotten his birthday, but I hadn't recalled it either. When we'd first dated—mere boys then— we'd stay up till midnight on the eves of our birthdays and share a toast or a kiss. But last night, I climbed into bed quietly, with no memory of his birthday, praying I wouldn't interrupt his sleep. This morning, however, my mission was clear: to reassure him I hadn't stopped loving or desiring or needing him.

My mission was hardly a grueling one. Sex with my husband is a pleasure. Easy too. Not boring or simple, just easy. What one might expect of anyone who has been studying the same material consistently for so many years. But if I were to tell you that I got lost in the moment and forgot you existed while my husband and I fucked this morning, I would be lying. Ben, you were there too. I wasn't fantasizing about you being in bed with us or even alone with me; I was merely talking to you. Another of the endless and wordless one-sided conversations I have been having for days. But the occasion of my first true love's birthday was not the time for soliloquizing. And so whenever it dawned on me that I was imagining a tête-à-tête with you while my husband was inside of me, I conjured up other scenarios: a foursome from a few years ago; the fantasy I have of my husband and I spit-roasting the short, curly-haired barista up the street; my high school boyfriend; Lee Pace; Colman Domingo; Lee Pace with Colman Domingo. Until suddenly, I was thinking of nothing but merely enjoying every second and every inch of my husband.

That's the turned corner I was referring to at the start of this email. Briefly, I flirted with a cute guy at a party, and I was able to have great, even if initially labored, sex with my husband. I suspect this means I'm on the road to recovery, or that recovery is possible.

Argentina won the World Cup. The match was brutal, amazing, and probably not something you care much about. Also, I glanced at your social media accounts and saw a picture of you and someone I don't recognize, a cute-enough man with a trim beard, in front of a theater marquee. It was the musical I'd wanted to text you about a few days ago. I didn't believe for one second you would have posted that picture if we'd been together still. It was an *I'm okay and having fun* picture. I understand. I have the same urge, to let you know I'm alive and still handsome, but I fear it'll come across as trying too hard to display that I'm alive and still handsome.

I hope you had fun, Ben. I hope you don't feel what I'm feeling. I hope I hope I hope is all I do these days. But please believe me when I say, whatever comfort I might derive from knowing we're both a mess is undone when I think of you alone and in pain, a pain to which I've contributed. I'm sorry.

—Me

PS: In 1942, the president asked a Republican-led Congress for a 100 percent tax on incomes over $25k (about $400k when adjusted for inflation today). One hundred percent. That's not a typo. The Republicans, to no one's surprise, balked, but FDR held firm, instead using the subsequent years to build popular support for his tax plan, cannily riding the pro-labor movement sweeping the country. Only then did he return to Congress, which acquiesced to a 94 percent tax on incomes over $200k (roughly $3M today). That tax rate remained in the 90 percent range until the early 1960s. It hovered around 70 percent until Reagan, when it dropped to 50 percent, and then 31 percent under the first Bush. Currently, the highest tax bracket is nearer to 37 percent. Think about that for a moment. When people talk about making America great again, they

MIDDLE SPOON

often mean the halcyon days of the 1950s, but many don't realize that our government was collecting a massive tax on the rich and redistributing it through public goods and infrastructure. To truly make America great would be to tax Elon Musk and the hundreds of other billionaires in the United States 100 percent on every dollar they earn over a billion. Imagine what we could achieve with that sort of tax revenue. Everything "universal"—basic income, college, pensions, health care, day care, pre-K, ADA compliance, internet—all the reparations, Land Back programs, a thirty-six-dollar minimum wage, arts funding, smaller classroom sizes, mobile mental health clinics, high-speed trains from Bangor to Baja, and more Q trains to south-central Brooklyn.

PPS: Earlier, I referenced the inefficient radiators in your apartment, but I'd be remiss if I didn't also acknowledge that these wrought iron relics were designed to give off an unbearable amount of heat so that the denizens of overcrowded apartments would be forced to open their windows during cold and flu seasons and thus increase airflow and reduce the risk of contagion. Tricking people into making positive health choices is a risky strategy, but sometimes it works.

PPPS: I gave some thought to Fred's encouragement about writing a screenplay but quickly realized I didn't have the patience or the desire. Instead, I jotted down some ideas in a journal, fanciful notions about us, and I have to admit that it's been fun to feel creative in the midst of all this pain.

Hey,

Tonight was the first night of Hanukkah, which means very little to me, but I know it's a tradition you keep. I'd planned to gift you a toothbrush, not as a passive-aggressive gesture but as a reparative token. On our last night together, after the all-white-people-except-for-me parties in Williamsburg and Bushwick, after the romantic back-patio dinner, where you and I shared the dan dan noodles and the gin martini that you loved and I didn't have the heart to tell you was too floral for my taste, after our drunken cabs and walks between parties and home, after you insisted I stay at your place, which was the first time you ever insisted, after I took my wedding band off and slipped it onto your finger, after you slipped your grandfather's ring onto my finger, after we walked back to your place married in our own way, after I lay on top of you while you lay on the floor of your living room, after you adhered to your bedtime ritual—brushing, flossing, face washing, moisturizing, water drinking, ibuprofen taking, back stretching—I asked if you had an extra toothbrush, since I hadn't intended to spend the night because of Nico's sore throat and low-grade fever and my guilt about leaving my husband with the sole responsibility for his care.

"You can use mine," you said. I didn't know if you were being generous, lazy, or kinky. What I do know is the brush had exceeded its life expectancy, bristles curved out like a dried-up bouquet of supermarket flowers, the kind I used to bring you every time I came to your place because the first time I brought you flowers you commented that no one had ever done so, and I got a kick out of bringing you one or two or three single-stem flowers—whatever was in the bucket at the market: roses,

MIDDLE SPOON

carnations, tulips, daffodils—so that you could keep adding them to the bouquet on your counter, a bouquet that only ever died one or two flowers at a time because of my constant replenishing, until, that is, you joked that I probably shouldn't bring you flowers any longer, which was fine by me because they were expensive, so I began gifting you fruit, usually bags of clementines, but sometimes grapes, and I truly don't know how you felt about that, but since you never complained I continued the ritual.

You offered to let me brush my teeth with your toothbrush, which surprised me, even in my inebriated state, because the gesture was so unlike you, the you who used to be turned off by my pecking you on the lips if I hadn't finished chewing whatever bite of food I hadn't yet swallowed. If such a minor act could rile you up, surely the sharing of a tool used to scrub the insides of our mouths was beyond the limits of your comfort. For what it's worth, I, too, was less than thrilled by the prospect of cleaning my mouth with your beat-up brush, but I wasn't turned off by it either, and as you watched me brush my teeth, you said, "This is maybe the most intimate thing that has ever happened to me," which is when it occurred to me that I had never intentionally brushed my teeth with my husband's toothbrush because, well, we've always had both of our toothbrushes handy. As a matter of fact, the few times I'd inadvertently begun to brush my teeth with my husband's toothbrush—twenty-two years is fertile ground for anything—I immediately withdrew it, spit, and gargled whatever I could find (mouthwash, hydrogen peroxide), which, in retrospect, couldn't be more absurd, considering where my tongue has been as it concerns the ins and outs of my husband's body. This isn't to say that my love for my husband is lesser or has never achieved the degree of intimacy you and I reached that toothbrush night. I guess I'm saying there was something special between you and me, something unique. Or maybe something powerful had gripped us. Both things could be true. Three things could as well: special, unique, powerful. And although one day we would have been boring and full of routines, the beautiful moments we had during our brief time together suggest to me that our voyage could have been long.

Have you ever seen *Jerry Maguire*? It's a terrible and wonderful '90s film with Tom Cruise and Renée Zellweger. It put her on the map and scored Cuba Gooding Jr. an Oscar, but more importantly, it gave Regina King her first mainstream canvas—I mean, white mainstream. Ben, when I think of how long it took the establishment to recognize King's work, I could scream. In fact, when she became an award-show stalwart a few years ago, I found it difficult to rejoice because I couldn't help but think of how she'd been great for nearly thirty years—thirty years!—and only then was she getting her due. (Yes, I can hold on to these sorts of grudges, but only when they don't concern me directly. I'm a very forgiving person otherwise.) In any case, the beleaguered, work-obsessed Maguire, played by Cruise, much too belatedly realizes that what he lacks in life is love; but as it happens, he already had love in the form of his wife, played by Zellweger, from whom he had recently separated. In one of the final scenes, he bursts into the living room of Zellweger's home, which she shares with her sister, played by Bonnie Hunt, another woefully underrated actor, and declares his undying, rather practical, and somewhat self-serving love. "You complete me," he says famously.

Well, you are, in a way, my Renée. No, I don't mean we are two halves of one whole; I mean I am composed of many parts, and I believe you were one of them. And knowing you exist in this world will make living in it more difficult than it already is if you're not with me, if you're not occupying the space I've been inadvertently reserving for you.

Happy Hanukkah,
Me

Hi,

Judging by Nico's horrid and infuriating mood this morning, I've concluded he's unhappy at school. Although there's nothing extraordinary about protesting the routine of Mondays, Nico's persistent grumbling about getting up, about getting dressed, about eating breakfast, and about going to school is a jarring transformation for a child who, until recently, couldn't wait to get to school. According to my mother, it's to be expected at the dawn of adolescence, the difficulty of transitioning between the freedom of weekend and the constrictions of weekday. "You were like that too," she told me recently. But I worry it's something else. What if he's afraid? What if something has happened?

As I poured Nico's cereal, he railed loudly against alarm clocks and Mondays and commuting and Ms. So-and-so and not having an iPhone and all things school related. My husband and I traded animated eyebrows, but we both resisted engagement with the child. After all, Nico's mutterings are an innocuous form of angst relief, even when they continue while he dresses and while he packs his bag and while he brushes his teeth—if he brushes his teeth—and while he puts on his shoes, as they did this morning. Nico, however, chose silence on the long walk to the bus stop, a silence I indulged because of my own mourning.

I was contemplating going to you after Nico got on the bus—cursed bus that adheres to its own schedule irrespective of what appears on the MTA app. My fantasy involved knocking on your door, coffees and egg sandwiches in hand. I don't know if you like egg sandwiches, but I know you love eggs because you eat them every day. They aid your weight-training regimen, you've explained. You also drink supplemental powders

· *105* ·

that I find suspect, probably because I've conflated them with performance-enhancing drugs.

"It's just whey protein," you said after sighing at my scrutiny.

"It's cheating."

"Cheating who? What?"

"I mean, it's like cutting corners. People have had exceptional physiques since the beginning of time, well before these highly unregulated powders existed. You don't need them."

"I don't have to spear my dinner or climb a tree for the perfect banana. But you're right, I don't *need* them. I *want* them. What's this about?"

"Nothing. I just want you to be healthy."

"That's literally what I'm doing."

What I didn't tell you was that the consistency with which you exert yourself feels excessively body conscious, as if the adolescent twerp inside of you were perpetually settling a score. What I didn't tell *myself* was that I can't walk past a mirror without pinching back my shoulders and tightening my abdomen, and your disciplined gym routine makes me feel old, flabby, lazy, and therefore out of your league. Also, I fear you're not lifting weights properly or at least not in a way that won't further exacerbate the chronic back pain in your life.

In any case, this morning, instead of reliving a year's worth of moments with you, I made an effort to remain focused, as it concerns parenting, and I did something unorthodox or maybe just unexpected—I included Nico.

"Kid," I said, "in the interest of transparency, I want to share that I've been low this past week. I'm going through something—grown-up stuff—but don't worry because I'm going to come out of this fog."

"Okay," he said without looking up.

"That's all any of us can do—keep going," I continued. "One foot in front of the other. Do you know what I mean?"

MIDDLE SPOON

Nico's solitary nod was unconvincing, so I kept at it. "For example, you're not happy about going to school today, and I don't fully understand why. You don't have to tell me—you can, if you want, but you don't have to. But if you keep pushing through these low moments, you'll find yourself in a better place. Let's believe that together, okay?"

Again, Nico remained quiet, and I probably should have trusted that he'd heard and understood me, but it was cold out and I was mesmerized by the visibility of my breath, so I insisted further—"Okay?"—to which he responded angrily, "Okay!"

By the time we'd walked the six garbage-strewn (bags, containers, food scraps) streets to the bus stop, the moment had passed, and Nico seemed in better spirits; his head was up, his eyes no longer trained on his shoes. A small win, I thought.

I'm a dad, not a jilted lover! might be today's mantra.

Last night, there was another holiday party—Eric's. Remember? He sent me a message yesterday afternoon, asking if I was going to attend, which of course made me wonder if you'd put him up to it. You wouldn't go to a party if you thought I'd be there. I told Eric I couldn't make it; then I told him about the breakup. His response consisted of a broken-heart emoji, and: "Ben's not coming to the party after all, but he didn't say anything about you two breaking up. Sorry."

Afterward, I concocted my own elaborate narrative: When you learned I wasn't going to the party, you decided to show up. To your surprise, I arrived there just as you were leaving, and I convinced you to grab a drink with me at the bar next door. It was awkward at first, but it took only half of our martinis for us to settle into our norm. I rested my hand on the table, allowed yours to rest atop mine. After we finished our drinks, I stood up and kissed you. "Let's go back to your place," I whispered into

· *107* ·

your mouth. On your couch, I ran my fingertips carefully along your bare shoulders and watched you tremble, a prelude to my lips running the length of your back, your favorite, and while I wanted that to be a prelude to more, you dozed off—you are not a night owl—and I rolled over to my side of your bed and passed out, hopefully not snoring, and around 1:45 in the morning—it's always 1:45 in the morning—I awoke, and somehow, you did also, and we kissed passionately for a few minutes, while rolling around, first you on me, then me on you, then both of us on our sides, tangled, before dozing off, and around 3:15—it's always 3:15—we did that again. This time, however, you went back to sleep, and I remained awake—our relationship has been abysmal for my sleep—fearing I'd oversleep and not get home in time to take Nico to the bus stop, not get home in time to slip into bed beside my husband, so that if Nico or Jules walked into our room at 6:30, they'd be none the wiser about my previous night's whereabouts, and so, at 5:45, I climbed over you, went to the bathroom, peed, didn't flush—the acoustics in your apartment leave something to be desired—got dressed, and then returned to you and your neck, which I kissed lovingly before settling onto your lips and whispering *I love you* into the room's darkness. This is exactly how our last night together had transpired, except, when I kissed your neck for the last time twelve days ago, before moving on to your lips, you preempted my declaration of love with your own. You had been somewhat frugal with those words, which never truly bothered me—they're just words, after all—but whenever you said them, I'd feel good. And it was on that cloud of goodness that I floated home, which is to say I biked over treacherous terrain (Brooklyn potholes) to my husband and kids, never once imagining it had been our final morning together, and it's how I would have made my way home this morning if we had both gone to Eric's holiday party last night.

It's going to be a cold day, Ben. I hope your radiators are working adequately. I hope your hectic Monday morning meeting goes well. I hope you have plans tonight so that you're not in your head. I hope you're not waiting until you're hangry to eat. I hope you're getting over me. I hope you never get over me.

My day, if you're curious, will consist of trying to convert the statistical analysis of the effects of wealth inequities on life expectancies into prose, of trying not to think of you, of visiting my friend Dee in the hospital—day seven and still no hospital bed; NYC has more billionaires than free hospital beds; we're all going to hell, Ben—of going to buy some pants for my husband, of dinner with my family, of drinks with a friend—another mutual friend, another curation of my emotional state so that this friend's interpretation of me to you makes me look good, aloof, strong.

What have I done to deserve this?

—Me

PS: The other day, Nico and I waited twenty-four minutes for the godforsaken bus. It's somehow both unconscionable and perfectly logical in our kleptocratic city. I happen to be an upper-middle-class person who prefers to ride the bus and subways, and consequently has minutes, goodwill, and critical analysis to spare, but most of the people who rely on buses are working-class and poor, with limited options, which is certainly why the buses run as they do, but how are we expected to stop driving cars if we can't rely on mass transit?

PPS: *What Have I Done to Deserve This?* is one of my favorite Pet Shop Boys songs and Pedro Almodóvar films. Same title, unrelated. I know for a fact you'd never heard of either because when I asked you what your favorite Almodóvar film was, you looked up to the ceiling before asking, "Who?" And when I played the Dusty Springfield–assisted track, your face curled up into an oblivious smirk. But you liked the song. And you liked *Bad Education*, the Almodóvar film that we watched in four parts across two weeks because you kept falling asleep.

> *I bought you drinks, I brought you flowers*
> *I read you books and talked for hours*
> *Every day, so many drinks*
> *Such pretty flowers, so tell me*
> *What have I, what have I, what have I done to deserve this?*
> *What have I, what have I, what have I done to deserve this?*

Dear Nico,

I went to therapy this morning, something I've been doing twice weekly for several years in the hopes of managing and one day overcoming my anxieties. During today's session, you were the topic of conversation, and Fred—one of my two therapists—suggested I try writing you an email.

"And say what?"

"Tell him what's going on."

"He's too young."

"Don't send it. Do as you've been doing up to now. Imagine yourself having a conversation with him. What would you want to say if there were no restrictions or taboo subjects or age-specific sentiments?"

And so, I came home, while you and Jules were at school and Pop was at the office, and I started writing.

I wonder how old you'll be when you read this email, or if you'll ever read it. Despite your age and the sensibilities that accompany that age, I've tried my best to be transparent with you. I haven't sugarcoated much, I haven't baby-talked to you, I haven't shied away from elaborating on complicated themes and ideas. And yet, there are limits to what you might understand and to how I should share information with a child. You knew, for example, that Ben was an important person in my life, but I never felt at peace telling you that I loved him or that I wanted him to be a part of our family. I wasn't ever affectionate with him in your presence, for fear of scaring you or Jules or of disrespecting Pop. I guess I'm writing to you now because when you're older, I'll want you to know what

111

was happening in our lives. I'll want you to know how I was feeling. And maybe if I'm forthcoming with you, you'll be the same with me.

"He's my dad's good friend."

That's how I heard you describe Ben. We were waiting on our stoop, you and your classmate a few steps below me, sitting just far enough apart on the reddish stone to avoid the dried pigeon poop between you. You'd both spent the afternoon in the living room working on a poster board that listed all the countries the US had invaded—a global studies assignment by Mrs. Hernandez, one of the few progressive teachers at your school. Ben was coming over for dinner, and as I waited for him and your friend's mom, I stood behind you, swatting away October's early evening mosquitoes, trying my best to give you privacy while simultaneously eavesdropping on your conversation with Etta or Gemma—I don't remember her name, only that she detests cheese sticks, and her mother is Panamanian.

"Who's that?" Etta-Gemma asked after Ben had waved to them, fistbumped you, and walked past to greet me. That's when you referred to him as my good friend.

My dad's good friend stuck with me because the *good* was unusual. You could have said *my dad's friend* or simply *Ben*, but you chose to give him a more vaunted stature. Perhaps it was your way of acknowledging the importance of my relationship. Your way of saying, *Dad, it's all good*. I admit I was touched as well as uneasy. I feared I'd made you an unwilling coconspirator in this caper and that you were left discomfited by your vague understanding of my relationship—due to my vague explanation of my relationship—giving you no choice but to overcompensate and employ the simplest, most elementary of adjectives: good.

MIDDLE SPOON

"Ben is more than a friend," I'd said to you a few weeks before the stoop incident with Etta-Gemma.

"What do you mean?" you responded.

"He's special," I said.

"Like Pop?" you asked. We were, as is our MO, waiting for the bus, pandemic masks around our chins, ears bent by the elastic loops.

"No, Pop is his own category, but Ben has become someone I care about. You've noticed, right?"

"Yeah," you said and lowered your head.

"Are you upset?"

"No!"

"Embarrassed?"

"A little, maybe."

"It's okay. We can talk about this whenever you're up for it."

The silence was short-lived: "Dad, are you going to leave Pop?"

"No! Absolutely not," I said, feeling like one of the many gum stains on the pavement beneath us.

My response took the starch out of your little face. You were relieved but refused eye contact. Without much of a plan, I opted for an extemporaneous primer on open relationships and polyamory.

After I'd ceased blathering, you said nothing immediately, but then surprised me with a question: "Are Abuelo and Abuela in an open relationship?"

"No."

"Are Uncle Lucas and Uncle Akil?"

"Yes, actually. They are."

That seemed to settle you, knowing our good friends were members of a club your dads had just joined. Afterward, you listed every couple you could think of—aunts, uncles, neighbors, schoolteachers, Marge and Homer—all of which were closed relationships. Again, I felt as if I were

· 113 ·

matriculating you and Jules into yet another minority group you hadn't asked to join.

"Are you okay?" I asked after I'd allowed impatience to interrupt your processing. You nodded. Then you looked up at me, eyes as large and as dark as puddles over pavement, which made me feel smaller than I'd already felt.

While I contemplated my next move, which surely necessitated something sage and confidence-boosting on my part, you said, "Can I play with my Switch when I get home?"

Despite our no-video-games-on-weekdays policy, I said, "Okay," but after you'd scurried off, I was left to wonder if you had manipulated the situation or if you simply needed something to comfort you.

We didn't talk much more about Ben in the months that followed because his transition from taboo concept to sentient being in our living room and occasionally around the dinner table happened quickly. You seemed to get along with him well enough—not as well as Jules, who was easily enthralled by the novelty of a new person, but your level of interest and respect were sufficient. I deduced that your momentary hesitations—that time you refused to return Ben's high five or when you closed the door in his face as we were bringing up groceries and claimed it was an accident—were merely your attempts at being protective of Pop. Whenever I asked if everything was all right, you'd say, "Dad, for the millionth time, it's no big deal. Can you please stop asking?"

I took you at your word, and yet, even if *my dad's good friend* suggested an advancement on the matter of Ben, it was proof, too, of lingering discomfort. After all, you could have explained to Gemma-Etta that I was dating Ben; instead you curtailed the conversation, in fact ending it before it was given the opportunity to begin. Gemma-Etta asked nothing more.

MIDDLE SPOON

With adolescence looming, you didn't need to shoulder the weight of your father's romantic entanglements. If my actions have made your life more difficult or unpleasant or, worse, unsafe, I'm sorry, my love. I wish we'd had more atypical families and pairings in our lives, so that we might have normalized all this for you and Jules, the way we had with mixed-race families, adoptive families, and queer families. But here we were again, in the undesirable position of vanguard, with its unique set of dangers and discomforts. I can attest that being both a pioneer and a minority isn't a pleasant way to traipse through this life, but neither is it devoid of merit. Those of us perched on the tips of branches have unique viewpoints of the forest. Those of us at the front of the march evolve thicker, less penetrable skins. This is hardly the inheritance I wished to leave you, but since life is merely slings, arrows, buffers, and coping mechanisms, I will feel successful if I have prepared you for all of the contingencies with at least some semblance of proportionality.

None of this is to say that we wouldn't have adapted. Our family could have withstood its own growth. Logic suggests it would have benefited from another person in the mix. Another set of hands. Another mind. Another storyteller. Another cook. Another friend. Society would have done its level best to disabuse us of our unorthodoxy, but we would have persevered. We might have even thrived.

This email, however, isn't meant to be about polyamory. It's meant to be about heartbreak. You probably won't remember this (hopefully brief) period of our lives clearly, but you might recall one day that *Dad* was sad. After all, you and Jules have taken to worrying about me—*Are you cranky, Daddy? Are you mad at me, Daddy?* I've responded by telling you that I'm distracted, busy with work thoughts, a little tired, or just hungry. The truth is, this pain has made basic functions difficult, never mind good parenting.

Or partnership.

I haven't been as attentive to Pop either. I'm making meals; I'm dropping you off at school; I'm tucking you in at night; I'm holding Pop's hand when I lie beside him in bed or on the couch. But the activities of daily living have become a painting-by-numbers exercise. I'm a robot, a very basic android.

By the time you read this, I will be on the other side of the pain. I hope, too, that after I returned to a better state mind, I made an effort to talk to you about this beast called love, what becomes of it when it has been slayed, and what becomes of the slayers. I hope I did it in a way that made life more interesting and appealing and not anxiety-inducing.

It's funny that I've spent all of your short life worrying about the various permutations of pain that might one day befall you, without it ever occurring to me to worry that you could be on the receiving end of this, a pain from which I cannot offer protection. I can implore you to wear a helmet and to look both ways when crossing the street and to not drive after drinking and to not accept drugs from unknown sources and to never go to Times Square on New Year's Eve and to not wear contact lenses in the pool and to not have unprotected sex and to not walk toward an explosion and to not turn your back to the ocean and to not flaunt wealth in an impoverished area, but there's no prevention for heartbreak. You'll simply have to weather it when your turn arrives.

Or perhaps not. There might very well be buffers and coping mechanisms for this situation. Perhaps our financial security has given your brain an elasticity that's absent in mine. Perhaps having a strong community of friends and family to help absorb your pain will aid in your recovery. It's possible, too, your ability to pair up with the right people is keener than mine because of the aforementioned differences in our constitutions.

I hope all of this to be true. And if it's not, call me. Please feel safe

MIDDLE SPOON

enough, which is to say free of judgment, to tell me about your pain. I wish that for us.

All my love,
Dad

PS: While you and your friend Gemma-Etta were working on your global studies assignment, which I agreed at your behest not to micromanage, I couldn't help but peruse the internet, where I came upon an article claiming there were only three countries in the world in which the United States has never had a military presence or launched an invasion: Bhutan, Liechtenstein, and Andorra. Only three.

I emailed Mrs. Hernandez, your teacher, with a link to that article. She didn't respond, but I hope she finds a way to tuck that fact into the curriculum.

Dear Ben,

I'm drunk. Legally, but not wildly. I had three ciders; John had three IPAs. Just a few hours ago, we met at a bar in Brooklyn, perchance the bar where I celebrated my thirtieth birthday. It's incredible that I was once thirty. Come to think of it, when I was thirty, you were twenty-one. When I was thirty, I didn't have children. When I was thirty, I thought polyamory was an untenable extravagance for unserious and possibly degenerate people.

The place was dark and wainscoted with a long oak bar along one wall. A jukebox and pinball machine sat at the far end near the bathrooms, anachronistically labeled *Gentlemen* and *Ladies*. It was a large space, made even larger by how few patrons were present when I arrived, the kind of bar with a small but consistent slate of denizens who walk through the door at 4:15, assume their perches, and have forgotten their afternoons before dinner, a habit they've been practicing daily since before they moved to Brooklyn, since before they were priced out of the East Village, since before the Lower East Side became the East Village, fellow New Yorkers in whose proximity I enjoy being but with whom I never converse past a few pleasantries because their moods are redolent of the climate one encounters near a mountain's peak, the kind that shifts and traps without warning.

I arrived before John, and in those minutes, I made a pact with myself: I wouldn't offer up anything about us. If he were to ask, I'd say, *Oh, well, that relationship is no longer. It was sad to say goodbye, but it was certainly for the best. I look forward to reconnecting with Ben when feelings have subsided.* That's what I'd hoped to say.

John isn't a dear friend; he's more of an online acquaintance I see in

MIDDLE SPOON

real life a few times a year, an arrangement that suits us. I met John at a public health conference a couple of years ago, and you briefly dated one of his friends when you first moved to the city. John's a considerate person who always asks about me, my job, and my family before he offers anything about himself. He's tall and waiflike despite his robust appetite; his hair is an unnaturally vibrant red, and he wears combat boots every season of the year. But I don't want to spend too much time talking about John because he's inconsequential to all this, apart from having the honor of being the first mutual friend I saw since you and I broke up.

At first, the conversation seemed to be going in my favor. We talked explicitly about work and politics, with no sign that *us* would enter the arena, but after we'd reviewed all of the ills of the world and the public health industrial complex, he asked about *us*. "Oh, we broke up not too long ago," I said with an affected stoicism. He gasped and began immediately to give condolences, not only with his words but with his eyebrows— John's very expressive face and demeanor would make him an excellent ASL interpreter. His response confirmed that the news about us hadn't yet traveled, which I must admit was partly what had led me to him: I wanted to know something about your current state.

We continued talking, sipping from rounded pint glasses, atop our stools, which were at risk of buckling under the weight of his overblown attentiveness and my faux nonchalance.

"Honestly, I am eager to learn about myself," I explained. "I am becoming fascinated, in a detached sort of way, with grief's physiological manifestations," I went on. "This is a research study waiting to be proposed."

"Grrrl, the pain is real," John responded when I'd stopped prattling.

John was, on the whole, incredibly sympathetic during that portion of our conversation, recounting at length his own breakups, one in particular that had left him mourning for years. Years, Ben. I can't fathom feeling this way for even another week.

· *119* ·

John's support didn't only consist of it-gets-better reassurances; he also offered himself. He began by throwing just enough subtle shade (again, the eyebrows) at our relationship and you—"Ben's wonderful, but she's a messy girl. You were correct to break up. No shade, but his artwork doesn't do anything for me." Then, just when we'd decided to leave, he placed his hand strategically on my inner thigh. "I can help you forget him, if you want," he said.

The tips of his fingers awakened something in me, but I wasn't sure if it was arousal or fear. I scanned the dim space and its remaining souls, none of whom were concerned with what John and I were or were not doing. It crossed my mind to lead John into the room marked *Gentlemen* and accept whatever he was offering. I chose instead to laugh off his advances, pretend his intention had been nothing more than humor. To John's credit, he joined in my laughter before disappearing toward *Gentlemen* alone. When he returned, we exchanged goodbyes. He managed to miss my cheek and plant his kiss square onto my lips.

John's less-than-flattering assessment of you and our relationship will allow me to sleep well tonight. I feel in this moment as if I dodged a bullet; you were an exquisite bit of steel with the potential to thoroughly pierce me. I've been grazed, nothing more.

Speaking of ammunition, my husband believes that instead of trying to outlaw guns, we should outlaw the bullets, which can't be 3D printed and aren't protected by the Second Amendment. Seems too simple to be feasible, or so simple it has already been given consideration.

—Me

PS: Today was the third nonconsecutive day of no crying.

MIDDLE SPOON

———

PPS: As I was biking home from the bar, I missed a turn and ended up careening down Flatbush Avenue—terrible idea, considering the potholes, the traffic, and my lack of helmet—and I couldn't help but notice the number of empty storefronts. It's something I've been chronicling silently for years. All my life, really. This phenomenon, while hastened during the pandemic, preceded it too. It's a touchstone of gentrification. Greedy landlords raise rents, knowing they can attract wealthier tenants, in the process evicting long-term business owners, even if there are no tenants ready to take over the new leases. As a result, many of these spaces remain empty for years, which can only mean that the exorbitant rents paid by future tenants must cover the three or four years of no rent. Otherwise the greedy landlords wouldn't do it, right? In our scenario, you're the landlord. Not greedy, but maybe shortsighted. I was there, ready and willing to make you happy. I believe I was making you quite happy. Wasn't I? But you were thinking solely of your future. Yes, practicality is a virtue, but so is love. So is kindness. Why did you have to raise the rent so suddenly? Couldn't it have gone up incrementally and with a bit of warning?

Dear Ben,

On a mendacity scale, the lies I tell my mother, while unpleasant, aren't of an extreme nature. In fact, it wouldn't be inaccurate to call them obfuscations. After all, I often *am* preoccupied with looming work deadlines. I *can* be moody if I haven't had my morning coffee. And preparing dinner *is* a distracting endeavor. These are the lies—obfuscations—I've been repeating while on my way to the train or the grocery store, after I've dropped my kids off at their respective points of adieu, during a lunch break, and before dinner while talking to my mother on the phone, which is probably why I've been avoiding her lately, a choice I find preferable to the lying—obfuscating—I've been doing for the better part of a year and more frequently since you left.

I don't want to confide in my mother about everything that happens in my life, but I don't want our communication to be defined by taboos. Keeping you a secret has an air of shame to it because neither of my parents would abide by the notion of any person having an extramarital relationship. It's cheating plain and simple. And cheating is a sin.

It's giving immorality. It's giving Sodom and Gomorrah. It's giving degenerate.

No matter if I told my mother that my husband was aware and unperturbed by it, supportive even, she'd disdain us and polyamory at large— she'd roll her eyes at the very word. She'd be furious with my husband, too, whom she loves dearly. She'd see him as weak or stupid, a cuckold, and me as selfish and disrespectful. She'd worry about the welfare of her grandchildren. It wouldn't change her mind if I told her I considered you more than a distraction or sex, that I loved you intensely and wanted you

MIDDLE SPOON

to be a part of my family, and that I wanted her to welcome you for the holidays and help me figure out how to incorporate you into our lives so that you'd never feel a moment of unwelcome. It wouldn't make a difference. Her mind is her mind.

The roots of this intransigence aren't easy to address and, lamentably, are not all that interesting to contemplate. It boils down to imagination, or the general lack of it, and a pervasive societal unhappiness, possibly because of said lack of imagination. Capitalism and its focus on production and profit at the expense of personal, never mind collective, liberation has forced us to believe there are limitations that don't exist, but which rather conveniently line up neatly with religious precepts that have shaped society's moral code, in the process making it near impossible for anything outside of normality's small sphere to survive, in turn reifying the norm because of all the failed departures from its center. If we're destined to fail, our failure will then serve as proof of why we're destined to fail. Ben, you and I aren't together because of this very lack of imagination, and a touch of puritanism, which in and of itself was probably the result of feudalism or a similar system and the lack of imagination of those times. You had trouble telling people in your life about us because of this lack of imagination. I can't tell my mother about us because of this lack of imagination. You couldn't tell your own mom about our circumstances because of this lack of imagination.

To your credit, at least you told her I existed.

"I hope to one day meet this guy who monopolizes all of my son's time," she said to you over the phone, as I was frying chicken thighs.

"Maybe the holidays," you said to the phone, which you'd left on speaker on the counter between us, almost daring me to join the conversation.

Later, when I told you we hadn't discussed that possibility, your face got rosy, and you told me you'd only offered the holidays to placate your mother. "I'll deflect when the time comes."

· *123* ·

I'm sorry I never told you that I thought it was a sweet idea.

On another occasion, your mother inquired about my marital status after she'd spotted my wedding band in a picture you'd sent her. "Honey, you wouldn't date a married man, would you?" she asked.

"No, Mom, I wouldn't," you replied. I happened to be lying next to you, doing my best to conquer Sunday's crossword, on a weekend when my husband was away for work and the kids were visiting my sister.

"Babe, that's a death knell for any future relationship between your parents and me. Lies can come later but not at the beginning," I argued.

"I'll explain everything when the time comes," you said and made your way to the kitchen in your briefs. "It has to happen piecemeal," you continued. "You're the first guy I've talked about this seriously. I don't want to ruin things."

I was suddenly less concerned with your parents than I was with that minor revelation. I followed you into the kitchen. "I'm the first guy you've been serious with?"

You turned away from me and opened the refrigerator. "Do you want eggs?"

"Have you never been in love?" I asked.

"Hmmm, two eggs or three?"

"Not once?"

"Nope," you responded. Then you turned away again, but not before your face became rosy.

I didn't believe you. A person in his thirties with your extensive dating history and propensity toward sweeping displays of emotion had certainly been in love before. But why lie? You hadn't blurted out your response like someone who was trying to please someone else, as if to make me feel more important than I was or in order to mask your own doubts about us. You must have been telling the truth, because you're a competitive

MIDDLE SPOON

person, and in effect, you were admitting you hadn't had an experience I'd had.

Pride, too, was at play. You told the person you loved that he was the first person you'd ever loved. You could claim something I couldn't. Now you had the advantage.

But that wasn't an entirely correct interpretation of the situation either. What you never understood was that my love for you was unique and unlike any I've ever experienced in my life, even for my husband. Our love occupied its own space, making you, in a way, my first love too. A point to me.

Come to think of it, maybe I'm the competitive one.

—Me

Dear Ben,

You didn't find anyone to go with to the Adrienne Kennedy play. Your plan was instead to scalp my ticket, but I caught you just before you did. The Times Square crowd parted, and there you were. I said nothing while I watched the pools in your eyes fill and tremble. Then we sat in emotionally variegated silence for ninety minutes, periodically distracted by the inhumanity of legroom on Broadway, doing our best to focus on the travesties of history being depicted on the stage. Our elbows took advantage of the darkness to graze each other; midway through the show, our hands did too. Afterward, we seemed to float over the tourists back to your place.

I dreamed this last night, and when I recounted it to Sandy, my other therapist, she waited—four, five, six, seven seconds, like she always does—until she was certain I'd finished saying my piece.

"Be strong," she said. "Take care of yourself and do your best to stop worrying about Ben's well-being." She spoke to me with the softness of a hospice nurse in the final hours. "Your analysis of the situation—Ben's faults, your anger, your less-than-optimistic future—is beginning to show signs of self-preservation. These aren't pleasant feelings, but find strength in them. You're going to come out the other side," she added before her screen froze and the video call dropped.

When we reconnected, I asked Sandy what it would be like to see you. "In five or six months, will I be anxious? Or will it be nice to run into him because we're no longer in love?"

(Unlike Fred, Sandy is more amenable to my imagination and seldom gets exasperated with my thought experiments.)

"Seeing him might still produce an effect, but my hope is by then your survival instincts will have taken over."

"Will I want to get back together?"

"You don't want to let this man back into your life. Not unless he's ready to make concessions. But he's not going to. It's unlikely he'd get to that place in such a short period of time."

I've never met Sandy in person because she came into my life during the pandemic, and our short distance—we're only two stops apart on the Q—has neither prompted us to meet nor prevented us from developing a relationship richer than most of the ones I've commenced in real life. In another win for racial and ethnic concordance, as it concerns the patient-provider relationship, Sandy is Latina and an amalgam of Indigenous and European, like me. Sandy, however, is Cuban, which led to some initial consternation on my part because I knew there was a chance she might be the kind of Cuban who blames communism for Cuba's ills but says nothing about the US embargo. For the first couple of months, I steered the conversation away from the topic of my political leanings because I worried they'd taint our relationship. My fears were allayed during our tenth session, when she knocked over a glass of water onto her desk. In the ensuing chaos, she lifted her laptop and the computer's camera briefly scanned her bookshelf, allowing me to glimpse *Che Guevara* on one of the spines.

"I've been crafting emails to myself. They're addressed to Ben, but I don't send them. I thought it would be a good way to let out what I have inside of me, while also chronicling this experience."

"That's a wonderful idea. In my day"—Sandy is about fifteen years older than me—"we used to journal our feelings. In fact, I still keep a diary."

"To be honest, it started because I wanted to contact Ben, but Fred encouraged me not to."

"Fred? Is he a friend?"

(I've never told Sandy that I have another therapist.)

"Yes, Fred's an old friend."

(That was the first time I'd ever lied to Sandy.)

"Can I send you the emails?"

"Me?"

"It makes me feel good to hit send. And maybe they'll inform our sessions."

"If that'll make you feel better, sure, but I must warn you I don't have much downtime these days. I can't promise I'll read them—how many are you writing?"

"One or four a day, depending on the day. Sometimes they're very short. Sometimes not."

"I see. Well, that would be fine, but if I may suggest, please don't spend too much time dwelling," she said. "Expression is one thing; dwelling is another, and as far as I know, wallowing in pain has never helped anyone."

"I'll do my best."

"How about your mother? Have you told her? Last time we spoke, you wanted to come clean about Ben."

During our previous appointment, talk of telling my mother had been about announcing my relationship. Now it would be more of an autopsy. "No."

"Would you still like to?"

"There's no point anymore."

For the remainder of our session, I didn't feel at ease talking to Sandy about how I felt because I couldn't see my feelings as anything but dwelling. Not only a verb; a noun too. All of my subjective, internalized reactions have become a shelter, an encasement of sorts. Sadness, in particular, has crossed over into the realm of the conceptual or the meta. I'm sad about being sad. I'm sad about watching the movie of two people who

· *128* ·

love each other but can't be together. I'm sad about the prospect of those two people seeing each other years later and being so changed they barely recognize each other. I'm sad about how much shit my parents endured so that I could be middle-class, and somehow, I've been felled by a millennial with nice legs.

I'm spiraling again. Typical of me to take a virtue like introspection or an active imagination and transform it into a liability.

Let me stick to the facts: today was rougher than yesterday. This morning began with tears—a natural relapse, I told myself. Actually, this morning began with my husband gripping the bedsheets and wincing—a migraine—and I was left to manage the morning routine alone. After I dropped the kids off, it made impact, the godforsaken sadness. I felt as if I were flying through the windshield of a car in which you and I were the passengers. I moved slowly through the air in an arc, but because of my trajectory, I had no idea what had become of you. Were you still in the car? Had you already hit the pavement? Had you rolled off onto the side of the road? None of it made sense because our metaphorical path had been straight, recently paved, and empty. And still, we crashed.

I couldn't make it up the stoop, so at eight thirty this morning, with my head in my hands, I bawled my eyes out because the loneliness was unbearable.

The fifth friend I called answered—Ileana, Ily for short; you met her and her family briefly in Prospect Park this summer. I could hear she was preparing her squawky toddler for day care—stern cajoling alternating with fruitless pleas—but I was too upset to be considerate and allow her to escape. Instead, I recounted the summer breakup, the reconciliation, the magical four months, the unexpected breakup, and the subsequent suffering, all the while sobbing. Ily did her best to console me, but her squawky kid was quickly transforming into a wailing kid. As a parent, I was able to commiserate; as a werewolf, I felt of a piece with the child.

· 129 ·

Throughout that four-and-a-half-minute phone call, sadness and shame were my ventriloquists, and I couldn't tell where they ended and I began. You see, Ily works at a police watchdog organization in New York City, and yet, there she was wrangling two crying humans while simultaneously readying herself for the day's grueling work.

"Banana feet! Put on the other shoe first, baby—"

"What?" I said.

"Oh, hon, I'm so sorry you're going through this. It's the absolute worst. I remember these feelings as if they happened to me yesterday."

"It'll pass, right?"

"No!"

"What?"

"*This* shoe on *this* foot—yes, of course it'll pass."

Perspective was what I needed. I had an army of good people on my side, deployed with the sole objective of coddling me. Days and days and days of coddling. I, a married father of two, was nursing the heartache caused by a paramour. You. A fucking sidepiece, I kept telling myself. I wasn't waiting for police officers to be convicted, fired, or even reprimanded for the murder of someone I loved. No, I was no one dealing with nothing.

I'm trying. I'm really trying to pull myself together. I can see my pain has a short shelf life and a limited reserve of empathy from my fellow humans. I know I have to heal before the support disappears.

—Me

PS: I must remember not to share the emails with Fred or Sandy that mention Fred or Sandy.

Dear Ben,

Last night, after giving a guest lecture in the epidemiology department of a local university, my host, a fellow professor, invited me out for dinner because he was embarrassed that the university's only compensation for my efforts had been two one-way subway passes and a bottle of tepid water.

We went to an Italian restaurant on the Upper West Side, where my options were few because of the menu's near total incorporation of dairy and gluten into every item. I was nevertheless content with the distraction of his company and the firmness of the sautéed calamari.

The epidemiologist, a stress researcher with a thin mustache and several earrings, proved funnier and more interesting in person than he'd been over email or during the class, where he'd merely introduced me and sporadically prompted the students to ask questions. Over dinner, he joked with the servers about my allergies—"Don't worry. He won't die immediately"—and he was as fluent in *The Real Housewives*—"an American fascination with seeing women battle one another; that's all"—as he was in the work of Balzac—"a realist who was good enough for the socialists."

The epidemiologist was originally from Seattle and had moved to New York because of his husband's job—a film scholar who was no longer his husband. "Initially, I was embarrassed to divorce after years of fighting for the right to marry, but we simply weren't compatible. He's a Scorpio, and I'm . . . not," he said before taking a sip from his 2017 Nebbiolo. "And we're both bottoms," he added after he'd swallowed.

In these sorts of social situations, I prefer to absorb rather than to emit, to listen instead of sharing the details of my life with someone whose character I've yet to ascertain. But on this occasion, I hadn't eaten much all day, and I, too, was sipping the Nebbiolo, so I told him everything. About us, that is.

The epidemiologist was enchanted the way a child is during story hour, eyes wide and still and through which I could see the gears turning in his mind.

"Your husband sounds like a saint," he said when I'd stopped speaking.

"He's an atheist."

"You know what I mean."

"He's very patient and naturally unfazed by most things."

"Has he also had sex with Ben?"

"No."

"Did he want to?"

"He said he didn't."

"Did Ben want to have sex with him?"

"I don't think so."

"Did you want them to have sex with each other?"

"It crossed my mind, but only fleetingly."

The truth is, I had envisioned you and my husband together, but it never seemed wise to broach the issue. I figured if you or he were interested in each other, you should be the ones to say so.

The epidemiologist had an endless trove of questions and curiosities. *Where did I get my energy? How was the sex? Had I always been vers, or was it a midlife mutation? What did the children think? What did our friends say? What happens if Ben or my husband brings someone else home?* And when it was all done, when the last bite of the tiramisu had vanished from his plate, he invited me back to his place for a nightcap.

Because I knew my husband and children were already asleep and because I wanted something, anything really, to distract me, and because I was drunk enough to be marginally less forlorn about you, I said yes.

• *132* •

MIDDLE SPOON

We sat on a gray couch dappled with cat hairs, our shoes and socks off, the top two buttons of our respective shirts undone. Periodically, which is to say, whenever they were three-quarters empty, he refilled the small crystal goblets he and his ex had bought at an estate sale upstate. The liqueur was Italian, familiar, and had a medicinal flavor and a name redolent of a Dumas tale: Amaro Montenegro, your favorite. The epidemiologist and his ex had spent their honeymoon in Bologna, where they'd gone to a distillery or winery or wherever it is that these liqueurs are made, and they'd had several cases of this amaro shipped home. "When we separated, he took all that remained except for four bottles," the epidemiologist explained before pouring us more. "This is the last of it."

"I don't want to drink up your reserves."

"No, it's fine. I learned recently that they sell it at a place in Williamsburg. Problem is I'm never in Williamsburg."

I thought of you immediately, and I was relieved this man didn't spend time in your neighborhood, despite his self-declared status of sexual bottom, because you'd undoubtedly see him on the apps, if he's on the apps, and you'd certainly ping him or woof at him or send him a nude, because that's your way and because this man is objectively attractive: tall, sinewy, gold chain around his neck that gives him a tough-guy aura, tattoos on his knuckles that bolster the tough-guy persona, dark-skinned, and a sexy gap between his two front teeth. I didn't want to imagine you having sex with my, in a way, colleague, so in a moment of absurd jealousy, after I'd become aware of something taking shape in his crotch, I considered placing my hand on his knee and then sliding it up his thigh until I'd have no choice but to take the bulge in my hand and make its acquaintance. Instead, I jumped up from the couch, in the process kicking the glass coffee table on which our drinks rested. "I'm sorry!" I shouted about the averted catastrophe.

"Are you okay?" he asked.

• *133* •

"Yes. I should get going. I have to be up early tomorrow."

"That's too bad," he said before squeezing his own bulge and looking me directly in the eyes. "I think we could have fun if you stayed."

"I have no doubt. But I—"

"I could help you forget your boy. Being slutty helped me when my ex left."

"I'm not ready," I half shouted. "But thank you for the offer."

My words hung between us for more than a reasonable amount of time because we both wanted them to. But soon they vanished.

The epidemiologist was gracious about the rejection, even offered me a ham sandwich: "You barely ate anything at dinner." While he disappeared to the bathroom, I perused the white built-in bookshelves that occupied an entire wall of his living room, half of which were stuffed with books; the other half held a mix of videotapes, DVDs, and Blu-ray discs. Hundreds of movies by some of my favorite filmmakers, and in alphabetical order: Allen, Almodóvar, Altman, Anderson (P. T. and Wes), Antonioni, Bahrani, Bergman, Bogdanovich, Bong, Brooks, Buñuel, Burnett, Fassbinder, Fellini, Ford, Forman, Fosse, Lean, Lee (Spike and Ang), Leigh, Leone, Linklater, Loach, Lynch . . .

"My ex took most of them," my host said when he saw me eyeing the shelves.

"Why are entire letters missing from the alphabet?" I asked. "And then they just stop abruptly at L."

"I took these from the moving truck when he wasn't looking."

"Sneaky."

"He took our entire music collection!"

"Bastard."

"You have no idea."

I continued running my fingers along the spines of the movies, while he observed me at a distance.

MIDDLE SPOON

"There aren't any women here."

"What?"

"No female directors."

"The motherfucker kept those separate. Women and Romanian new wave directors occupied their own shelves. I couldn't find them on the truck," he explained while walking toward me. "See anything you want? To borrow, that is."

I shook my head.

Later, I regretted not accepting his offer, which in hindsight probably had an ulterior motive. It was his way of keeping in touch, something that might prove useful if ever I get over you, or if things become even more desperate and I require a new experience to wipe my slate clean of you.

—Me

Dear Mom,

Perhaps I haven't given you an opportunity to show me who you truly are. Who, after all, says love has to be endearing and transformational for the participants alone? Why not for the spectator too? If I'd explained about Ben and me, you might've simply rolled your eyes at the sheer complication of polyamory but ultimately surmised that *Gays really have this figured out better than the rest of us*—you'd equate poly with gay, the way you equate trans with gay and drag with gay and Richard Gere with gay.

"I've never seen two people respect each other and communicate like those two. Maybe it's because they're gays."

You whispered this to Dad in the kitchen years ago, after overhearing us discuss something mundane related to Nico's day care schedule. Your observation, which exited your mouth reflexively, like a yawn or hiccup, became a starting point for my theorizing. If there's truth in what you said, a truth to be extrapolated, I have a hypothesis: removing hierarchy (in this case gender) from a relationship—which isn't to say there aren't gendered differences between two guys (or gals)—increases its equity quotient.

A romantic partnership, not unlike a friendship or a society, cannot thrive in a state of disparity, and this is precisely why straight relationships are, as you suggested, at a disadvantage. One half of a hetero pairing will always be on a rung higher than his other half, whether they want to be or not. The other half is gaslit from the beginning; girls are told they're princesses, queens, goddesses, diamonds, pearls, precious in every way, but they're subjugated in as many ways too. At least [insert every other oppressed group here] are treated like shit and told they're shit, but

· *136* ·

MIDDLE SPOON

women get offered a seat on the subway and then raped on the walk home. This cruelty finds its way into everything.

You and Dad couldn't achieve the sort of parity you witnessed in my marriage because you were locked in a power struggle influenced by this societal illness. The stress of being undesirable immigrants didn't help— if you'd been rich, white, and born here, your marriage might have been nearer to what you wanted it to be. You, too, might have dabbled in polyamory if you'd been able to pay the electricity bill. Who knows?

None of this is to say my marriage is perfect or that our race and class differences are easily surmounted, but when two people are on the same plane, honesty isn't as painful or scary.

Maybe Ben and I weren't on the same plane.

"Ben? I knew it! I told your father something was happening!"

"Mom—"

"I'm so disappointed in you. I can't believe you would do something this dishonorable. I—I don't know what to say. I hope this was the medicine you needed to cure yourself."

"Cure? Love isn't dishonorable or an illness."

"Love? It seems to me you know nothing about honor or love. How can you treat your husband this way?"

"Mom! I've learned a lot about myself over the last year—"

"A year! Oh my God! You've been unfaithful for a year?"

"It's not like that!"

"It's true, all men are dogs!"

"I'm not a dog, Dad's not a dog, and this has nothing to do with pets. My relationship with Ben was a real relationship between two people— actually, three—and although it didn't work out, I'm grateful to have learned something about myself."

"Three people? ¡Ay, Dios santo! ¡Qué degenerados!"

· *137* ·

"No! I didn't mean the three of us were in a relationship. I meant the three of us consented to our current situation."

"I don't understand, and I don't want to understand. If that *situation* is what you needed, be glad it happened. Now, focus on your family, and don't play games anymore. You're a father, too, not just a husband."

"Mom, I know this may be hard for you to believe, but I think I'm a better person for having explored life with Ben, for trying to meet my needs outside of what society tells me is acceptable, for doing it all while respecting my husband, my children, my boyfriend, and myself. It wasn't always easy, but I did it, and I'm devastated it's over. Really hurting."

"Respect? We have very different ideas of what that means. I didn't expect this from you."

"Mom, I need you. Why isn't that more important than anything else?"

"Okay."

"Okay, what?"

"My baby, I wish I was there so I could wrap my arms around you and tell you I love you, and that this will pass, and that life is full of ups and downs, and that despite not having had the freedom to experience life to its fullest, I don't resent your experiences. I feel so connected to you that I, in my own way, live your life with you, and as you continue finding yourself, I will always be happy for you because it means I am happy for myself and proud I played a role in creating the person who you have become . . . Is that better?"

"Yes, but I would have settled for *I'm sorry*."

"¡Ay! Deja de joder."

"Sorry, that was beautiful. Thank you, Mom. Did you mean any of it?"

"Give me a break. Who talks like that?"

"Thank you for saying it anyway."

MIDDLE SPOON

"Baby?"

"Yes?"

"Did you wear condoms?"

"Mom!"

"Well, did you?"

"At first, yes, but I'd lose my erection whenever I put on a condom, so I got a Viagra prescription, but one time, I took too small of a dose— those pills are expensive, I had to break them into thirds—and the condom ruined everything, so we had sex without a condom, and it was pretty fantastic, and so I went straight to my doctor and got a prescription for PrEP, which Ben had already been taking rather dutifully for years, rendering my need to take PrEP futile, scientifically speaking, since he is my only sex partner apart from my husband, who, as you've probably guessed, is about as monogamous as they come, usually, but since I have forty years' worth of antigay (and pro-gay, to be fair) public health messages swirling about my mind, and since I have trouble trusting men, I took my own PrEP, which protects against only one illness, so I also did my best to dissuade Ben from having sex with other guys while we were dating, which I believe I succeeded in doing, but not without ramifications. You see, Mom, my desire to keep him all to myself might have precipitated our downfall. He soon wanted me all to himself, too, and well, that was never going to be."

"Oh, honey. You're not all that different from your own insecure mother. And your grandfather was also a jealous man. It's a family curse. Is this something you can talk about in therapy?"

"I do. I'm working on it."

"Good. Keep at it. Your children will be less insecure than you, and their children will be even less so. And one day, this thread will disintegrate."

"I hope so."

"Oh, honey."

"What?"

"What is he like, this *Ben*?"

"Special."

"What does *special* mean?"

"Well, he's handsome—really attractive. And he has eyes—"

"Everyone has eyes, mi'jo."

"Mom, I know. I'm saying he has the ability to look at me and make me feel great. But also terrible."

"Sounds manipulative."

"He's not manipulative."

"Does he make you laugh?"

"Yes, he is quick-witted, finds humor in almost everything. You'd love him."

"Is he good to you?"

"Except for currently causing me the worst pain I've ever felt, yes, he was. He used to run his fingers through my hair to help me get to sleep, and whenever we'd go out to eat, he'd make sure to order food that was gluten- and dairy-free because he wanted me to be able to eat off his plate."

"That's sweet. But this could be only infatuation. Maybe you want him because you know you can't have him."

"Can't it be both love and infatuation?"

"Anything is possible."

"He's also smart, hardworking, intuitive about people, and surprisingly practical for his age."

"How much younger?"

"Nine years."

"Oh."

"Is that a lot?"

"Between men and women, maybe. But it might be different between two men."

"I don't think so, Mom."

"Baby?"

"Yes?"

"Is this *Ben* the reason why you don't visit us more often?"

"Mom, please."

This is the sort of conversation I would like to have with you, not one where I ask you to agree with my choices, but instead one where I shoulder some of your disappointments and prejudices, so long as you are ultimately supportive. And yet, I choose to sidestep the complications to our relationship that might arise from speaking an unvarnished truth, a truth unconcerned with history or culture or reality. In fact, a scenario in which we never discuss Ben, but you're cordial, hospitable even, and everyone does their best to pretend, might suffice. Old-school gay.

The problem is, I don't want to be old school in this regard. There's an evolution to all this, and I don't want to leave you behind. Join me.

Te quiero,
Tu hijo

Dear Ben,

I wasn't born this way. None of us were. We were taught not to cry. I know because I teach my children to hide their feelings. Sometimes through encouragement, sometimes cajoling, at times, sanctions.

There's no weakness to speak of as it concerns the act of crying. And yet, I've recently found myself trying to suppress this most human of behaviors. When that's failed, which has been more often the case, I run.

That's not hyperbole. I bolted off the subway yesterday at Spring Street, just before the doors closed and shortly after I'd felt my face transforming into a Dalí. My escape originated in a frying pan and culminated in a fire. SoHo, it turns out, is a much less forgiving environment as it concerns hiding places than the penultimate car of the C train, where I could have at the very least survived the moment by burying my face in my hands or my head in my lap. At the intersection of 6th and Spring, however, there was no such escape. Every nook or shadow within sprinting distance smelled of urine or was being actively used as a bathroom or an opium den or both. I was left with little choice but to do what a prideful eight-year-old might have done in a similar situation: I turned to face a wall, in this case the side of an enormous building, which I realized almost immediately was the headquarters of an HIV/AIDS organization where I had volunteered many years ago, right out of graduate school, or more accurately, where I had gone to a handful of volunteer orientation meetings but then never returned. And so, yesterday afternoon, I was a gay man crying at a slab of concrete likely in the same spot where scores of gay men had cried at some point over the previous thirty years, a not altogether discomfiting scenario, and so I allowed myself to sob about the

· *142* ·

MIDDLE SPOON

death of our relationship without feeling pressure to hide my face, and only when I was done, or when the worst of it had passed, did I realize an elderly woman in a long camel-colored coat and a large yellow scarf draped over most of it was standing beside me, waiting for me to finish so that she might extend her hand, at the end of which was a neatly folded pink tissue that I accepted and instantly put to use.

"Thank you," I said as I cleaned my face and stared at hers, her poorly drawn lips and magenta-caked cheeks, the surrealism of which left me wondering if she was the victim of a shaky hand and poor eyesight or untreated mental illness.

"It's good to get it all out. You'll sleep better tonight. Mark my words," she said.

When I finished cleaning my face, I looked up and didn't see her anywhere. It was tempting to believe she'd been an apparition, the ghost of someone mythical I hadn't recognized or my own grandmother. I allowed myself to believe the fiction for a few minutes, until I saw her coming out of the pizza place near Thompson, a greasy paper plate and a flurry of thin napkins in her hands.

I can't pinpoint one formative lesson or one incident. It was likely an accumulation of moments and subliminal messages, in addition to the more direct proscriptions, that taught me crying was excessive, embarrassing, emasculating, and altogether wrong, a rather unfortunate revelation in the context of youth, especially one constricted by smallness of home, town, and perspectives.

All this to say, as a youngster, I cried often and a lot.

Until adolescence—what an inopportune time to abandon an essential egress for emotion—when I began to correlate my vulnerability with my sexuality. To cry was in effect to be girlie and to be girlie was to be a

· 143 ·

fag and to be a fag was to be ostracized by family, friends, and the god of big things. Suppression was prudent and tantamount to survival.

Suppression was also easier to achieve with practice. Learning to swallow the lump until its bitterness became something innocuous, if not sweet, was a triumph. Becoming adept at devaluing the very triggers of emotion, stripping them of urgency and importance, until even the emotions of others became targets for ridicule, condescension, and anger, until even freeness felt threatening, was also a triumph.

Those hard-earned defenses are nowhere to be found now. Perhaps this breakup has liberated me, transported me to my youth, before the Great Suppression began. Perhaps rejection was a portal I needed to walk through. Perhaps this has less to do with you than I'd realized.

—Me

PS: If I've portrayed my upbringing negatively, spare a thought for the powder keg in which our family lived. As any child might, I sought the attentions of my parents, without realizing I was after something scarce. Their rejections only engendered behaviors on my part that brought about more anger and volatility in all of us. I don't blame myself or my parents because we were downstream. I blame capitalism. I blame US imperialism. I blame racism. I blame the deregulation and the regressive tax structure that disempowered the middle class and merged the working and poverty classes. My tears were Reagan's fault as much as anyone else's.

PPS: Fred emailed me after reading the PS, and he said I sounded defensive. And I responded that I am defensive of my family because I detest

MIDDLE SPOON

judging matters at face value without discussing what's beneath—or above. He said it was possible to judge both.

PPPS: I emailed Sandy after my exchange with Fred and asked her if she thought I sounded defensive in my PS. She responded, "My family also chased the Dream. They moved us out of the city to the suburbs, and I can relate to your desire to defend them, if not their actions. But yes, a little defensive."

Note to self: stop telling my kids not to cry, even if I say it nicely. Let them have their feelings. Stop projecting my discomfort onto them. Try being a children's guide to heartbreak that you never had.

Dear Ben,

I've taken to investing my erratic ennui into journaling, and those transcriptions of my daydreams, in an ironic twist, read like a story on which a screenplay could be based:

A man, not unlike myself, travels back in time—fine, it's me, I travel back in time. I do so in order to find you before I meet my husband so that you and I can be together. I drive to your hometown soon after I graduate from college. I park my car across the street from your parents' home, a large colonial with a four-columned portico, at least eight front-facing windows, and a two-car garage. I spot you immediately. You're helping your father landscape—I assume the tall, dark-haired man wearing safety goggles and earmuffs is your father. You're sitting on the lawn mower drawing squares of your enormous front yard, while he traces the edges of the driveway with a long, sticklike gardening implement. Your back is mostly to me, the me in a baseball cap who slides down subtly in the front seat of his car, but periodically your face becomes clear. It takes only a few glances to remember that you're fourteen, which instantly mortifies me. I'm suddenly a gay man who believes a child is his future romantic partner. In my defense, there is nothing untoward running through my mind. I'm simply gathering information and trying to change the events of time and space to better suit our future needs. Logic sets in, and I give up on the plan to rewrite history. I drive back to college and try to find my husband, but he's gone. A mutual friend tells me he's accepted his Peace Corps assignment in the Ivory Coast; without me in his life, there are no second thoughts about the baked-in imperialism of the US-funded program and certainly no opting out of his assignment in order to

MIDDLE SPOON

stay with me because there was/is no me in his life. Despite my manic levels of gumption, I don't travel to western Africa to look for him. I remain in New York instead, waiting, dating, and working. I go to the Film Forum often, and I meet friends for drinks at Kenny's Castaways on Bleecker and Frank's on Fulton and Grassroots on St. Marks and Tile Bar on 1st and O'Connor's on 5th and Eastern Bloc on 6th and Metropolitan on Lorimer and the Phoenix on 13th and Nowhere on 14th and Scratcher on 5th and Art Bar on 8th and White Horse Tavern on Hudson and Alibi on DeKalb and Washington Commons on Washington and Weather Up on Vanderbilt and Diner on Broadway and Dick and Jane's on Adelphi and C'mon Everybody on Franklin and Txikito on 9th and, once, the Chelsea Hotel on 23rd. I drink too much. Periodically I check on my husband, who I learn lives in the Bay Area, not far from your art school, the art school that gave you a sizable scholarship that was publicized in your town paper's website. I continue dating. I get gonorrhea no fewer than three times; chlamydia twice. I have three HIV scares. I drink too much. I never leave New York, but I still end up studying public health. I have lots of gay male friends and go to boozy brunches both days of the weekend. In fact, I drink every day because there's always a friend or a date or a date who becomes a friend, seldom the other way around. I work out often; I have the abs and thighs of an underwear model. I remain as insecure as I ever was. It seems much of my psychological stability and personal growth stemmed from having a partner who quietly deflected and absorbed my anxieties and grounded me in ways I'd never known prior. Over the years, I enter into two long-term (not simultaneous) relationships with volatile men who bring out the volatility I'd long tried to suppress. Neither ends well. You finally move to New York, and I find you online. You still have crooked teeth and liberal politics. We go out twice—the Taiwanese place we visited often in real life and a bar down the street from your apartment. The physical attraction is there,

· 147 ·

but I can't quite connect with you. I don't feel the emotional spark that I expected (and frankly, was no longer after). Our sex feels equal parts exciting and transactional but without attachment. All of the sex I have feels that way. Professionally, I'm a superstar: tenure in record time, three textbooks under my belt, keynote speeches out the wazoo. I'm also the favorite uncle to all my nieces and nephews. I host Friendsgiving every year. I visit six continents at least twice (Antarctica only once). One year, I attend all four tennis Grand Slams. I take a trapeze class on Wednesdays. I lead a fine and fulfilling life, but it's not the life I want. It's not the life I almost had.

—Me

Dear Ben,

I've been rereading some of the correspondence I had with friends during our previous breakup, and I was surprised to find I was a mess then too. I expected the breakups to differ in dimension and intensity. At the very least, the first heartache should have served as a primer—no, an airbag—no! a vaccine—for the subsequent heartache. I would have been content for it to prevent death and hospitalization, like a COVID vaccine does, and not the illness itself, like the measles vaccine. But the previous breakup seems to have prevented absolutely nothing and might have even made the current pain more acute. Apparently, heartache as an inoculator doesn't function like the COVID or measles vaccine but instead like the flu vaccine: every season is different.

I'm beginning to wonder if this is why you have as much sex as I think you do. Or why you treat your pain with sex. Casual sex might not only serve as treatment but as prevention, a booster to build your defenses, in the process rendering human contact less meaningful. I'm not passing judgment; I'm simply noting I have many fewer defenses.

This afternoon, I asked Sandy what she thought of the latest batch of emails, and she waited her usual, interminable seconds to respond.

"As I was reading them," she said finally, "I felt you weren't sympathetic enough to the Ben character, not enough to warrant your affections. Why, I kept asking myself, would he jeopardize his current life for someone with whom he isn't all that compatible?"

The truth is, your dimensionality has been the casualty of my anger. I've found it cathartic to diminish you.

"I thought the last email, the multiverse one, was kind of cool," I said.

"It's very creative. And I appreciated your analysis of the effects of formative stress on your psyche, as well as how you acknowledge what your husband has brought to your life. I also laughed several times throughout."

"Which parts?"

"I'd have to revisit the document to be certain," she said rather lethargically.

"Sandy, how many pastimes will I have to take up to forget him? How many emails do I have to write? How many days will this last? Do any of your other patients lose their minds like I have? What do you tell them? Do some people never recover?"

Again, she hesitated to respond.

"How do I get better?" I pushed. "Sandy?"

It seemed our connection had frozen, and she remained stuck in time, her elbow propped up on her desk, her chin cradled in her hand, her eyes closed, mid-blink.

"If you can hear me, Sandy, I'm going to sign out of the session and then sign back in."

That's when her eyes opened. That's also when I realized our connection was fine and that she'd fallen asleep.

"Like I said, time heals all," she said almost mindlessly, as if she kept pithy declarations at the ready for people like me or for situations like mine or for when she was sleep-deprived. "You cannot rush time."

No shit, I thought. *But time is endless*, I also thought. Time has become nothing more than an infinite collection of instances. Time is like the clock of the heart. Time after time. If I could turn back time. Morris Day and the Time. Time to make the doughnuts. *Time* magazine.

—Me

To Whom It May Concern at the National Institutes of Health:

I am a trained public health worker with decades of research experience, and I believe we haven't adequately explored a pervasive problem, a crisis really.

The public health implications of heartache are, for lack of a more meaningful word, astounding, and possibly immeasurable. But as stewards of the population's well-being, it is our duty to address this phenomenon in order to adequately treat it and prevent its most deleterious effects.

It behooves us to begin with the questions we want to answer:

1. How many of us are heartbroken exactly? Millions? Billions?

2. Of those, how many of us are dealing with acute-onset heartache?

3. For how many has the problem become a chronic condition?

4. Is heartache distributed evenly among a population, or are there risk factors to consider?

5. What roles do the social determinants of health play on the severity of the condition?

6. What are the long-term consequences of heartbreak, both to the persons affected and to society at large?

The collective effect of everyone's pain as a result of a romantic disentanglement is an epidemic ripe for exploration. Or is this a pandemic? Upon further reflection, it's neither, because it's not spreading quickly, and it's not specific to one region. Heartbreak-induced grief is endemic to the planet. And the way it scrapes out our insides must have cumulative effects. It might bear out in the economic outcomes of a given municipality, for example. Perhaps it correlates to other illnesses and to life expectancy. It might explain the people who don't share the sidewalk while also accounting for the people who put up their feet on the subway seats. Perhaps it's the root cause for the abundance of dog excrement on the streets of Brooklyn, Paris, and Buenos Aires. Or why so many hedge fund managers do what they do. We might find a statistically significant correlation between heartbreak and many of our societal evils.

In a species that depends on social cohesion for survival, vis-à-vis better health outcomes, heartbreak might be the great undoer of the ties that bind, as simple as why so many of us don't make eye contact. Along with racism, it might account for the lion's share of unfriendliness in the world. The possibilities are endless.

The irony of course is we, the heartbroken, are desperate for human contact. It's the pain that tips our heads downward and trains our gazes to the ground until we begin to believe we're alone.

I offer this encounter with my own mother as an example of what heartache does to the mind and to human interactions:

"Are you listening?" she asked, one recent morning. "Is everything okay?"

Countless times in the last few days, she's posed some variation of these questions because of my clear inability to remain engaged in our conversations. But it's not only on the phone that I've vanished. It's on the street. On the subway. At my desk. At the dinner table. I am unable to participate in anything unrelated to my grief, and consequently I am incapable of being productive.

"I'm fine, just a lot of work on my mind," I responded.

"Hmmm," she offered.

Hmmm is correct. To experience grief is to live in a state of hmmm, and I can only imagine how many other humans find themselves in a similar place. The collective weight is why we must investigate.

MIDDLE SPOON

Unlike clinicians who concern themselves with the health of individuals, public health workers are driven by the well-being of populations. We are trained to look at health data in aggregate and not to generalize solitary or outlier cases. A broader view allows us to tackle the preponderance of poor health cases at once—through prevention and treatment—in order to lessen the illness burden on society. And yet, individual cases are often representative of the norm. I have put forth my own experience as an example of what I believe to be a prevalent problem.

This email does not constitute a detailed proposal but is instead meant to signal my intentions and to elicit exploratory feedback. I've only begun to brainstorm study designs, but I suspect that this sort of phenomenon would benefit from multiple data collection sites. To get a clearer sense of the global implications, we'd need a worldwide sample. A few thousand people from each country. Or from each region. Including a variety of government types. And economies. After all, US heartbreak might differ from Ecuadorian or Sri Lankan heartbreak. Über-capitalism could very well lead to more devastation because it happens to an already damaged people in an inhospitable setting. Danish and Japanese heartaches are possibly more manageable because egalitarian policies, a thriving middle class, and the room for individuality produce stronger, more secure citizens who are sustained by a durable social fabric and safety net. Cuban and Chinese heartbreak is probably milder still because the forced collectivism and the flatter hierarchies make for a level playing field characterized by transparency, respect, and possibly tempered emotions.

Or perhaps pain is pain. And grief, much like death, is the great leveler.

I'm eager to explore these hypotheses, the study of which has the potential to both enlighten humanity and reduce its disease burden.

I await your reply.

· *153* ·

Dutifully,

, PhD
Department of Sociobehavioral Studies
██████████ University

PS: Cuba and China are not the same as it concerns communism, but I'm not sufficiently versed in political ideologies to adequately explain their differences. The size of the countries must play a role. As does culture. And their proximity to anti-communist interests. After all, without the United States' embargo, Cuba might have been the admirable version of communism that was originally put forth.

PPS: After further consideration, it occurs to me that what constitutes individuality in Denmark is perhaps different from that in Japan. These are important distinctions to draw and certainly oblige us to include anthropologists, historians, and geopolitical scholars in our research team.

Dear Ben,

There's something we never got around to discussing that we certainly alluded to and that I probably have no business broaching because I don't have anything particularly insightful to say on the matter. In fact, I fear my opinions won't advance the conversation, if there is a conversation to be had, and will instead serve to reveal my latent conservatism and internalized homophobia, and possibly *promote* my latent conservatism and internalized homophobia, as well as the deep-seated misogyny in both. But here I go . . .

I'm a top, and you're a bottom, and that should mean very little in terms of human relations, but I've come to believe it means a great deal. I should back up a little—no pun intended. I'm versatile, as it concerns sex and penetration, but in our relationship, I was explicitly the top, which meant you were on the receiving end of me; it also came to mean you went nowhere near my ass, never massaged my shoulders, and seldom picked up the tab at an expensive place. This made sense to me because, in a way, I'd been you. For nearly twenty years, I was the bottom in a relationship with someone who has never been one for the intricacies of receptive anal sex; pressure, or even a modicum of pain in that area of my husband's body, takes him out of the experience. I, however, manage pain and discomfort rather well, in small part because I find it arousing, but I've also wondered if my tolerance is owed to the servile and insecure nature fomented during my formative years and whether that nature was nurtured by parents whose internecine tensions of being part colonizer and part colonized were habitually boiling over and splattering onto their children.

I feel obliged to pause here and state the obvious: being penetrated anally is actually quite spectacular and isn't all about gritting teeth and bearing pain—you know—but I'm also not going to pretend there isn't a nonnegligible amount of wincing that accompanies the act. As such, bottoms should receive extra care for our/their efforts, which is why I had no qualms—the opposite of qualms, even—tending to your needs more than you did mine. Caring for you constituted one of my greatest pleasures and one of my least understood needs.

But I remain curious about the geopolitical forces at play in the bedroom. The consequences of having been a brown, prequeer gay son of immigrants whose aspirations took him away from the multicultural community of an urban setting to working-class Catholic white suburbia cannot be discounted. The dissection of these forces is no less a requirement for understanding the blueprints of sex than it is for knowing oneself and society at large. That's how these terrible categories work, isn't it? They make their way into all the crevices of life—again, no pun planned. I'm not ashamed of any of my identities or facets thereof, but periodically, and especially since becoming a parent who is concerned with the imparting and parsing of human relations for the benefit of his own children's socialization, I have become aware of how utterly stupid it is for humans to be assigned to categories for the purposes of distributing power and resources and, furthermore, for me to have to teach these differences as if they were in anyway meaningful, never mind deterministic of human potential, when the culprit is a system of control and faux scarcity (yes, yes, capitalism) that imposes these identities vis-à-vis the repackaging of differences as barriers and reasons for distrust, when they are verifiably neither, which is further complicated by the fact that these very categories have now become important, sometimes essential, and, at other times, beautiful unifiers for otherwise disempowered members of

MIDDLE SPOON

society who need the strength of numbers to counterbalance the weight of oppression.

See what I did there? I delved into the political in that rather didactic way I tend toward in my research, which has been the source of much criticism from some of my colleagues and the public health community writ large. But you know what, Ben, to hell with my critics. The world is on fire.

In any case, I thoroughly enjoyed your ass and the moaning that ensued as a result of my efforts, but what I'm trying to impress upon you is that the act of penetration has connoted for me a sort of power struggle, in which the top is, if not the winner, the incumbent, and I suspect this imbalance has everything to do with the intrinsic inequities brought to bear in a heteronormative and patriarchal society. Men penetrate women, men make more money, men run corporations and countries, men punch, men blow things up, men own everything, men control. Women don't. Or at least didn't during the period of my life when I was making the associations and drawing the conclusions that would forever mark my worldview, which, in turn, led me to believe that who and how one fucks comes with an assignation of power.

In my youth, whenever I imagined two guys having sex, which wasn't infrequent, I must have, without meaning to, applied that same template of power. The guy who got penetrated was the weaker, more feminine one who probably made dinner and washed the dishes. And the top was the one who paid the bills and scared the children.

These ignorant—through no fault of my own, I say again—notions were then the basis on which I saw my own relationship. I was the bottom, my husband made more money than I did, I was more emotional, I enjoyed being taken care of, I liked having my back rubbed and my coffee made, and so on.

Wait!

First contradiction: Why is my husband making the coffee if I am his bottom? Shouldn't I be the homemaker in this rendering of gay domesticity? Why, too, is he the more patient one who rarely loses his temper with the kids if he's the caveman and I'm the damsel? Why has he never been led by jealousy or cortisol? Why doesn't he shy away from asking for directions?

Perhaps this is where the category of power bottom should receive attention. It's possible I am someone who enjoys getting fucked, so long as I am holding the metaphorical reins throughout. Perhaps I get off on controlling my husband and precipitating his loss of control during sex. Maybe the joy I derived from being provided for wasn't a gene expression linking homosexuality and female fecundity, as has been posited elsewhere, but simply the realization that playing the submissive role came with built-in power.

Or maybe the practice of sex has nothing to do with preordained roles, but with preordained personalities. I've simply adapted to my husband's proclivities because I'm naturally accommodating, and he makes me coffee because he likes to feel useful. Life might be little more than predeterminations and categories, like Plinko, the *Price Is Right* game. We, too, are just slots. I, for example, am the slot that likes all the permutations of sex; my husband is the slot that likes to hit it from behind; and you're the slot that likes to ride it.

Or perhaps the power dynamic between my husband and me was exacerbated by our political identities. I allowed myself to be dominated by a white man in the bedroom because at least there it was consensual, unlike in the outside world, where, truth be told, I detest when others assume my husband is the provider or the decision-maker—at restaurants, at the lawyer's office, at the airport, etc. Everywhere but in private I like to be in control, and with you, Ben, I felt this desire in private as well.

This brings up another contradiction: you're white and resolutely the bottom, which isn't to say I'm incredulous about the notion that white

MIDDLE SPOON

men bottom. It's that I've often felt white men try to take power from me or relish lording it over me. I know that sounds conspiratorial, but you'll just have to trust me and the near-decade more experience I have. There's no way around it; people above you in the hierarchy are very uncomfortable with giving up their spots, ergo, I was surprised at how much dominance I had over you. I wasn't, however, disappointed. The physical and social control awakened something in me that had lain dormant for nearly twenty years, a provider-caveman who'd been hibernating. I enjoyed taking care of you. I felt powerful when you got emotional and I remained stoic. I found it titillating when you encouraged me to order for you at restaurants. I suppressed a grin whenever you'd pretend to be focused elsewhere as the server slid the bill onto the table. All of it made me stronger, more confident, secure.

Or.

Or did I have power at all? You might very well have been in control from the start, biding your time, giving me just enough room to make me feel as if I were in the lead, when all the while you were in charge. You understood well that dominance, power, and control weren't synonyms. On the other hand, if I knew you were pulling the strings, wasn't I then in control? Or if you knew that I knew, and consequently, I knew that you knew that I knew, were you then in charge? Or was I in charge again? Did it matter?

From each according to his ability, to each according to his need has a true and solemn ring to it. In every arena of life, I believe this adage, but that doesn't mean I don't want to better *understand* our abilities and needs, as well as our motivations, which is probably why I overanalyze power structures.

I fear I've belabored a simple point: I like to bottom, and I like to top. I married someone who only likes to top and feels secure enough in our marriage to allow me to seek what I'm missing elsewhere. In the process,

· *159* ·

I fell in love with someone who only likes to bottom, and I don't want to let go of either person because I realize I don't only want both—I need both. I may not have any answers about why there are tops and why there are bottoms in this gay world, but I've learned at least this about myself. I've also learned I'm terrible at disentangling sex from emotion. This might be my Plinko slot.

—Me

PS: I've given more thought to the top-bottom debate, and I have arrived at the conclusion that we gays are much more inclined—these puns write themselves—to bottom than to top. My theory is predicated on the fact that bottoms are more likely to acquire sexually transmitted infections, including HIV, because of the microtears and surface area of the anus and rectum relative to the penis (i.e., bottoming is riskier). This reasoning got me thinking that the first wave of the AIDS epidemic in the US must have killed bottoms at a much higher rate than tops. At least one generation of bottoms died. And yet, if you log on to the dating and cruising apps, you'll see the majority of squares in the grid identify as bottoms, which tracks with the real-life demographic I've encountered in my lifetime. In other words, the proclivity to bottom must predominate, maybe even have a genetic or epigenetic component, which aligns with the fecundity research. Notice I said proclivity, not ability. Most anyone can bottom. But some of us truly enjoy and crave it. Or maybe we gays have learned to bottom, our way of performing societal subjugation if you will.

PPS: I told my friend Lisa, a behavioral health researcher, my theory on the heart and its non-role in heartbreak, and she told me there's a new

MIDDLE SPOON

book about heartbreak by someone whose divorce left them rather traumatized. The book argues that the heart—the actual organ—can be damaged by the dissolution of a relationship if the dissolution rises to the point of serious adverse event. In other words, even a person without crusty arteries, which are the common precursors to a heart attack, can have a cardiac event if the stress of the metaphorical heartbreak is severe enough.

Hearing this makes me want to avoid you.

The book is called *Heartbreak: A Personal and Scientific Journey*. It's by Florence Williams.

PPPS: I've returned to this draft email because of something pertinent I learned last night during dinner. We were at the new Thai place around the corner—we almost went there one night, but I was worried they wouldn't have gluten-free options, remember? It turns out they do. In any case, our friend Akil's friend, Rosalie, both of whom joined us for dinner, introduced a word I'd never heard of: *circlusion*. The term was coined a few years ago by the German writer and feminist Bini Adamczak. In brief, circlusion is the opposite of penetration. But the implication of this antonym is greater than just syntax. Circlusion gives action to the historically passive.

I've argued (above and elsewhere) that bottoming, at best, is a reactive action or role; it happens *to* someone (the receptive partner), and therefore the bottom is dependent on the top. Circlusion, however, argues an enveloping, a swallowing, if you will, where the bottom is a bottom in name only. Just one part of the puzzle. Jonah, after all, wasn't penetrating the whale.

Similarly, your hole, your canal, your mouth, didn't only receive my cock, it welcomed it, squeezed it, trapped it, constricted it. Seen that way,

· *161* ·

a bottom is in control as much as or more so than the top. This makes perfect sense, because in my previously limited understanding of these dynamics, penetrative sex between penis (or other appendage) and vagina (or other orifice) would have been defined by an insurmountable imbalance, one perpetuated by society, in particular those of us with limited imaginations. There wouldn't be the possibility for the receptive partner to have power, even in a postrevolutionary society where women had achieved an equitable status. I was so caught up in two cis dudes getting it on, I didn't consider how these power dynamics could be extrapolated to all sexual configurations.

This cluelessness reminds me of an undergraduate class I taught a few years ago—the Ties Between Diabetes and Colonization—where student A (she/her, straight-identified), during a discussion about discrimination, asked student B (he/him, queer-identified) about his earliest memory of homophobia, and student B recounted the times adults, usually his father, his aunts, his uncles, had asked him, by way of a greeting, how many girlfriends he had. Simple inquiries that transformed into fraught preoccupations in the adolescent mind. While I listened to the conversation between my students, I was reminded that I, too, had been asked this question often enough in my youth, a question that made me scramble and left me little choice but to join in the charade.

I have so many girlfriends, I've lost count.

Ha, ha, ha went the room.

After student B had finished sharing the moments of not-so-subtle indoctrination from his youth, student C (she/they, queer-identified) chimed in, "My relatives used to do that to my brother, too, and I remember thinking, *Wow, boys can have many of us girls, but we can only have one of them.*" Student C's interjection went off like a small stick of *Looney Tunes* dynamite in my chest. Before that, I'd never considered what my sister must have internalized when she heard our relatives inquire about my

MIDDLE SPOON

sexual prowess. Years of witnessing this misogynistic ritual without anyone to interrupt it—not a protective rebuttal or a commiserating eye roll from any adult in the room—must have sent the sort of subliminal messages one can only repel after they've become aware of their existence.

I can't quite explain it, but I think I've done the same thing with my top-bottom discourse. I've discounted most of humanity with my assumptions and preconceived notions. By making this all about me, I didn't stop to think about anyone else.

Dear Ben,

This week the number one song in the country is Mariah Carey's perennial Christmas hit. I don't know if you know this, but holiday songs reappearing annually on the music charts is a relatively new phenomenon in US metrics. The British charts have allowed it for years, but the music industry in the US, until recently, has relied on holiday-specific charts to prevent the renewed success of bygone tunes from interfering with the chart success of new music. On the other hand, if the purpose of weekly music charts is to measure the mode, these holiday songs are the fashion of the last five weeks of every year and, therefore, should compete with newer fare. I don't mind it in the least. I like Carey, and this chart metric evolution will extend her grip on the number one position in perpetuity, well after she's stopped creating new music, which is only fair because it's difficult to imagine a catchier holiday song being written to replace hers, even if I do wish Wham!'s "Last Christmas" could have a week at the summit.

As far as pop music paragons go, George Michael lived at the intersection of cat's pajamas, saint, and gorgeous babysitter. I loved his music. I loved him. I met him once. I'm sure I didn't mention it because I didn't think you'd care and because it's not something I think about often. Sometimes years pass without the memory of that meeting coming to the fore, and when it does, I wonder if it actually happened or if it's the detritus of a long-ago dream.

I was nine or ten, and he was eating at the chic French restaurant where my dad worked in the '80s and early '90s. I happened to be there because I had strep throat, and that was the era when parents staying

MIDDLE SPOON

home with sick children had to clear a higher hurdle than slightly swollen tonsils. The restaurant's employee locker room served as my all-day infirmary and rec room but for a brief time in the afternoon when I went up to the dining room for an off-hours lunch of off-menu chicken consommé that my dad had asked one of the Colombian cooks to prepare for me. I recall, too, a heaping plate of french fries because my dad's coworkers had ribbed him about giving his sad, gray-pallored kid fancy soup instead of fancy fries. These fries were more than just elegant potatoes; at one point, they were hailed in various publications as the best fries in New York City. Thin like the ones at McDonald's, these very French french fries were gilded, crisp, and salted to perfection.

Anyway, as I ate my meal, my dad, unbeknownst to me, was serving George Michael in a separate dining room reserved for guests who required more privacy than the velvet curtains at the restaurant's entrance and the steep menu prices had already guaranteed. I would have remained unaware of Michael if my dad hadn't brought him over to my booth, the one closest to the kitchen, the most incognito of the main dining room, where staff typically ate during their breaks, and where I was swiping my fries through a heap of ketchup, mustard, and mayonnaise. My dad and the megastar heartthrob approached me so casually, I assumed at first it was a prank, a performer my dad had brought in from the kitchen or the street to cheer me up.

There he was, quite bearded, wearing small sunglasses unlike the aviators he wore in the videos, as well as a drop earring, which may or may not have been a crucifix. He also wore a baseball cap emblazoned with the Yankees insignia. The internet claims George was six feet tall, but on that day, he was nothing short of ten.

"This is my second," my dad said, referring to my place in the birth order. I could tell from the gleam in his eyes he was proud of himself for having gifted me an experience of this caliber, and still, my father spoke

· 165 ·

dispassionately, like someone unimpressed by celebrity. By that point, he'd met everyone. Name a famous person, and my father has, on multiple occasions, uncorked their wine, folded their napkin, and set a steak knife beside their plate. To him, humans either tipped enough to help him pay the mortgage, or they didn't. The rest was inconsequential.

"He's a fan. Show him your moves! Show him!" my dad prodded while nodding at me, as if I were a trained street urchin. I was mortified for all the ostensible reasons, in addition to some inconspicuous ones, primary of which was that I didn't know how to dance like George Michael. In my mind, he wasn't known for his dancing. Yes, George Michael danced, quite freely, if memory serves, but I suspect my father was thinking of Michael Jackson, whom my brother and I mimicked often at his behest— I guess all fathers have a bit of Joe Jackson in them.

In that posh, carpeted dining room full of waist-high squares and circles draped in white tablecloths, George Michael must have taken pity on me, or he was eager to carry on with his day, because in the most mellifluous of British voices, he said to my father, "He'll show me next time." Then he turned to me: "How about we snap a picture?"

My memory of that day is generally vague. What clothes was Michael wearing? Was he alone? Why hadn't I stayed with my aunt in Queens instead of going to the restaurant? But I recall some details vividly, in particular the phrasing of Michael's question, because after that day, I began using the phrase *snap a picture*.

A camera materialized, and someone (I don't recall) stood a few feet away and did exactly as George Michael had suggested. (A photograph I've never seen.) He then shook my dad's hand, and, before I could extend mine, said, "How about a hug?"

As I saw it, I had two options before me: lose consciousness or combust spontaneously, urges that must have neutralized each other and rendered me temporarily mute. So consumed was I by my own stress response, I couldn't decode the anger or dismay in my dad's stare. Later, he would tell my mom I looked as if I'd seen the devil, a humorous interpretation because Michael was more god to me than God was.

"What about my strep throat?" I managed to utter in my father's direction, but he swatted away my conscientiousness with the folded napkin that had been until that point draped over his forearm—my dad's arm was for nearly forty years a towel rack for the rich and famous. "My kids are clowns," he said, somewhat flustered. It was then that George Michael hugged me—briefly, truthfully—infusing my olfactory receptors with a tonic of expensive cologne, body odor, and cigarettes, a scent that occupied the entire spectrum between orgasmic and unpleasant.

Around that time, *Faith* won Album of the Year, beating Tracy Chapman's eponymous debut in the process, in the same year Anita Baker's *Giving You the Best That I Got* wasn't nominated—the Grammys have always been stupid, Ben. But with *Faith*, they did all right. Michael's signature album produced four number one songs, which could have easily been six: "I Want Your Sex" and "Kissing a Fool" were robbed. The remaining tracks on the album, "Hand to Mouth," "Hard Day," and "Look at Your Hands," would have been top ten if they'd been released as singles.

The late '80s were undeniably Michael's artistic heyday, but I was drawn to more than just his music. You see, I knew he was gay before I knew what gay was and before I knew I was. That lone, ostentatious earring. That silk scarf of a voice. That please-love-me smile. But more telling was the ache in his eyes, the timidity in his manner. Whereas Prince proudly projected something illicit, alluring, and interpretable, at the outset of his career, George Michael intimated something shrouded, unspeakable. We were torn from the same leather jacket. He was a working-class ethnic minority with a trace of melanin and passable rhythm in a majority white society. Check. Check. Check. Check. A patron saint. Or a yellow brick road.

This is all to say, "Last Christmas," a ballad about being left by a lover who retains their hold, is a small treasure that transformed longing sadness into charming pop. "Last Christmas" is also about steeling oneself to see that lover again. How odd to be identifying with a George Michael song at this point in my life.

Things have been getting easier. The drowning and suffocating feelings have diffused into a numbing. The quotient of melodrama in each day has lessened, a welcome development not least of all because Fred and Sandy are both taking the holiday week off. Today, however, is one of those relapse days that makes me wonder if everything has been reset, if the worst is about to resurface. Without having consumed a drop of alcohol last night, I woke up hungover this morning, scattered, possibly the consequence of abbreviated sleep. What little I slept was fitful, possibly the consequence of you. At three a.m., I made my way into the living room and tried to read a manuscript for a textbook about wealth inequality's effect on societal happiness for which I'd been asked to write an introduction. The first couple of chapters were a slog, in part because I was nodding off, which was no fault of the book or its writer—a fellow faculty member—and in part because these chapters were incredibly overwritten, entirely the fault of the book, its editor, and possibly the writer, who seemed, in every one of his words, to be trying to prove something beyond what he was telling us. Until suddenly, the book found its way. It's yet too early to give my verdict, but there may be something honest and interesting to say about it. After all, the growing research showing that unequal societies aren't only unhappier but also unhealthier is becoming irrefutable.

Ben, I've done my best to not reach out, to not tell you what I'm feeling, after months and months and months of telling you everything. At times, the very effort to not contact you is a futile and inhuman task.

MIDDLE SPOON

Unfair too. You called things off, after all. *You* should be the one to reach out to tell *me* you miss me, to tell *me* you want to make this work, to tell *me* you know it won't be easy to break with heteronormative conventions, but if anyone can do it, it's queer people. Or maybe you're not queer. Maybe you're just gay—I was still trying to figure that out about you. I'm not, in case you're wondering, suggesting all queer people must embrace polyamory, but I am suggesting queer people have to question institutions. That's one of the few requirements to being queer.

I was at Jules's holiday concert this morning, subtly responding *they/them/their* to the parents and staff members who said *he/him/his*, when the grief and desperation began coiling around my chest, at first like slow-growing vines, but then like a corset.

Grief and *desperation* don't do justice to the feelings. The apt words exist, but they're out of my reach, which only layers the pain with frustration. Being incapable of describing my own goddamn emotions heightens the ambiguity at a time when I desire preciseness even more than I desire you. And I cannot help but layer this frustration over my frustration with the inadequate education system in this country and its contribution to my shallow reservoir of words. A series of evocations is what I've become: scenes and landscapes but few adjectives.

Today, I felt like a fog crawling [noun + verb] across a British countryside—*British* because I associate that part of the world with drabness; the verdant fields and the pop music all happen beneath gray skies as far as I can tell. The auditorium of the elementary school, however, was a cross section of gentrification: imagine all the races, ethnicities, and classes of this city, but not in direct proportion to the community outside or the city at large. I was in a public school that was simultaneously a looking glass and a trip into the past.

· *169* ·

An abundance of holiday reds and greens decorating the cavernous hall did nothing to alleviate the technologically inept and disastrously awkward transitions between student performances. What should have been a thirty-minute concert lasted nearly two hours. The children sang off-key. The parents occupied the aisles, phones in raised hands, obstructing views—a collection of individuals performing their rendition of a community. It was the life I'd chosen, a mundane existence that had once given me great pleasure, even in these tedious moments. But no longer. Now, whenever something veers toward unpleasant, I long for you.

What that previous declaration lacks in romance, it compensates for with devotion and delusion. The lionization of the departed is a principal precept of grief, I've gathered. This is the reason I have found it near impossible to ascribe to you any negative attributes since our breakup. I can intellectualize the red flags, and to that end, I've made lists of failings and incompatibilities, but I don't feel them.

Ben, you were, by turns, emotionally unavailable, politically naive, empathy deficient, immature, socially awkward, selfish with our shared meals, and occasionally tacky, stylistically speaking. You had an inflated sense of your ability to compromise. And if we're being entirely honest, I never fully trusted you. Something about the way you moved in this world—how you ogled men, how you never gave me the code to your building, even though you had a key to mine—belied your assurances. I had the sense you were biding your time for someone else; I was merely a well-appointed waiting room. And in the process of waiting, you found comfort. I may have won you over, but I never rid myself of the suspicion that your attentions were elsewhere.

Anyway, there I was sitting at that miserable holiday concert this morning, trying not to think about the failure of race relations in our neighborhood, trying to find joy in my eight-year-old's joy, trying to

MIDDLE SPOON

laugh when everyone else laughed, clap when everyone else did, accept my fate, but I kept thinking of you.

Fa-la-la-la-la, la-la-la-la.

Love,
Me

PS: It's not entirely true what I said about your style. I quite like it. You were always freer—colors, patterns, cuts—with your wardrobe than I've ever been. I was initially critical because I was projecting my own insecurities. There's nothing tacky about it; in fact, it was inspiring—by the way, you left a fishnet tank top at my place, and I plan to wear it this summer.

Ben,

I don't want to give David undue importance in all this—he's just a friend after all—but he happened to be the person who saw me at my worst, twice, and in retrospect, I've found his reactions (supportive, then cruel) to be indicative of the responses most people have to polyamory.

You met David briefly at the farmers market in the fall, remember? He had a bag of lemon sole fillets in hand and a loaf of sourdough under an arm. I'm certain of that because on many occasions he's complained to me that these are the only two things worth buying at the farmers market—he prefers to have everything else delivered. If you remember that Saturday morning encounter, you probably also recall that David is white, tall, shaggy-haired, a little goofy, and has an uncanny resemblance to John Ritter, the actor. (Do you know who John Ritter is? *Three's Company*?) David is also affable and wealthy, some of it generational—like me, he's a homeowner in a sought-after neighborhood in Brooklyn. David and I have been friends for nearly twenty years, but it hadn't occurred to me to mention you or open relationships or polyamory until I had no choice.

Last July, I was on my way to the bodega to buy a lottery ticket and baking powder for pancakes. David was after coffee and toilet paper. It was the day after you'd dumped me in the parking lot of the Walgreens in Williamsburg, the first time we broke up. I was still reeling and had no business participating in small talk, even with a good friend, because all I knew in that moment was big, existential talk. As is customary with David, our encounter began with a gust of forwardness.

"You look like your grandmother died," he said.

MIDDLE SPOON

When I offered nothing in response, he continued, "Oh shit, man. Did your grandmother actually die?"

"Yes," I said. "Years ago."

After an extended laugh that teetered on catharsis, I told him everything. That my husband and I had briefly opened up our marriage, that I'd met you, that we'd had an intense, short-lived affair, and that I was feeling low because you'd decided to end things suddenly.

"Say something," I said after I'd finished. By this point, we were standing in the shade of the bodega's awning, cradling our loose purchases.

"I'm shocked," he said. "I didn't expect this from you guys. I thought everything was going well."

"Everything is going well. There's nothing wrong with us. I just . . . met someone."

"Wow. I'd kill to be gay," he said, almost to himself.

David didn't browbeat me or utter a judgmental word, no doubt disarmed by the hollow in my eyes and the softness to my posture—there is no better way to describe how I felt: hollow and soft. If he disapproved of anything I'd shared, he did so secretly and quickly before pivoting toward kindness. More kindness than I'd come to expect from him. On that terrible July morning, David even offered to buy me a coffee, all the while offering reassurances: "This'll pass, man. Give it a few days. I think it's cool you guys allowed yourself to have this."

David's support, however, must have ended then and there, after we'd discarded our disposable cups, because when we saw each other earlier this month, he took a different tack.

I was walking home through the park with my dry cleaning in hand. It was cold, but it was the tolerable cold of recent inconvenient-truth Decembers. The park was dotted with only a few characters: nannies and their charges; off-leash dogs and their intrepid owners; and David. I followed slowly behind him, never saying a word, hoping I could avoid the

· *173* ·

encounter, but there was little chance of that since we live on the same block. When he reached his stoop, he turned. "How's it going?" he called out.

"Hey!" I shouted.

He pulled the small, white earbuds from his ears and placed them in their little, white case. "What's wrong?"

I deflected. I spoke broadly about friends and the state of the city, but when that ended, he inquired again, "What's wrong?"

The thought of crying in front of David embarrassed me. "Nothing" was all I could muster that wouldn't unleash a deluge.

"Is it your guy—the boyfriend?" he said while affecting quotation marks.

"That's over," I responded before turning away to readjust the shirts and hangers in my hand. When I looked back, David was staring at me with the blank-eyed expression I've come to associate with underprepared clinicians, which only made his subsequent reaction all the more shocking.

"Good," he said rather pointedly, "I'm glad. You should have let it die last summer."

David is the sort of person who'll ask anyone (best friend, complete stranger) anywhere (in the middle of a party or street) if the blemish on their face is herpes, so it shouldn't have surprised me he would say what he felt on the matter. What surprised me was that he felt as strongly as he did, and that he hadn't blunted his reaction for my sake.

"Honestly," he continued, "it was weird and unnecessary. It's for the best."

I could think of nothing to respond that wouldn't have caused a confrontation, so I walked away, despite the conversation having had no firm conclusion, and despite the sudden burst of wind that blew my pressed shirts and their thin plastic sheets into the air, making them unwieldy and my exit graceless.

MIDDLE SPOON

"Oh, c'mon, man!" David called out. "I'm sorry. I'm sorry you're down."

"It's all good. You're probably right," I said without stopping or looking back.

David's assessment could very well have been the correct one. I sensed it was, and I was grateful to have a friend who cared so much about my marriage and my husband, and possibly me, to be as frank as he'd been. But on that day, I was reeling from the surreality of our breakup, and I couldn't appreciate David or his godforsaken probity or his devotion to my family. I wanted only to hear something reassuring, something that might explain or arrest the cataclysmic events in me. I would have settled for an arm around my shoulders. David is, after all, a tall person with the wingspan of an Olympic swimmer; a bit of affection from him might have been enough. For the love of God, why is it so difficult to receive compassion? Furthermore, why is it so difficult to ask for compassion? I could have said, *David, shut up and hug me!* But I didn't. I walked away, even more dejected, and simultaneously afraid David had been a bellwether. Maybe I wouldn't receive sympathy from anyone. I was (I am), after all, the very picture of a charmed existence—health, family, happiness, professional success, wealth, man. It was I who played with fire and (to possibly no one's surprise) got burned. I, too, would have had trouble sympathizing with that protagonist—I'm having trouble now.

These last weeks have proven me wrong; compassion hasn't been in short supply. But every day is a new day with an accumulation of the days that preceded it, and I can hear a distance growing in the voices of my friends. There's an efficiency to their sympathies and reassurances—calls are shorter; texts are fewer. I have no choice but to get over you.

—Me

Dear Academy of Motion Picture Arts and Sciences, Television Academy, and Recording Academy,

I recently watched Martin McDonagh's *The Banshees of Inisherin*, and I have thoughts I'd like to bring to your attention, not about the film per se but about films in general and about the current state of mainstream art.

I hadn't seen McDonagh's previous outing, the one with Frances McDormand, in part because of my diminished appreciation for McDormand, but primarily, I avoided the Irish director's film because of my disdain for non-US directors who come to work in the US. In fact, it's distrust more than disdain, which, come to think of it, is probably why my appreciation and respect for Pedro Almodóvar has remained intact all these years, even if he did make that short film with Tilda Swinton last year, and even if she becomes his muse in subsequent films—yes, I know Tilda isn't from the US, but the same principle applies. My hang-up is simple: I find it tacky, and borderline traitorous, when filmmakers make a name for themselves in their respective countries of origin with actors and crews from those same countries, typically with funding from their governments, and then, after achieving an above average degree of notoriety, they jump ship and hire a cast and crew of nonnationals, in particular, from the US, to burnish their résumés or to make money or to . . . what? Be able to claim some sort of achievement for working within the US context? It's a brain drain and, frankly, a bad idea, not least of all because those movies tend to suck. Did you see the Blueberry one with Norah Jones from Wong Kar-wai? (I don't think anyone did.) Then again, Alfonso Cuarón crossed over, and his Harry Potter installment was big-budget brilliance. Then again, that was the UK.

· *176* ·

MIDDLE SPOON

As for Tilda Swinton, I'm not a fan of her either. And no, I'm not one of these people who dislikes beloved celebrities simply to be contrarian. Okay, fine, I'm often skeptical of fads—what glory, after all, is there in piling on?—but I hardly go out of my way to dislike folks. Consider the case of Taylor Swift. I genuinely disliked her music from the get-go. I saw her perform with Stevie Nicks at the Grammys in the year when Swift won her first Album of the Year—don't get me started on her having multiple of those coveted trophies when so many other worthy musicians don't have even one Album of the Year—ahem Jazmine Sullivan, ahem Pearl Jam, ahem Bruce, ahem Janet, ahem Madonna, AHEM Prince. In any case, when I saw Swift perform alongside Nicks, my first thought was, *Who on God's green Earth approved this?* She was a mere mortal beside Nicks. A high schooler completely unprepared for the moment. This is all to say, I didn't board the Swiftie train for legitimate reasons, not because I derive pleasure in manufacturing hatred for people I don't know who are more popular or successful than me, which I believe is a common reason for hating people we don't know: envy. But I'm not envious of Swift. In fact, I've come to appreciate her music. Sometimes, I even like her. Not that she needs me to like her. She doesn't need a damn thing. And while I remain firm in my belief that her musical prowess is overvalued, there are many worse people out there, and if I give it some thought, she's actually not bad at all. I'll even admit I love "Lover." Song par excellence. Genius pop. It's also worth noting that the very notion I should have an opinion about this performer, a youngish woman, doesn't feel right or, even more important, necessary. There are plenty of truly terrible humans to criticize in this world. Majority of them men—Jon Voight, Kanye West, Henry Kissinger, Jared Kushner. So many unearned, testosterone-laden privileges to fold into paper planes and fling into the Pacific or Vesuvius. Taylor Swift should not be my or anyone else's target. Neither should Tilda or Frances, but since I've already begun . . .

• *177* •

Tilda is a fine actor who deserves her plaudits, in particular the Oscar for her *Michael Clayton* performance, whose barely contained lunacy was nothing short of magnificent, plus the accent. On the other hand, that was the year you could have recognized Ruby Dee for a career that went largely unnoticed by your members. I'm not, it should be clear, advocating for a policy in which actors are bestowed prizes for their life's work in lieu of their nominated performances, but since it happens often enough for white actors—Alan Arkin over Eddie Murphy is a recent example—it's only fair your collective guilt should serve non-white actors too, no? (Full disclosure: I didn't watch *Dreamgirls* or the movie for which Ruby Dee didn't win.)

As for Tilda, I dislike her not because she inadvertently deprived Ms. Dee of an Oscar—should she and all the supporting actors that year not have submitted their names for consideration? Should Adele, in an act of solidarity, not have submitted a subpar *25* for Album of the Year in deference to *Lemonade*? No, I don't blame Tilda for Ms. Dee's injustices. I dislike Tilda because of an anecdote I once heard Margaret Cho tell. Apparently, Tilda reached out to Margaret during the fallout over Tilda being cast as the Ancient One in *Doctor Strange*, a role written as an East Asian character in the source material. To avoid blowback, Tilda wanted Margaret to endorse her, as if to say, *This Asian doesn't care if I'm cast in this role!* which Margaret didn't. The conversation, as recounted by Cho, soured my feelings on Swinton and further confirmed the racial obliviousness of Europeans.

While we're on the topic of Cho, I don't think she's ever been utilized to her fullest potential. Not every stand-up comedian has a Marlon Brando inside of them, but I have no doubt Cho has a fountain of emotion and a spectrum of nuance that could be honed by a skilled director. Her riches remain untapped because of all the rampant [insert *-isms* here] in Hollywood. This, in my opinion, is the major failing of the Me Too

MIDDLE SPOON

movement: its inability to repair the more egregious and outward-facing instances of sexism. Yes, the institutions need to be scrubbed clean of the patriarchy, but let's also see some concrete results. Cho, like Annabella Sciorra, like Mira Sorvino, like all the people whose lives were ruined by powerful men, should have the right of first refusal on the next ten jobs she wants. Casting directors should start with a list of Me Too survivors.

My problem with Frances McDormand is my problem with Swift is my problem with Swinton. I've been a die-hard fan of McDormand for many years, but once she started winning third and fourth Academy Awards, the achievement bar inched up, and what I've observed is McDormand no longer transforms into anything. The human who animatedly accepts Oscars is indistinguishable from the spunky characters she plays in her movies. In other words, her acting is merely a heightened version of herself, which isn't necessarily not acting or bad acting; it's Tom Cruise acting. McDormand's role in the Zhao film was, admittedly, much subtler than her usual fare, but even then, she didn't deserve an Oscar over Viola Davis's performance in *Ma Rainey*.

That's the other problem with overdoing the accolades for a handful of folks: the opportunity costs. Actors doing great work, even better work, are being passed over because of the familiarity, fame, and fawning over these incumbent performers, which, it must be said, are white. And before you call me out on vaunting flamboyance over subtlety (i.e., Davis's Ma Rainey over McDormand's trailer park denizen)—no. Not at all. This isn't about that; Davis was a marvel. And if your members truly valued delicate, felt performances, they wouldn't have ignored Alfre Woodard in *Clemency* in the year Zellweger won her second Oscar and ScarJo was nominated twice.

To address these irregularities and injustices, I encourage you to look no further than the Emmys, which inadvertently proposed a remedy a

· *179* ·

few years ago, the year the *Saturday Night Live* writers hosted the show, the year of the reparations skit, in which they handed out Emmys to Black actors who'd been previously snubbed. It was meant as a funny, albeit pointed, interlude, but they righted some wrongs that night by simply recognizing the contributions of Marla Gibbs, Kadeem Hardison, Jaleel White, John Witherspoon, Tichina Arnold, and Jimmie Walker. I wish all award shows would do something similar—that is, acknowledge deserving performances that were overlooked in their time. The very notion of redress promotes humility, engenders a desire for truth and justice, and comes with a degree of catharsis. The annual award could be named Best Overlooked Performance, and it would have to be aired during the live ceremony.

How did I get to this point? Oh, right, McDonagh! The new movie was fantastic. A return to form. And, it must be said, a return to Ireland. I'm not sure if I fully understood it all, but I couldn't look away from the screen. On the surface, the film is an absurdist tale about small people in a small place becoming sick of one another, about the end of kindness, but it also seems there's an allegorical component, apart from the war in Ireland, about the danger of inaction and complacency. Maybe it was meant as a critique of art or an attack on those who didn't support Irish independence, choosing instead the idyllic comforts of their green hills. Whatever the intention, the performances were mesmerizing. I would be perfectly happy to live in a world in which Colin Farrell is an Oscar winner. I mean, if Matthew McConaughey gets to have one, everyone should, no?

Sincerely,

PS: I hope you won't receive this as presumptuous, but I've been meaning to suggest other ideas about your acting awards. As society moves toward

MIDDLE SPOON

eliminating, collapsing, and expanding gender, I propose adding two more performance categories to the Oscars: Best Acting in a Featured Role and Best Acting in a Voice-over Role. These two would be in addition to the more traditional categories, Best Acting in a Leading Role and Best Acting in a Supporting Role. In other words, there would still be four acting winners, but they would be genderless awards. To be clear, the distinction between Supporting and Featured Roles is primarily one of screen time, but possibly of importance too. In *Ghost*, for example, Whoopi Goldberg would remain a supporting actor, and a scene-stealing performer like Vincent Schiavelli (the tormented subway spirit) would be nominated in the Featured category, alongside the likes of Martin Short in *Father of the Bride* or Rosie Perez in *Do the Right Thing* or Anthony Heald in *The Silence of the Lambs* or John Witherspoon in *Friday* or Kathryn Hunter in anything.

PPS: Since I have your attention. At the Oscars, the Best Original Song should be one that appears in the movie and is integral to the story. That award has become nothing more than an EGOT box-checker. Writing a pop song and then affixing it to the credits should not translate into film award credentials. With all due respect to the rhythmless tracks that bookend the Bond films, *Encanto*'s Lin-Manuel Miranda was robbed. Billie Eilish and her brother are great and should win armfuls of Grammys, and the performances of their songs on their respective award show broadcasts, if deemed spectacular, should be considered for Emmys, but not for Oscars.

PPPS: On second thought, Martin Short in *Father of the Bride* might very well meet the criteria for Supporting.

· *181* ·

Dear Ben,

This afternoon, I met with my sister for lunch in the West Village. She was visiting from Albany, where she works as a legislative aide for a state senator who was recently accused of accepting bribes during his years on the city council. The senator was my sister's professor in college, and he contacted her almost ten years ago when he made the leap from academia to politics. "He's too mild-mannered and idealistic to get caught up in bribes," my sister whispered, as we settled into our table and tied up the conversation that had consumed most of our walk over from the subway. "I know it sounds simple, but he's not like that. And you know me, I'm a good judge of character," she said while perusing the wine list. "We think it's a ploy by the guy who wants to unseat him next November."

The restaurant was a splendid one, on a charming street lined with trees, vagrants, and sex shops. I'd been to it several times, but never with you. Despite it being Italian, the staff accommodated my dietary restrictions with near ebullient degrees of pride and attentiveness: "But of course we can do that, sir." "I'd be happy to substitute the polenta for fries made in a fryer that we keep free of gluten." "For dessert, the chef has offered to make you a meringue with a coconut cream and a homemade jam."

My sister and I shared the house salad, an abundant plate of greens, in fact the most abundant I'd ever been served: leaf atop leaf atop leaf in a chaotic mound that resembled a pile of crumpled money drizzled with sherry vinaigrette, which seemed a bit too on the nose considering the menu's prices. We also ordered the grilled artichokes doused in aioli and a plate of perfectly roasted chicken in a green sauce that managed to be both comforting and antagonistic. By the time the bill arrived, which I

· 182 ·

MIDDLE SPOON

snatched from the server's hands before my sister could, we'd drunk the equivalent of a bottle and a half of wine, the cost-inefficiency of which the server was quick to point out: "Next time, a bottle of the Cab Franc would make more sense," she said before committing to an exaggerated wink.

It was as we waited for the server to return that I began working up the nerve to broach you, but my sister's sixth sense preempted me.

"What's going on here?" she said while circling a tipsy finger in my direction.

I was tired of saying *Nothing*, so I exhaled forcefully instead.

"Oh, this is big, huh?" she said.

"Kinda."

"Would it help to say it quickly?"

"Maybe."

She placed her hands over mine. "Go ahead. Like when we were kids. Close your eyes and just say it fast."

I did just that. I closed my eyes, and everything came out. I told her your name. I told her about our age difference. I told her about our racial discordance. About how the kids had met you, at which point I felt her hands leave mine. I told her how it had all been unplanned. About how my husband was game. About the first breakup. About the most recent. About Fred. About Sandy. For good measure, I came out as the parent of a nonbinary child.

When I was done, I opened my eyes and found my sister recoiled into her chair. Her arms were crossed in the international sign of unhappiness, and the squint of her eyes communicated something between *You're disgusting* and *WTF*. It took her much too long to say anything. I was about to recriminate her for encouraging me to be so vulnerable and then abandoning me, but just then the server showed up with the receipt for me to sign.

"Thank you for dining with us," she announced. "We hope you had a pleasant experience and that you'll come back again soon."

· *183* ·

"Actually," my sister offered without invitation, "I have a minor critique."

"Oh," said the server. "Absolutely. We value your feedback, and we'd be—"

"Since you opened the bottle of wine for us and served it all before opening another for our third round, it would have been nice of you to charge us for the first bottle and not for the individual glasses."

The server's eyes shrunk to nearly nothing, and her long, thin fingers clamped her waist—international sign for simmering teapot. "I will share your suggestion at the next staff meeting," the worker managed to say before walking away.

"Are you kidding me? Another white guy?" my sister asked.

"What?"

"All you ever do is complain about the whiteness in your life—at the university, at the kids' schools, in your neighborhood. Why bring another white person into the mix? What about the kids? They would have two white dads and you?"

"Ben wasn't their dad. And Latino isn't a race; it's an ethnicity."

"You missed me with that. You know exactly what I mean."

"It doesn't matter. The relationship is over. Now, can you dig into your purse and see if you have any gum and sympathy to spare?"

"I'm sorry you're hurting. But also, this is just like you."

"What are you talking about? I've never done anything like this before."

"Not this, but all your life you've been impatient and indecisive."

"I absolutely haven't."

"I have at least forty texts from you about possible restaurant options for today's lunch."

"I wanted you to have a great meal. Sue me!"

"In college, you were premed, then drama, then government, and finally public health."

MIDDLE SPOON

"Oh, excuse me for taking advantage of a fine liberal arts education."

"Before you got married, you told me you wanted to bail and take a trip to Bolivia instead."

"What Evo Morales did for the Indigenous population is unheard of. Chomsky called it the closest society to a true democracy. Besides, am I not allowed to have wedding jitters?"

"When you were a kid, you'd get upset if we had to leave the supermarket. Mom says if you spent more than twenty minutes anywhere, you'd have trouble leaving."

"Okay, so I'm not good with transitions."

"You tried to get your high school friends to move to Cancún with you after a five-day graduation trip."

"It was a fun time, and we weren't well-traveled people."

"Life isn't only about fun and new experiences."

"You sound like a dorm poster."

"And you sound like an anxious person with perpetual FOMO going through a midlife crisis."

"I ask again, can I have some sympathy? This has been a miserable experience. When I'm not drunk and sad, I'm sober and scared. Say something encouraging. Please."

My sister rolled her eyes and shook her head, flipping her hair in the process: a shampoo commercial. "I'm sorry you're going through this. I've been there, and I know you'll be okay."

My sister is not known for that sort of sincerity or kindness, so I was—

"But for real, I'm fucking glad this didn't work out. I'm all for poly blah blah, but you have kids and the best husband in the world, and a pretty great life. Introducing a younger man into the picture is just . . . way too off-the-grid. And my God, Mom and Dad would have lost their minds. Please never tell them."

"Do you really believe that?"

· *185* ·

"One thousand percent. I still haven't shown them my tattoo, and it's been fifteen years. Just let them die without another American Dream nightmare—and don't expect me to cozy up to this Ben person if you get back together."

"We're not getting back together."

On the walk to the subway, my sister pretended to bump into me several times, her way of making peace. When I said nothing, she sneaked her hand into mine. "I'm here if you need me," she whispered. I smelled the wine and garlic on her breath, which I knew were on mine too. I squeezed her hand.

If anyone could be simultaneously right and wrong, it was my sister.

When I was almost home, I received a text: "Jules is so nonbinary. No child has ever straddled the line so perfectly," she wrote and then affixed a yellow, white, purple, and black flag GIF, which I hadn't realized was the nonbinary flag.

All in all, not a bad coming out for any of us.

—Me

Hi,

The cyclical nature of art is one of the benefits of living in New York City. Good art returns, usually. Yesterday, for example, I saw a play I'd missed twenty years earlier, one of those major works everyone told me to see and that I had every intention of seeing when I was twenty-two, but, for one reason or another, dragged my feet and missed.

I went to the matinee of *Topdog/Underdog*. It was on the list of shows we made on your couch a few weeks before we broke up. Remember? We'd just showered. My hair was still wet. You were wearing small briefs and putting on long striped socks. It was a short list—two Broadway shows, one off-Broadway, two off-off-Broadway—because we both agreed ticket prices had become untenable, in a way that neither inflation nor worker salaries could justify, something we both felt entitled to assert because of our various friends in the theater world who are egregiously underpaid for their efforts. Our goal was to buy the tickets before the start of spring—we looked at a calendar and chose March 21 as our deadline, despite a mild disagreement about whether the date of the equinox had changed as a result of the quarter day or eighth of a day that gets tallied annually but that neither of us understood well. *Topdog* was near the top of our list.

To say Suzan-Lori Parks's play is a masterpiece would be both obvious and unoriginal. It's a two-hander by two shape-shifters—Corey Hawkins and Yahya Abdul-Mateen. I'd seen these actors in other shows and movies, but they were unrecognizable in this. If the awards gods were just, these two actors would split all the pertinent trophies this season, which, in my opinion, doesn't happen enough. The sharing of awards, that is. There are performances so symbiotic that considering them independently is a slight to the intrinsic nature of the roles and to the very skill (nay, art!) of collaboration. Imagine living in a society that nominates two actors in one slot. The very notion implies a respect for cooperation and collectivity that, frankly, we don't have and that we cannot achieve without more, well, cooperation and collectivity. Tom Hulce and F. Murray Abraham would have both won Oscars for *Amadeus*. Susan Sarandon and Geena Davis might have both won for *Thelma & Louise*. Bill and Hillary could have ruled as one, officially. As it concerns *Topdog*, however, it's fairer to say there were three entities on the stage: the two protagonists and the pain they lobbed between each other. The trauma of their youth became the currency of their adulthood. Their humor, their language, their demeanors, their choices: all of them, manifestations of pain. What a tremendous indictment of our society! To communicate something so global through something so interpersonal is the greatness of art, and I was lucky to have experienced it.

And yet, during one of the most mesmerizing stage works I'd seen in years, I was still thinking about you. The actors and stage crafters did their very best to enrapture me, but periodically I'd wake and realize I hadn't been paying attention to one of the greatest American dramas of the last century. It was like driving on a highway and suddenly becoming aware you've been on autopilot for God knows how long—seconds? Minutes? Entire states?—a terribly frightening sort of somnambulance that, on Broadway, is a tremendous waste of money, as well as a little bit frightening. If Suzan-Lori Parks can't keep my mind from drifting, what chance do I have?

When I woke yesterday, I sensed I was in for a difficult afternoon. Instead of getting out of bed, I chose to remain under the covers and to curl up as tightly as possible, like a rodent fetus or one of those useless fiddleheads that appear in the farmers market every spring, my eyes squeezed shut, my bent knees pressed against each other, my head under a pillow. I felt as if I'd entered a second wave of this sickness, the pain renewed and fresh, as barbed and electric as it was on the first day. I went to the *Topdog*

MIDDLE SPOON

matinee in part because I believed theater would serve as immersive palliative care. But from the moment I arrived, until the moment the curtain went up, I had to dig deep into my reserves of willpower not to text you.

Draft 1: "Can I come by after the show,
before picking up Nico from school?"

I was proposing the sort of late-afternoon visit I'd made dozens and dozens of times over the previous year. Yesterday, however, what was once expected and comforting would have been fraught. These whims, Ben! These near-actions built on desperate desires—as if nothing were remotely wrong—somehow trick me into believing everything will go back to normal if I pretend everything is normal.

I came close to sending you that message several times; instead, I busied myself studying the mix of matinee-goers—tourists, theater students on class trips, retirees—funneling into the regal red room with gilded fixtures and truly abysmal legroom. Then the lights flickered, and the ushers hurried to their stations. That was the moment to message you because I was seconds from turning off my phone, which would have remained off until intermission, giving you plenty of time to respond. In fact, I was on the verge of hitting send when the realization arrived: I wouldn't have had enough time to see you before picking up Nico from school because I hadn't accounted accurately for the Midtown-to-Brooklyn trajectory. At the tail end of this epiphany, the theater's lights began to dim, so I panicked and typed something else, an attempt at humor.

Draft 2: "You over me yet?"

But before I could commit to sending those four words, it occurred to me that they might land poorly, and possibly painfully, so I tried again.

· *189* ·

Draft 3: "This is really hard. I miss you.
What are we doing?"

I was milliseconds from sending that existential missive, but then I imagined you responding after I'd turned off my phone and being insulted I'd waited ninety minutes to reply. You'd think I was playing games even though I wasn't playing games. Just then, the short usher with short hair and big eyeglasses, who bore a striking resemblance to Martin Scorsese, waved at me furiously to turn off my phone, which I did without hitting send, forcing me to subdue my desire to text you throughout the show, even during intermission, throughout every second of that gut-wrenching bravura final act, during my commute to Nico's school, throughout Nico's birthday dinner (what kind of shitty parent is thinking about his ex-boyfriend when he should be celebrating his child?), throughout the evening, including the final episode of *Ramy*—gosh, that season was uneven—until I went to sleep. It gnawed at me like an infected wound, a damaged spleen, or something similarly internal and obsolete.

Blah blah I'm hurt. Blah blah I'm miserable. Blah blah I'm repetitive. Blah blah blah blah blah I've been dumped and so has everyone else on Earth and throughout history I need to grow the hell up and move on and forget you we were never going to last anyway and you're out there getting fucked by all the tops in Williamsburg are there any tops in Williamsburg you probably go to Bushwick for tops good luck to you Ben.

—Me

PS: There is precedent for nominating two actors in the same slot. *Side Show*'s Alice Ripley and Emily Skinner were co-nominated for a Tony for lead actress in a musical. They played conjoined twins.

Dear Ben,

Today, the downstairs neighbors moved out after only two years. They'd bought the two-bedroom, one-bath apartment from the ornery couple with the three cats who'd hightailed out of the city just weeks after the pandemic became undeniable and who'd settled somewhere along the Hudson, in a bucolic town whose residents regularly get profiled in *The New York Times* for doing all manner of artistic things. The couple who bought the place from the ornery people—ornery in part because they complained whenever anyone left their own umbrellas or their own shoes on their own welcome mat or whenever someone hadn't closed the dryer doors properly. It must be said, the haranguing (it was certainly not gracious) always took place over email; in person they were aggressively polite and engaging. Anyway, the couple who bought the apartment from this ornery couple was also ornery, off-putting over email and in person, in the sort of way that someone might label spectrum-y—direct, unfriendly, and unaware—if such a label were acceptable. But while the first couple seemed to relish putting the rest of us in our place, much like our galoshes, the second couple, the one who moved out today, the one who moved in barely two years ago, didn't appear to take any joy in telling the rest of us that "someone should do something about the terrible stench in the garbage bins" or that they found it "very distressing that the front door was left ajar in this current climate." It felt to me as if not chiding us or not naming the obvious things in a passive-aggressive fashion caused them harm, and self-harm at that—they had no choice. By the way, the climate they referred to was not meteorological but instead socioeconomic—our resplendent, tree-lined, historically landmarked block abuts the second-poorest census tract in New York City—but the second ornery couple could never bring themselves to say such a thing or, to be fair, didn't know about such things. Instead, they spent a year living in a sublet in a less economically undesirable part of the city, while they renovated their home—completely gutted the apartment downstairs—and allowed their contractor and his team to consistently leave *both* front doors ajar, while the rest of us rolled our eyes and worried quietly about the climate. I don't know to where the latest couple is moving, only that the newest couple, who arrives next week, paid a price so exorbitant for the two-bedroom, now-two-bath, it was written up in the local press. And yet, I don't think the couple who moved out today profited as greatly as one might deduce from the real estate announcement, because their renovation was of a caliber that could not have cost less than four years of an Ivy League education—easily. Their profit, however, was still well greater than a year's living wage for a family of six in the city. But I don't think their primary concern was money. It was safety: the husband of the most recently departed couple was mugged one week before they decided to list the apartment. He was left physically intact, but the experience, in addition to the lack of elevator in our modest brownstone town house, was incentive enough to flee. The couple prior to the ornery ones who now live upstate (with their cats) had also gutted the apartment and left after only four years because the wife in the (not ornery at all) couple— four pairs ago, if you've lost track—fell in love with another man in the neighborhood who also walked his dog in the park at six thirty a.m., which didn't surprise me at all because whoever volunteers to leave their home so early every morning in order to walk their dog is in some way or another unsatisfied at home.

I haven't, with any confidence or conviction, liked or disliked the various couples who have lived in the unit below, but when each of them announced their intentions to move, a pit developed in my stomach, a

MIDDLE SPOON

trepidation that lies dormant in anyone who lives in a shared building in a liberal city of transplants and generational wealth, the uncertainty of who will be joining the human experiment. Might they at last be the ones who make living in my home unpleasant? Miserable? Might they be the greatest people I've ever known? One has to live to tell it.

The ease with which people choose to leave their homes in this city is quite unsettling given all the people who've left without a choice, those who ended up far from the place where they had lived, sometimes for their entire lives. It isn't only the arrival of new folks that accelerates the injustice; it's their departures too. Only then is the vaunted value of the home marked in the record of time, increasing the cost of housing for everyone else. There would be no occasion to reappraise value if the home weren't vacated, and no one would know what a home currently costs if it weren't listed.

On the other hand, moving periodically probably makes one more adaptable to life's situations. An eighty-year-old person who has lived in her home for fifty-five years, for example, will have a much more difficult time adjusting to a nursing home than the ornery couples who move every two, five, or seven years.

I've thought, too, about how invigorating and possibly life-affirming it would be for me to get up and go somewhere, anywhere. And how I would if I were alone in this world. And if it were easier to find reasonably priced housing in New York.

—Me

Dear Ben,

Near the end, things were getting rough. In bed, that is. You liked me to be firm with you, a firmness that teetered on violence. You wanted me to press my hand onto the back of your head until there was little air between your face and the pillow. You liked teeth. You absorbed a well-timed shove. You loved an unforgiving grip on your flesh. A languorous slap across your back or ass made you yelp with curiosity, a wounded thing intrigued by his assailant. I did my best to meet your desires, to inhabit the character you wanted in the bedroom, in the kitchen, in the shower, in an empty subway car, but I couldn't help second-guessing myself—*Did that hurt? Was that too rough? Are we going to get arrested?*—and consequently overthinking the visceral moments. I became the personification of a nagging cough or a ringing cell phone during a night of theater. I sensed your frustration—*I'll tell you when it hurts!*—but I was much too concerned with crossing lines and causing harm to fully commit. Whether my apprehensions are the natural consequence of a youth peppered with violence or simply another characteristic of my Plinko slot is difficult to know.

Did I ever tell you about my volunteer gig during grad school? For a brief time, I delivered food to people living with AIDS, all of whom were quite far along in their opportunistic infection trajectories and therefore deemed too unwell to go out in search of nourishment or to prepare their own meals at home. In some cases, the physical deteriorations led to psychological burdens that kept them indoors; they were afraid of facing the world as they were. I didn't know enough about the progression of AIDS to understand why, with the availability of antiretroviral therapies—it was the early aughts after all—they were in such poor shape, but they were.

To be clear, I didn't seek out the job because I was a good guy, although I'm not a bad guy, or because I operated under the assumption that altruism is an unimpeachable attribute; I did it because I wanted to be a good guy, and I knew I couldn't be one while holding on to my prejudices.

You see, I'd come of age during the first wave of the AIDS epidemic, and I, like so many gays socialized during an era marked by desperate uncertainty—or maybe just the Catholic ones—was petrified of getting infected. I couldn't disentangle my basic desires from assured death, probably because *AIDS is a punishment from God* had been an oft-repeated admonishment—at home, in church, on TV—that served as both warning and divination, and while I don't know if I was ever swayed into believing God (THE God, the bearded one) had nothing better to do than infect humans with illness, I became convinced the gays—all of us— wouldn't escape infection. A matter of if, not when. In fact, I was so afraid of getting HIV, I steered clear of penetrative sex until I met my husband.

It's worth noting that the lack of anal sex in my repertoire did nothing to prevent me from getting tested regularly. Kissing a boy with significant stubble that left my face chafed was reason enough to visit the clinic. This is all to say, I've had fear-based attitudes about sex, and about life in general, for most of my time on this Earth. I wasn't only afraid of getting HIV through sex or basic touch with a fellow gay; I was one of those after-school-special, daytime-talk-show-audience people who was afraid of being in proximity to HIV—handshakes, water fountains, subway cars.

Ignorance, nothing more, nothing less.

Ben, I have to admit I often felt the decade of life between us was to

· 195 ·

our disadvantage. We'd never be able to discover life's monuments together because I'd be visiting them for a second or third time. I would spend our lives observing your reactions to the new things, the way I do my children's. But this—HIV/AIDS—is one context in which your age undoubtedly served as an advantage. You never knew to be afraid of sex the way I'd been. You were unfazed by prophylactic pill regimens. You didn't mind your ass being a pin cushion for injectable treatments. In fact, you'd had several sexual partners with HIV. This lack of hang-ups and the humanity that accompanied it were an enviable collection of freedoms I couldn't fathom.

It should be said that in the period of my life where I held ignorant attitudes about HIV, I never voiced (never mind defended) them to anyone. I was afraid and yet somehow self-aware enough to be embarrassed, and as I matured, the fear and embarrassment remained, but to my surprise, a penchant for enlightenment also took shape. Twenty-two-year-old me was determined to baby-step his way toward a more human consciousness, and he believed his path was a route, one delivering food to people living with the illness he most feared—or, to be scientifically accurate, a group of illnesses brought about by a depleted immune system.

The long, sprawling route of about twenty drop-offs took place over the course of a few hours on Thursday evenings in the suburbs of Seattle, where I lived during graduate school. At each stop, I'd announce myself— a knock, a buzz, a shout through an open window—and usually, someone came to the door. When they didn't, my predicament became about what I would do with the food I couldn't deliver. Because of the fresh produce and dairy, I'd been directed not to leave packages outside. Sometimes, I gave the last clients on the route—that was their official designation, *clients*—double meals. Sometimes, I brought the remaining bags of produce and oven-ready meals home with me and salvaged the fresh fruit but discarded the rest. Often, I gifted them to homeless people. One time

MIDDLE SPOON

I hadn't eaten lunch, and I ate cold, microwave-ready meat loaf in the parking lot of the housing complex where I'd just attempted a drop-off. Come to think of it, I did that a few times.

All of my clients were memorable for one reason or another: their homes, their degrees of wariness, their facial hair patterns, the unique damages to their bodies. Nearly everyone was nice, eager for companionship, a companionship I wanted to give but couldn't at the outset because of what their illnesses represented to me. A few of the clients kept their distance, *Thank you* and *Goodbye*, sometimes not answering the door and instead asking me to leave the food *Just outside, please!* But primarily the clients were happy to see another person and to exchange pleasantries. My first stop each week was at the house of an inquisitive man (*How long have you been doing this? Where are you from? What are you studying?*) in his late fifties or early sixties, gray domed, but also tall and broad shouldered with large arms. In fact, *he* was a couple. What I mean is, I should have delivered food only to his very ill partner, but the service agency that coordinated the food drop-offs acquiesced to delivering to both of them despite the healthier partner with HIV not meeting the agency's threshold for delivery: a rare instance of efficiency and compassion overlapping. It was the healthier partner—the brawny, garrulous man—to whom I handed the food each week at the door, but during the fifth or sixth week of volunteering I brought the groceries inside—a kindness the service agency had left to our discretion—because the front door was open when I arrived, and because he'd called out, "I'm in the kitchen!"

I recall the inside of the house was perfectly unremarkable—a couch, a wall-mounted television set, a table, possibly a few tables, paintings, books, a bit of chaos—apart from one unusual object: a massive sling that hung from the center of the living room's ceiling. I had to walk past this leather-and-metal contraption to reach the kitchen and more importantly the kitchen counter, where he'd instructed me to set the bags. The

· 197 ·

juxtaposition of a suburban living room and sex furniture led to a momentary dissonance. In my brief life, I'd already wandered into a few sex clubs, the sort of seedy venues that are often tucked into the industrial parts of the suburbs where one grows up or the third floors of multipurpose office buildings in the heart of a city where one moves after college. I'd also watched plenty of porn with sling set pieces. So while it was momentarily odd to be in proximity to something out of its expected context, it didn't require too much effort to affect indifference. "Here?" I asked pointing to the empty spot on the counter. "Thank you," he responded.

The following week, the door was again ajar at the sling house. "Hello?"

"We're in the kitchen," he shouted.

We, I assumed, meant him and his partner, the sicker man whom I'd yet to meet. But as I approached the kitchen counter—cluttered and light blue—I discovered *we* meant someone else altogether: a tall—taller than the refrigerator—man, bald and also muscular, as well as completely naked but for a studded leather cock ring. I pretended not to see anything, "Where do you want these?" I asked because I couldn't think of anything else to say.

The transition into something like shock was rapid. My heart was in my ears, and I could feel my blood flowing. My reaction wasn't exclusively in response to the unexpected man or his size or his absence of clothes; I was also acutely afraid because seconds earlier, while I'd made my way into the kitchen, I'd heard something behind me, which I now assumed was someone locking me into the house.

It was in those micro-moments of hysterical supposition that a heavy and rather calloused hand appeared on my neck. This flesh weapon wasn't attempting to choke but to transport, and the destination was the naked man standing before us, the refrigerator-sized man who could have snapped me in half if he'd so desired.

MIDDLE SPOON

My resistance was at first subtle, silent, and oddly involuntary. My neck found a posture I've only ever envied in others, and one of my legs inched backward, as if my body were endeavoring to do what my voice couldn't. But my efforts were ineffective and possibly counterproductive because the pressure on the back of my head mounted, and before I knew it, my face had made contact with the unknown man's bare, moist chest, his scent becoming one with my breath—*Wait! What's that other smell? Faint at first, but now stronger.* A chemical odor I associated with the back rooms of bars and the shadowy landmarks of my youth wafted into my nasal passages, and that was when I realized that the hitherto-garrulous man, the man I'd known for nearly two months' worth of Thursdays, had now coiled his gargantuan arm around me in the sort of headlock my brother had applied countless times in our childhood bedroom, while the naked man's long fingers brought a small bottle of poppers nearer to my face. Only then did I begin to struggle with force. Only then did I find my voice—*No. No! NO! NO! NO!*—and broke free and turned around and walked fast, then faster because running felt like an escalation, and I could almost hear the adults screaming at me to *Stop running!* as an off-leash dog chased seven-year-old me across an endless field of Flushing Meadows, but in that suburban Seattle sex dungeon, I might not have possessed the ability to run because my body was mid-thaw, somewhere between frozen, frightened, and full flight, and just as I approached the door, the probably locked door—this nothing-special door that was suddenly a portal to freedom—I realized my fate, not unlike the door, had been sealed, and so I simultaneously scanned the room for a window and something with which to shatter that window—I don't believe in fate, Ben—but instead what I saw was a man, a frail man, only his silhouette, a vision or a subject in a painting, something starkly baroque but not lavish. It was the sicker partner, the one I'd never met. He was lying on a gurney or a cot, tucked behind a very thin, transparent curtain, gossamer if ever there was a gossamer fabric, and I didn't know if he'd always been there or if he was a figment of my imagination or simply an audience. All I know is my hand gripped the doorknob and, to my ever-loving relief, it turned with the sort of ease only angels and genies can grant, and the nothing-special door opened with a similar facility, allowing me to step out into what remained of the autumn's evening light and experience one of the grandest moments of relief in my life.

Only then did I run. To my car, which was parked on the street, no more than fifty feet away, all the while fumbling for my keys before then fumbling *with* my keys, and after I managed to get inside and lock the car's doors—a minor miracle because my hands were two shapeless tuning forks that had just been whacked—I did my best to chill the fuck out because my legs, too, trembled, in a way that wouldn't have allowed me to drive. And as I sat there, keenly aware I was still too close to the epicenter of what had just happened, I called my then-boyfriend, now-husband, who told me to get out of there and drive a few blocks and park somewhere else, before telling me he had a meeting in a few minutes—"Can I call you back?" he asked. "Sure," I responded, but not before taking his advice and driving a few blocks and parking along a more visible road, where I did my best to breathe and stop vibrating. Then I called the agency, where I encountered a dumbfounded volunteer coordinator who had no idea how to respond and who managed after an interminable silence to say, "Are you sure?" a question that, despite its petiteness, filled all the unfilled spaces and signaled to me that nothing particularly horrific had happened and that I should pull myself together and continue my route because one bad apple shouldn't spoil the orchard or however that saying goes. And then a few minutes later my husband called back and said he was worried about me and I should go home, but I resisted because I was afraid of being afraid, and—"Can I call you back? The agency is calling," to ask if I was okay and to say they were very sorry and

MIDDLE SPOON

everyone there was worried about me. I guess everyone has delayed reactions to trauma, even when they're secondhand traumas, which is both useless for the endurer of the original trauma, but hopeful, too, in a way, for humanity because it suggests some people are still unfamiliar enough with trauma to develop systems to process it, which isn't to say we couldn't be a hopeful society with firm contingency plans, but there is something optimistic about not expecting the worst.

On that day, I delivered meals to the rest of the clients because violence and its vanguard, the threat of violence, weren't unfamiliar to me. The encounter in the kitchen was unimpeachably terrifying—yes—but I could place it on a spectrum and tell myself, *It was worse than this but not worse than that. Worse but not the worst. Bad but not the baddest. Terrible but not the most terrible.* This, while cynical in some regards, is also hopeful.

The next few months were difficult primarily because I wasn't capable of developing relationships with the clients, making the experience less fulfilling in a way, but then again, I was a delivery guy, not a friend. It was helpful to be reminded that this wasn't about me. The next few months were also difficult because I learned from the agency that the client who'd placed his hand on my neck and whose delivery service they'd discontinued was a retired cop, which left me with a nagging fear that he might try to retaliate for my complaint because, well, that's the sort of vindictive, morally bankrupt thing cops are known to do, and so for months, I looked over my shoulder more.

Those post–Sling House encounter months were difficult in yet another regard: I had to do some internal work to disentangle *violence* from *HIV* and *violence* from *gay*, tasks that proved difficult despite the very absurdity of the pairings. The experience, nevertheless, resonated with the prejudices I'd held all my life and that I'd hoped to exorcise at that very volunteer job.

· *201* ·

ALEJANDRO VARELA

Disentangling violence from whiteness proved even more onerous. I had trouble unseeing myself as a brown boy being taken advantage of by older white men who believed they had the right to treat me as they saw fit. Mistreat. All my life, white men had been doing it. And gay men had been some of the worst, but to be fair, most of the white-on-brown mistreatment had come from straight white men.

Ben, how muddled all of this is. You, a white man. My husband, a white man. Me, a brown man. If you'd stuck around, what would we have learned about our power dynamics? What would you have done to retain your power? Why do I put myself in these situations?

Seriously, what is happening inside that warren of flesh encased by my cranium?

I continued that delivery route for another year, and one Thursday, months after the incident, another client invited me inside his home. "I'm sorry," I said, "but I can't. I'm running late." He, too, was a friendly person. An urban cowboy—I called him that because every week he wore a Stetson, leather boots and vest, and suede chaps over his blue jeans. Midday, in the suburbs of Seattle. (All power to him!) Prior to the cowboy's invitation, our monthslong small talk had taken place on the stoop of his modest, red clapboard house, where we seldom faced each other but instead stared out at his barren lawn with its chain-link perimeter while exchanging pleasantries. At another time or in a parallel universe where I hadn't been accosted recently, I might have accepted his invitation. But *No, thank you* had now become my default stance on these matters. And yet, I labored to walk away. Isn't that rich? No matter my fears, I wanted to connect with this human, and I certainly didn't want him to think I was saying no because he was a man living with AIDS or because he was a Black man living with AIDS, never mind a Black cowboy living with AIDS, and so, moments after I'd rejected his invitation, I doubled back

· 202 ·

MIDDLE SPOON

and explained why. You see, Ben, I have always been an oversharer. You've marveled in the past about my ability to communicate freely, and I wish I could say it was a concerted effort on my part to be honest or my intrinsic respect for the truth, but it's much less calculated than that: I just can't help myself.

The cowboy sat down on his steps, and when I told him what had happened in the Sling House, a few tears pooled in his eyes before traveling the length of his face. Real cowboy tears. Then he lambasted humanity, particularly its most terrible components. "You didn't deserve that," he said. "I'm sorry they did that to you."

"You don't have to apologize," I told him. "Besides, I'm not afraid anymore. The worst of it is over."

"There's always one dipstick who ruins it for the rest of us."

Why, Ben, am I telling you this? Well, in part because I like telling you things about myself. I liked learning about you too—your basketball days in high school, your bathhouse predilection in your twenties, your penchant for falling asleep on a moving train and waking up several stations past home. I'm also telling you because I knew you wanted me to be rougher with you, and I found it difficult to comply. I feel a tension about performing violence during sex. It's thrilling, for sure, but separating it from real violence hasn't been a seamless process for me. Yes, there are entire niche communities of people who practice this type of sexual aggression in safe and consensual ways, but I wanted to know you better before I could give myself fully to the moment. I wasn't yet sure how to draw the distinctions between what we wanted for pleasure and what we were performing as a consequence of what we'd experienced in this life. It took my husband and me many years to explore this part of our sex life, and I still don't know if I've engaged in it for the right reasons, which is to say, I fear I'm reinforcing beliefs about myself that I've yet to unearth.

· 203 ·

To further complicate matters, our aforementioned racial discordance. Pain is one thing, but pain at the hands of, well, you know, is another thing altogether, and so I kept a degree of skepticism throughout our relationship. I'm no longer talking about BDSM. I'm talking about simply being with you.

—Me

Dear Ben,

You once told me a story about the first guy you kissed. I admit we'd had several drinks, and I don't recall if you recounted the tale at a bar or restaurant or on your couch, but I'm certain you were sitting close enough for me to put my hand on yours and close enough to feel that the mere recollections moved you.

The summer before college, you worked at a catering hall. "Mostly weddings," you explained. One of your coworkers was a Polish guy named Camile who was only a few years older than you. Tall and beautiful, he had an accent that disarmed everyone because of how it seemed to cradle every sound he uttered, but most of all, he was friendly. "He was also confident," you said. "Whenever someone—even our boss—called him Cam, he was quick to stand his ground. 'Cah-MEAL,' he'd say, but always friendly." Everyone loved Camile, and, frankly, he loved everyone in return, which is why you didn't place much importance on his habit of running his fingers through your hair or massaging your shoulders whenever the others were hiding behind the flower-delivery van smoking cigarettes.

"It didn't turn you on?" I asked.

"I wasn't out to myself then," you explained. "I enjoyed being around him, but I didn't think it was more than friendship. I thought that was how he was with everyone."

It wasn't until the week before you left for school that something unambiguous happened. You'd locked your keys inside of your car, and it had gotten too late to call your parents: "I'll take you," Camile said louder than everyone else who was offering to drive you home. "You're on my way," he explained. But you weren't on his way.

· 205 ·

When he pulled into your driveway, he turned the car off but said nothing, even after you'd thanked him. "He had a big grin on his face," you explained. "And I was all 'What?' but he kept smiling like I was supposed to know. That's when he put his hand on my leg and squeezed my thigh. If he had done that at work, I wouldn't have thought twice, but in the car, it wasn't playful. It was different, something I'd never experienced before."

"That was you first encounter with a guy?" I asked.

"I remember play-wrestling with one of my friends once and realizing afterward that I'd gotten hard. But I'd never done anything with anyone except kiss a girl once freshman year. It's weird to explain, but before Camile, everything was unclear and not particularly urgent. After . . . everything changed."

You and Camile kissed for a while before he undid your pants and blew you.

"I was just about to finish when I saw a light turn on in the house. It was my parents' bathroom, and I didn't move until the light went off. Then Camile offered to drive us to an empty lot a few blocks away. All these years later, I still can't believe I had the nerve to say yes."

"What became of Camile?"

"We worked together for one more week, but I was young and nervous, and of course immature me avoided him as much as I could. It took that entire week before I could get the smell of him out of my nose and the taste out of my mouth. Even though it was sexy, it felt shameful too."

"Poor Camile."

"I called him before I left for school, but I didn't recognize the person who answered, so I panicked and hung up. The wild thing is when I got to school, I had to come up with a password for my email account, so I scrambled up his name and phone number. For four years, every time I

MIDDLE SPOON

had to use my password, I thought of him. One Thanksgiving, while I was home, I got drunk and called him, but I hung up after one ring."

You got quiet after recounting that story, as if Camile had been someone very meaningful.

"He wasn't that important," you explained, "but he was the first guy. I think I carried that around with me for a long time. I didn't come out for another year or so. It was at least another year after that before I hooked up with another guy. Camile was the only person in the world who knew me intimately, and he was the only person I knew in that way."

"Have you ever looked him up?"

"It's kind of fun to think about that experience from time to time, but I never pined after him. But I guess—I don't know."

"What?"

"I've wondered what it would have been like if there had never been any pressure to hide anything. If everything were normal. My parents met just before college, at a summer camp where they were both counselors. And they're still together. Maybe in the multiverse, Camile and I have been together for almost twenty years, and we have kids and a house somewhere."

Again you got quiet, but you had the appearance of someone who was thinking or possibly lamenting. I realized then that you were more of a romantic than I'd allowed myself to believe, and that maybe my presence in your life was preventing you from a simpler, happier existence.

"Probably not," you continued, "but maybe."

Love,
Me

Dear Ben,

This morning, Traci called me earlier than I've come to expect. Her name typically flashes on my phone at eleven a.m.—she's on the West Coast—but today it was nearer to nine thirty. I've known Traci since graduate school, but the urgency of our breakup has imbued the friendship with a sense of renewal. For the last few weeks, we've talked every day, often twice a day, three times on a few days, which is why I didn't think anything of her earlier call. But this morning had nothing to do with me.

"The police knocked on my door at two a.m. They said I was involved in a hit-and-run."

"Are you kidding?"

"No, they said I hit another car, and the driver of that car followed me home, and then went to the police and reported me."

"Is this a joke?"

"I know! They said they have video."

"Who? The police or the person who accused you?"

"I don't know. The police said they've seen the video."

"Is this even remotely possible?"

"No! Hell no! I'd know if I was in a car accident!"

"Are they saying the person was hurt?"

"No. They're not saying anything. They just wanted me to know."

"They didn't arrest you?"

"No. Thank God. Apparently, I have to wait a few days for the report."

"That was all?"

MIDDLE SPOON

"They asked if they could come into my house. I told them no."

"Good. And that was it?"

"Then they went and checked out my car. But I don't know what they did. It was two a.m.! I was half asleep."

"Are you okay?"

"I'm shaking. Literally shaking. I think I was in shock when they told me, but now I'm freaking out. What am I going to do?"

"This sounds like a case of mistaken identity to me. Were you drinking?"

"NO! I mean, yes, but I had a drink at dinner, and then one before the show started. That was like three hours before I drove home."

"Are you sure that was it?"

"Since my DUI, I'm very careful. I space my drinks apart, I drink water, and I wait a long-ass time before getting in the car."

"So you don't remember anything out of the ordinary? Is it possible you forgot? Or that you had more to drink than you remember?"

"At one point, about halfway home, I remember a car stopped short in front of me, and I had to hit the brakes, but nothing happened. It was one of those *Phew, Traci, that was close* moments. That's all. Then I continued listening to my book on tape, and that was that."

"What book?"

"*The Years.*"

"Oh, is it good?"

"So good."

"Cool. Is it possible you tapped the car in front of you, and they're the litigious sort that's taking advantage of the situation?"

"I mean, I'd have to be blackout drunk not to realize I'd hit a car, no?"

"Listen, I'm sure it's just a mistake. The guy probably followed the wrong person home."

"What if it's like an intersection camera?"

· *209* ·

"If you didn't hit anything, then it doesn't matter. They can't have caught you doing anything."

"But what if I had a stroke and don't remember?"

"Traci, how much did you drink?"

"The drink at dinner."

"What about the one at the concert?"

"Oh, right! That one too. But that was it, and I only had a sip of that drink. I didn't finish it. I didn't leave the venue for another two hours after that sip. I wasn't drunk!"

"Why are you driving after drinking at all?"

"You know Seattle. Everyone drinks and drives here. Just have to be careful about how much. If I'd had three drinks or if I'd had to leave sooner, I would have taken a cab—I'm freaking the fuck out!"

"Okay, okay. But try to be chill. Wait for the report. In the meantime, find a lawyer. I know a couple of people who might be able to help."

"Lawyer? You think I need a lawyer? How can I afford that?"

"We can help."

"Fuck's sake. How did I get myself into this mess? Why am I always getting myself into messes? I've been making mistakes for like forty years. Who does this kinda shit? What's wrong with me?"

Traci and I were both socialized in the space where poverty and the working class (they used to be two separate classes) meet, and that volatile, albeit formative, experience engendered a striking number of similarities between us. I understand her mind. I understand her impulses and insecurities. I understand the inclination to rely solely on emotion and to make bad decisions in the dark one would never make in the light. I've spent most of my adult life suppressing urges I was hardwired to have and questioning beliefs and assumptions that were indoctrinated in my youth and now run contrary to my worldview. It's a lifetime of psychological toil. Sometimes in upper-middle-class spaces, which constitute most

MIDDLE SPOON

of my spaces these days, I have to remind myself not to react to abuse the way I might have in my youth. I have to remind myself that these new people wouldn't consider their actions abusive at all, just honest, that they don't see me as inferior and are merely contending with their own ignorance, or they do see me as inferior, and in a perverse manner, their actions make sense because they're predicated on ignorance. I can't quite describe my state of mind in those moments of stress, but it's akin to a train leaving a station. The train's engine is never off, and the train's initial departure, too, is often out of my control. As a result, I've had to become adept at slowing it down. On some occasions, I've been able to stop the train altogether, and, even rarer still, have it return to the station. The nature of this beast is that I carry around with me a foreboding, the fear of this neurochemical locomotive. In fact, I spend an inordinate amount of time and energy imagining situations that are likely never to happen, just so I can stay ahead of my unwieldy emotions. To be clear, my charmed life means (a) I rarely find myself in circumstances where the train needs to leave the station, and (b) I can preempt situations at a distance and therefore seldom approach the metaphorical station.

I fear I'm blowing this out of proportion, or, by examining my mental machinations, I'm pathologizing something unexceptional, harmless. I'm not, after all, a physically violent person—I've never been in a physical altercation in my life. But I have been known to escalate small encounters when I feel attacked or trapped. I have been known to fly off the handle after a few drinks. Many times, I've killed with off-kilter kindness, and my silences are of a potent variety, of the kind only powerful, angry women and their queer sons have—this is how I was raised to deal with disrespect. When I think back, I shouldn't have gotten this far. In life, I mean. There were enough youthful episodes that could have turned out quite poorly, egregiously poor, if not for happenstance. Drunk nights, road rages, tense exchanges. Ben, have you ever read *Crime and Punishment*?

· 211 ·

Reading it was a harrowing experience for me because I identified with Raskolnikov much more than I should have. I felt his delusion and regret in my bones, and for years after reading the Russian classic, I had recurring nightmares. In the most frequent one, I'd robbed a bank; in another, I'd killed someone; in both, I got away with my misdeeds but was left debilitated by the guilt. I never dreamed of the acts themselves; my dreams were situated in the aftermath of my crimes, already part of a dream archive. These oneiric deeds remained in me throughout my youth and into adulthood. I'd wake terrorized, needing to convince myself I was innocent, and yet afraid to share my nightmares with anyone for fear I was actually guilty of something. These old dreams sometimes appear in my new dreams even now. My subconscious is convinced I've done sinister things I've never actually done. I believe this is what happens to a brain that develops under duress, under undesirable conditions.

When Traci told me about the cops at her door and the accusation, I envisioned myself in her situation. The terroristic twinge of being caught, of being taken away. I felt a change in my limbic system. I wasn't only worried about my friend; I was also afraid for myself. What was I capable of?

I suspect you'd say I'm not giving myself enough credit. I am, after all, a thoughtful human without much catalyzing struggle to speak of. But that doesn't change the fact that when stress arises I am more likely to become Traci or Raskolnikov than I am Gandhi or whoever else is notable for their equanimity in the face of great adversity, which isn't to say that Traci's offense is akin to murder *or* that she even committed an offense *or* that Gandhi isn't guilty of his own violences—violence doesn't have to be physical to be damaging. It's merely to point out that reaching the standard of functioning, productive, graceful member of society isn't the same road for everyone, and even when someone has climbed out of the pits of precarity and trauma, they're still beholden to their neuro-

MIDDLE SPOON

logical pathways and their coping mechanisms. Simply put, it's a lot harder to just exist. Traci, it must be said, has faced some serious economic and health woes in recent years. I'd sensed in previous calls that she was at the end of her tether, which makes the careless drinking and the subsequent hit-and-run narrative viable, but I didn't have the heart to tell her that.

Being with you was a reminder that I don't do well when stressors arise, when I feel trapped, when I feel abandoned, when I feel rejected, when I feel scared, even when I feel loved. Of course, everyone has reactions to these feelings, but as it concerns emotional elasticity, some people are rubber bands, and some people are anchors. My husband, for example, bounces right back, leaving scant evidence that he'd been even briefly taut. I, however, am perpetually at the bottom of the sea, covered in barnacles, lodged between the exposed parts of whatever sank before me. Getting back to shore can be an exhausting endeavor. More strength, more precision, more know-how, more effort. Do you see what I mean?

I think you do see, because I saw a bit of that fire in you. You struck me as someone who also works to suppress urges. And although you're doing pretty well, I've seen it in your stained-glass eyes and heard it in your quavering voice. Like that time you thought I was flirting with your coworker, and you got upset. You wouldn't even look at me. Your jaw made angles of your already narrow face. And the anger twisted your mouth into a knot, an adorable knot, but a knot nonetheless. I recognized that anger. I was reared in that anger. I'm not saying you weren't wrong to be upset, but it was a misunderstanding—I don't find your coworker even remotely attractive.

The myriad misunderstandings and endless doubts and now this godforsaken breakup haven't produced anger in me, not a sustainable one, but they've made me desperate and afraid. I want to claw my way out of this, but I'm not sure if I'm crawling my way out of the relationship's wreckage or out of the uncertainty—damned uncertainty—that plagued me whenever I didn't understand how you felt about me, about us, whenever I didn't know what was coming next, whenever I imagined what was coming next. It's been eighteen days since you left, and I feel it still.

—Me

Dear Ben,

I have OCD. I've suspected as much for years, but today Fred was unequivocal in his assessment. After I sent the last batch of emails, he responded, "My holiday plans are in flux, and I have our usual hour free tomorrow. If you can come in, I would like to see you."

When I got to his office, he wasted very little time getting to the point. "It would be prudent for you to talk to a psychiatrist, so they can evaluate you for obsessive-compulsive disorder. I'm certain you meet the criteria," he said without breaking eye contact.

When I didn't respond, he pressed, "How does that make you feel?"

"I don't know. Relieved. A little scared."

"Are you surprised?"

"When I was a kid, I avoided the cracks on the sidewalk."

"All of them?"

"No, but if I accidentally stepped on one, I'd double back an entire block and begin again. And if I wasn't alone and couldn't repeat the block, I'd remain uneasy about it. I also remember mindlessly tapping my lips with the tip of a finger, and then feeling compelled to tap them with the other nine."

"I'm sure you can think of dozens of these sorts of compulsions."

"Yes, but none of them felt terrible. Or debilitating."

"I believe your turmoil surrounding this breakup is being aggravated immensely by your obsessive thinking patterns and compulsions." Fred calmly sidled up to the edge of his deep-buttoned leather chair and leaned toward me, elbows on his knees. "There are OCD-specific treatments," he said. "It's different from our talk therapy."

"Pills?"

· 215 ·

"Not necessarily. But possibly."

"Do we stop seeing each other?"

"It depends. Sometimes one type of treatment can interfere with another."

"Why not continue working on my problems with you? Just as we always have. I leave here with a sense of relief and hope."

"I may inadvertently be validating your obsessions. Our very meetings might be compulsive behavior."

"So now therapy is bad for me?"

"I've been seeing you for anxiety, not for OCD. You may very well have both, but it would be useful to know. I'll send you names for psychiatric clinicians."

I should have been relieved or optimistic about my new avenue for self-improvement, especially if it meant breaking out of the cycle of thoughts about you, but I felt burdened and weak. I was no longer damaged; I was broken. I'd spent weeks feeling broken, but now the designation was on the verge of becoming official.

"Before you go"—Fred remained seated as I shook out my scarf and wrapped it loosely around my neck—"I want to apologize if I was too clinical or cold. It dawned on me yesterday that I have been making your situation worse these last couple of years. And I want to put you on the right path. I don't want to see you suffering like this. I've had clients undergo OCD counseling, and they make incredible progress."

Here's hoping.

—Me

PS: I didn't see Susan Sarandon again today. Just before I went up to see Fred, I stood at the same spot where I always stand when I see her. I

MIDDLE SPOON

wasn't late. It wasn't raining. In fact, it was Tony Kushner–style crazy cold sun weather. Perhaps she's not feeling well. Or maybe she's on location filming something mediocre that doesn't deserve her. Maybe she was visiting one of her children. Or she'd taken her Oscar statuette to get professionally polished.

After therapy, I took a walk around the block, reading through Sarandon's IMDb page for forthcoming projects, all the while sneaking glimpses at the plethora of sophisticated women of a certain age who were holding leashes. When the scouring proved fruitless, I considered increasing my search radius, one more block east, one more block south, and one more north, but as I made my way toward 5th Avenue, it occurred to me that I'd spent fifteen minutes looking for someone I didn't know, whom I had no interest in knowing, whom I only wanted to glimpse. At that point, I made my way back west, toward the C train.

Dear Ben,

It seems the world isn't quite ready for nonbinary humans. Over the last week alone, Jules got in trouble at school because they confronted a minor bully; a man on the subway roared at us for allowing Jules to wear a pink bag; and a passerby looked at Jules's hot-pink tights and then at me, and then back at the tights, and then at the plastic tiara in Jules's hair, and then back at me, before saying, "It's sick what you people do to children."

In all three cases, I did my best to engage, defend, or dispel because it felt like my duty as a parent and because I have trouble walking away from an argument and because I wanted Jules to feel protected, but I'd be lying to you and, more importantly, to myself and Jules if I didn't admit that other people's fears, irrespective of how rooted they are in ignorance, do have an effect on me.

"Are you letting a boy wear a fucking purse?" shouted the middle-aged man on the crowded Q train, en route home from the MoMA on Sunday. The four of us were standing over him, my husband and I gripping the horizontal bar above the seated man; our children, attached to the vertical one in front of him. None of the other passengers displayed anything resembling alarm, curiosity, or even a rudimentary awareness of the verbal lashing; the children continued gazing up at the advertisements above us all, as if they'd heard nothing. My stress response, however, kicked in immediately. I was both afraid of a physical altercation and worried about the psychological damage on Jules. I was also growing more embarrassed with each passing second for not having immediately defended them.

MIDDLE SPOON

For his part, the enraged man remained quiet between 57th and Times Square, but I felt something simmering. I searched in vain for a sympathetic figure who might come to our rescue if the one-sided confrontation were to envelop us, but whoever might have contemplated coming to our aid was now lost to the various stimuli that constitute a crowded train and a complicated brain.

"Let's get off at the next stop," I whispered to my husband, hoping to preempt another tirade, but the train's slow crawl into the station foiled our escape. "I can't believe a boy is wearing a fucking purse!" shouted the man. Again, he did so without making eye contact. A few of the passengers looked briefly in our direction. The angry man's face was etched with a lifetime's worth of anger, all too easily unleashed by my parenting choices.

Just as I'd resigned myself to an unsatisfying conclusion, Jules spoke up. "Actually, sir, I'm nonbinary, and this"—my baby pointed to the bag strapped across their chest—"is a fanny pack, not a purse." The man's eyes instantly doubled in size as if it was the only way for him to see Jules clearly.

Emboldened by my eight-year-old, I added, "Why do you care what my kid wears?" It was all I could think to say that might give him pause without thickening the tension.

And that was it. We remained on the platform while the train pulled away.

Something else must have remained because this morning, I spent an inordinate amount of time trying to dissuade Jules from wearing their violet leggings and the off-the-shoulder sweater that you'd helped them make a few months ago by cutting a wider neckline. I kept thinking of the neighbors, the passersby, the judgmental nannies and schoolteachers, the other kids who would spend the day questioning Jules. I'd briefly weighed the various harms to Jules and concluded that thwarting their

• 219 •

self-expression paled in comparison to other people's judgments, but when Jules stomped away from me, I came to my senses.

They wore the leggings and the revealing sweater. As a trade-off, I spent the walk to school averting my gaze, pretending Jules and I were the only two people on the street and maybe even in Brooklyn. Protecting oneself suddenly seemed a surefire way to destroy a community.

I'm going to give this more thought.

—Me

Ben,

Fuck it, I'm coming over. I'm on the L, on my way to your place. This is either the bravest, most correct thing I've ever done, or a runaway train headed toward a collapsed bridge.

Wish me luck,
Me

Dear Ben,

In an unexpected turn of events, I saw you this afternoon, twenty-one days after the last time I saw you. I came to your apartment unannounced around two. I was nervous but also resolute—hell or high water, I was going to make my way into your place. Apparently, I could have done with less gumption because you let me in without even asking who had buzzed, a misguided knack I attribute to you not being from New York.

Once inside your building, my resolve faltered. Instead of racing up those rickety stairs, I remained frozen on the ground floor's landing, that dreaded meeting place for fear, anxiety, and love. I contemplated leaving before you could see me, but I heard your apartment door and your foot-steps. I looked up and saw you peering down at me.

"Oh, God! Come up." Your faux-exasperated voice was all the permis-sion I needed to bound up the stairs two at a time.

"I'm headed to the airport in fifteen minutes," you said after I'd stepped inside.

I knew you were traveling south for the year-end holidays, but I couldn't recall when, and in the last couple of days, this uncertainty had fed my desire to contact you. The act of leaving town is ponderous and stakes-raising. To be grieving a handful of stations apart is one thing; to be on opposing sides of the Mason-Dixon while nursing broken hearts is an acceleration of the clock and a decisive turning of the page. And yet, I'd stuck to my guns. I'd chosen abstinence and safeguarded my misery here, in the drafts folder of my email and in the inboxes of my therapists. I'd done what I was told to do.

Until I received your email.

MIDDLE SPOON

I was at a gluten-free café on the Upper East Side, not only miserable about you, but also hungry—worse, angry at not being able to eat anything. As it happened, the secret ingredient to the sandwich café's gluten-free breads was my other nutritional kryptonite—cow's milk—so I ordered a salad, in the process elevating my already elevated ire; no one in their right mind wants leafy greens sprinkled with quinoa when they're starving. If it were possible to feel the intricacies of one's own metabolic processes, I'd say misery and hunger had formed a crucible of bile that was lapping onto my viscera, like the turbid autumn surf onto a poorly constructed bulkhead.

Your email was long, said plenty—you missed me, you loved me, you couldn't stop thinking about me—but offered nothing. "I just needed you to know how I felt," you wrote at the closing. What the hell was I meant to do with that declaration? Could you have been more selfish? And what to make of the subject line: "Hey, hey, hey . . ." That alone should have sent you to my junk folder. But you were also recalcitrant: "Sorry for sending this when I know it breaks our rules, but I was sitting here thinking that you were thinking you didn't mean anything to me, that it had all been in your head. And it wasn't. You meant everything to me."

I was suddenly, and for the first time in weeks, alive, which is to say, my emotions were unambiguous. My hunger, which had been a source of pain, was now a beacon of pleasure. I was happy too. As well as horny. And relieved.

"What is it?" asked my husband, who until that moment had felt foolish for having chosen the café and helpless for not being able to cure me of you.

"He emailed."

My husband's face managed to fall and widen at the same time. He wanted this all to be over, but he, too, was caught up in the soap opera.

· 223 ·

As he read the email, I became aware of the grin across my face—the salad was spectacular. My reactions were reminders of how much lies outside of one's control. Mine was the sort of instantaneous metamorphosis I associated with addiction, and your email had been the fix. Dopamine, oxytocin, adrenaline, and endorphins were behaving as pinballs inside of me. But what was the illicit substance? Was it You, my love for You, or the validation I felt whenever You reciprocated anything?

I did my best to stay focused on your arrogance and your lack of creativity, but I sensed I was doomed. In short order, I'd be back to waiting. A pawn ready to revive his queen or to be sacrificed in her defense. To stave off purgatory, I kept the phone in my pocket for as long as I could manage—thirty-eight minutes. By that point, my husband and I had gone into the Guggenheim, which I am embarrassed to say I had never before visited. Perhaps there's nothing particularly noteworthy about this admission, but since I am a lifelong New Yorker, a fan of contemporary art, and a bit of a pocket art critic, and since the Guggenheim is a world-renowned museum—whatever the hell that means in the era of synthetic desert cities built with oil money on the backs of migrants—not visiting the museum had felt like a gaping and inexcusable hole in my résumé. The good thing about art, however, isn't only that it cycles; it also travels: if you miss it here, you'll catch it there. And yesterday, while I was employing every last shredded fiber of my being not to respond to you, I ascended the museum's spiral design, and in the process, entered the lives and minds of Alex Katz and Nick Cave. I wasn't familiar with Katz's oeuvre, but I had many years before seen Cave's exhibit at the Seattle Art Museum. Katz's output was principally a collection of landscapes and portraits—people in his life, mostly other artists and writers, including his wife or partner, a simple and elegant muse who appeared throughout. The sheer volume of his work, spread across the walls of the entire helix, made me feel as if I were traipsing the mid-twentieth-century timeline,

MIDDLE SPOON

which seemed to unfold primarily in his living room in the 1960s: tapered polyester, horn-rimmed eyeglasses, martinis. I felt as if I were both cruising and being cruised by his subjects. Cave's pieces were of another medium, sculptures of collage, human-sized, headless, frocked in layers of colorful clothing and jewelry, all of which called out, *Look at me! Don't look at me!* (I knew exactly what he meant.) The repetition in both oeuvres evoked obsession—careful, thoughtful obsession. (I understood this too.)

Mid-ascent I sent you a message—not a reply, a message: "I miss you. Let's talk." But the farther I climbed the museum, the less phone reception I had and the more consumed I became with your response. My life was again terrible, and I must have been wearing the disillusion when my husband approached me in the gift shop. "Why don't you talk this out with him? Face-to-face," he said as I unfolded an overpriced floral-print hoodie. "I don't want you to be depressed anymore."

"I've been thinking about this," he continued. "We've always been on the margins, no? Gay couple. Mixed-race couple. Married gay couple. Adopted children. And now blended polyamorous family—why not? What we have is special. I don't believe adding someone to the equation will ruin anything."

I said nothing because I felt I was doing something entirely for me, not for us, and certainly not for him. I squeezed his shoulder, hoping the gesture would communicate gratitude. "I love you," I said.

At Union Square, I said goodbye and hopped off the train, like an anvil might hop, leaden with guilt and muddled thoughts, wondering how to characterize my choice to abandon a great partner and father and friend on the subway:

A. allegorical

B. metaphorical

C. a portent

D. a harbinger

E. terrible

F. selfish

G. correct

"Don't feel guilty," he'd said a few minutes before. "I have work this afternoon. It's not like we were going to be spending time together anyway."

Rich. That's what this is. The love of my life was at my side, supporting me in every possible way one human can support another, willing to entertain the logistics of my leaving him so that I might also be happy with you, willing to invite you into our lives so that he wouldn't lose me, willing to lose me rather than see me undergo another emotional tailspin. And you? Where are you, Ben? At the first sign of trouble, you disappeared. This is when you're supposed to fight; this is the moment in a relationship when the path before us begins to take shape. And you're not here beside me. What kind of craven monster leaves his husband on the 5 train for this?

I got to your apartment, rang, came up, and eventually migrated toward your couch, where you sat beside me, just far enough away for touch to remain out of reach, only words, including a rehash of the case you'd made when we broke up last summer and again twenty-one days earlier, namely that you hadn't expected to love me so much, and now that you did, you were certain you wanted me all to yourself, but you could never ask me to leave my husband, until you did, a few minutes later: "Will you divorce him and be with me?" And I explained the following:

- You were asking me to leave someone who'd been by my side for more than half my life.

- You and I had known each other for a year, only the previous four months of which had been consecutively happy.

· *226* ·

MIDDLE SPOON

- I loved my husband and you at the same time but differently.

- I would continue making room in my life in order for you to never feel second best.

- We could continue to learn about each other, so that I could make you happy.

- I enjoyed making you happy.

- I had no plans to stop making you happy.

- We should continue to be happy together.

- We should not destroy something so beautiful and rare because of a possible future that isn't guaranteed for any of us.

- We'd never have predicted six months earlier that we would have all of this love between us; therefore, we don't know what's in store for us, and we should keep going.

As I was saying this, you opened your mouth to speak many times because you have always found it difficult to let me complete a sentence, never mind an argument. But this time, you restrained yourself and waited patiently on your end of the couch, legs folded to one side, feet bare, until I'd finished.

"You're implying you might one day leave your husband, which is only leading me on, and that isn't fair." That was your tearful response once I'd stopped speaking.

I couldn't articulate the distinction between leading you on and hope, so I said nothing. Instead, I crawled across the gray cushions in search of an embrace and whispered, "I don't want to say goodbye again and regret not holding you." By that point, you were crying, and the hopelessness in your chest was unmistakable against mine.

You ended our reverie quickly. "I have to call a cab," you said.

And as you tapped away at your phone, I said, "This is like a romantic comedy, which means the odds are on our side."

You laughed and inhaled noisily.

What I didn't say was that maybe the romantic center of this comedy—dramedy, really—was my husband and me. I didn't say that because, to begin with, I wasn't thinking that until just now and because it would have been cruel to say such a thing, and well, it might not be true. It's possible you and I are the protagonists of this tale, which doesn't guarantee a happy ending. But I believe this could have a happy ending, and that was the case I attempted to make in your living room yesterday.

When I was done, your phone dinged, and you walked over to your shoes. I told you I'd be here in a few days when you returned from visiting your family, and you said, "No, I'm trying to get over you," and I argued we were both in that boat—the USS *Same*—but that you had broken the rules with your email, and now I felt freer to try to win you back.

"If you won't see me next week, then I'm getting in the cab with you, and we're finishing this conversation today."

"Are you joking?"

You were incredulous but not very incredulous. I'd made the sort of romantic gesture you loved: your man fighting for you, taking big swings. And so I took that cab with you to LaGuardia, that endless, traffic-addled ride through a half dozen socioeconomic classes and no fewer than 250 language diasporas, during which we held hands, both of us happier than we'd been since the breakup, despite your ensuing tears and my internal misery and all the talk of how this was truly the end. We smiled the entire way because we were together, and that, I have to say, is why we need to stick it out. We have an uncommon connection, and to deny it is to deny love and hope and, in a way, life. But you were a shotgun of counter-

MIDDLE SPOON

arguments: society doesn't support polyamory; your parents wouldn't approve of you being with a married man; your friends would pity you; television shows wouldn't ever reflect us back to us.

"Ben, it's a lack of imagination," I said with a decibel increase that caught the attention of the driver, who was now peering at us in his rearview mirror.

"You're oversimplifying this," you responded.

"It is simple. We of all people should be willing to do something daring and uncomfortable for love, or at least not be constrained by conservatism and tradition."

The driver raised one brow.

"That's unfair," Ben responded. "Sometimes, you have to think and not just feel."

"Think about this: all your heteronormative friends who judge you or us will one day divorce or separate or cheat on their spouses or be cheated on by their spouses, but *crazy Ben* with the married partner will still be in that *weird* relationship. And guess what? We will be a model of stability and love and freedom for our community. The world will catch up!"

My pontificating, it turned out, might have dented your resolve, and possibly the driver's, whose head I thought I saw move up and down with approval. I took the tears in your eyes as a signal to stop talking, but if I'd kept going, I would have said, *I will one day take a sabbatical and work on a research study that extols the benefits of polyamory and depicts our relationship in a way that makes you (and me and my husband and our kids and communities) feel validated.* I wanted to say this, but the truth is, life with me would serve as validation enough, and you wouldn't need population-level data to do it for you. Besides, I don't know if I could get anyone to fund that research. It's also worth noting this is all new to me too. I'm not asking you to join my world; I'm inviting you to create a new world with me.

· *229* ·

The final five minutes of the ride transpired in silence, but you never let go of my hand. "Are you coming in?" you asked when we'd reached the tailgating line at departures. I nodded and then made my way to the trunk of the car, where I accepted your bag from the driver, who I swear did everything humanly possible with his eyes to tell me he'd been impressed with my performance.

Ben, I fear you've confused conviction with impatience. You want an answer now about the rest of your life, and that's not fair to me or you. But you win because you have the weight of society behind you, telling you the only healthy path is a partnership between two people and that your partner must be completely beholden to you and without linkages to other people. I, too, live in that world, and I, too, feel that pressure, and I, too, will have a lot of explaining to do and knitted brows to smoothen, but you're worth it. That's all I went to say yesterday. What we have is worth all of it. Possibly more. To further thicken the broth, don't forget that nontraditional configurations of love and family exist in this world and have existed in this world probably since . . . always. There are blueprints for us.

I attempted to say this, no doubt ineloquently, as we stood somewhere between the ticketing kiosks and the entrance to security. I know you heard me because one of your knees bent slightly and you set your bags down. Because you stepped toward me and kissed me once, quick and soft, with all of your lips. Because we held eye contact for the entire time. I didn't feel great about being the softener of your stance, for fear I was manipulating you—I swear I want you to come back to me of your own volition—but I also wanted to win you back.

Just before you walked away, toward the two angry, disheveled airport workers, who somehow managed to be imperious and hapless at the same time, standing at the entrance of a bright, futuristic cavern—it should be

MIDDLE SPOON

said that the renovation of LaGuardia is marvelous; if only the city would do that with everything else—you said, "What if this is it?"

"The end?" I asked.

"No, what if you're the one for me?"

Yes. Yes, I am. I feel that in my bones, but I also don't believe my bones have any predictive powers. It might be more accurate to say I want to be the one for you.

You kissed me again.

"Can I message you?" I asked.

"Yes," you responded.

And then you walked away, but I remained in place long enough to watch you turn around four times before you disappeared. Four times.

Four.

And now you're gone for eight days.

Eight.

The traffic on the ride home was even worse than on the way there. Nico was already standing outside his school, backpack slung over one arm, water bottle in hand, when the car pulled up. *In the nick of time* is effectively my relationship with New York. And today, it was my relationship with you. If I had been twenty minutes more indecisive about seeing you, you would have already left.

My husband had messaged me a couple of times while I was with you. He wanted to know how it was going. And if I was okay. On my way to Nico's school, I'd called him. "I'm not sure how it went," I said. "It's weird. I feel optimistic about our future and, at the same time, like I might have gotten some closure. It could go either way."

· 231 ·

The driver, who was carrying on his own phone conversation, couldn't have been less interested in mine.

"I love you, and I always will," I said. "Please don't give up on me."

"I have no plan to," responded my husband. "It's you who might leave me."

"I have no plan to."

—Me

Dear Ben,

I had my annual physical yesterday, and I told my doctor about you and about my OCD.

"I could have told you that," he said about the diagnosis.

"Then why didn't you?"

"I've suggested before that you consider antianxiety medication."

"I thought you were just pushing pills because I don't handle stress well."

"You email me a dozen times a year convinced you have every illness—cancer, HIV, herpes, shingles, strep throat, crabs, Parkinson's—and it's usually a viral cold, eczema, or anxiety. A few times, it's been all three."

"I thought I had mild hypochondria."

"Half dozen of one; six of another."

"What?"

"It's all the same," he said.

Dr. B has been my PCP for nearly fifteen years. He's gay, treats mostly gay patients, and knows my health history. He's also brown. With all the things that go wrong in this world, having this refreshing degree of resonance with a person who monitors my cholesterol levels is a gift.

"As for the boyfriend dilemma, I suggest having sex with more men."

"What?"

"More men," Dr. B repeated after I'd hopped off the scale, before lowering my underwear. Dr. B often has to repeat himself because his lips tend to stay together when he speaks, leaving me first to wonder what he's said and second to ask him to repeat himself.

Conversations with my doctor about extramarital sex have always been shaped by what I believed was a fear of illness. His advice has been to caution me against opening up my marriage in general and against condom-less sex specifically, even if I were to take a prophylaxis. But yesterday, Dr. B's tune changed.

"A few different men," he explained while he pressed my left testicle between his fingers. "That's how you move on from this—testicles are normal, no need for an ultrasound this year."

"*Different* men?"

"Turn around, elbows on the table—yes, a few guys. The one you're infatuated with now is an unknown quantity. Don't end your marriage for him, not without first trying this—prostate: no sign of inflammation," he said before removing his plastic gloves, handing me a few stiff napkins, and leaving the exam room.

"Were you being serious?" I asked after I'd dressed and taken a seat across from Dr. B at his desk.

"About?"

"About fooling around with other men?"

"Absolutely. I suspect sex with one or two bottoms, or even three, will help you move on more easily. You've found pleasure in playing a role you haven't in a long time. This happens more often than you think. It's an age thing. Explore it. Should I send the PrEP refill to the Walgreens or to the other pharmacy in your file?"

Ben, it's not only my doctor; Fred ("It might help you to disentangle emotion from sex"), Lucas and Akil ("After the third guy, you won't give a fuck about Ben"), and even my husband ("Maybe everyone has a point") have all suggested I do the thing you're probably doing right now, probably with that guy you hook up with whenever you visit your family.

It's Christmas Eve, and I'm in my childhood home, trying to enjoy the moment or the collection of moments that constitute the occasion of re-

MIDDLE SPOON

union, but it's not working. I'm thinking instead about how the few text messages we've exchanged since LaGuardia were all initiated by me, and how your responses have felt less than enthusiastic, flat even, and how that might be because you're busy, trying to forget me, or annoyed that I'm messaging at all, and there's no way for me to know the cause because we're not actually communicating, instead skirting the edges of communication. Perhaps our rekindled love is circling the baggage carousel in Terminal C.

I detest this uncertainty, and since I've never had it with my husband, I'm back to believing you and I are not really compatible or the practical version of *meant to be*. I'm also wondering if I should be on antianxiety meds. And I'm thinking of Whitney Houston.

Yes, Whitney.

You see, even before I learned she was closeted, I sensed something was off. During her early years in the spotlight—"You Give Good Love," "Saving All My Love," "I Wanna Dance with Somebody"—she appeared happy. Before becoming high and bitter, she was ebullient and sweet. Whether she was performing on a stage or sitting for an interview, her smile, a luminous and authentic ornament that was nowhere to be found in the later years, was second only to her voice. By the time *The Bodyguard* came around, and possibly by the end of the *I'm Your Baby Tonight* era, she'd changed, as if she were a reluctant guest at her own surprise party. The smile remained, but it had the camber and plasticity of a mask, a kill-them-with-kindness grin bereft of genuine happiness or compassion, one she couldn't wait to peel off. It would have been safe, and not altogether incorrect, to assume Houston's transformation was the natural outcome of being Black and a woman and a Black woman in this world and specifically in the entertainment industry. After all, how much chronic disrespect can one person stomach before their demeanor is forever altered? But I couldn't square that with her wealth and popularity, which

· 235 ·

should have buffered her from the worst this world lobbed in her direction, at least through the nadir of her success. With no other cause, drug use became the believable culprit for Houston's perceived woes. After her death, when Robyn Crawford's role as friend-lover-assistant came to light, Houston's transformation made sense, the drugs made sense, the veneer made sense, Bobby made sense.

I am capable of living a charmed existence dappled with anger, but not regret and not sadness. I don't want to play out a queer version of *The Bridges of Madison County*; Whitney and Robyn already did that for us. We don't face their obstacles. We could be in Afghanistan or in a frat house or in NYC before the Stonewall Riots or at the dawn of the Industrial Age or on the trading floor of a bank on 53rd Street between Park and Madison or in Spain during the Franco regime or in a Tarantino movie or even in the early Obama years. No, our barriers are our own, maybe not of our making, but neither are they solely external. And they're certainly not insurmountable.

Children are hovering around a meticulously decorated tree of red and gold bows, silver tinsel, and homemade ornaments; each picks a box with their name and shakes it. Various adults call out for them to be gentler. My mother is in the kitchen stirring a soup that accommodates a household of dietary restrictions. My brother is on his phone playing a slot machine game. My father is shuffling a deck of cards, while my sister, brother-in-law, and husband wait for their hands. Periodically, my sister produces a surreptitious thumb at her side and toggles it between up and down, to which I respond with a flat, horizontal hand that I roll side to side. I'm burritoed in a throw on a sofa chair, attempting to calculate overdue student grades for a class I'd completely forgotten—Health Services 521: Wealth Inequality as a Risk Factor for Poor Health Outcomes—and that

MIDDLE SPOON

was brought to my attention by way of an email from the dean of our school: "Very unlike you to be tardy with your grades." That's what I'm meant to be doing, instead of thinking of you and quietly bracing myself for the pain I'll feel when we see each other again.

I might very well be ready to take the psychotropics that help people deal with sadness, because I don't know what else to do to manage this grief. You see, I did the one thing I was advised by everyone in my life not to do: be in touch with you. Now, I'm embarrassed to seek counsel from the people who've been urging me to stay away, to stay strong, to call them instead of calling you, to text them instead of texting you, to write letters but never send them. Just yesterday, Traci texted me after not answering my morning calls: "Honey, I'm sorry you're going through this, but I'm dealing with a lot of shit right now. I promise this will pass. Merry Xmas!" I've lost credibility, and whatever I'm going through at the moment is no longer of your doing but of my own. I could have ignored your email. (You selfish asshole.) I could have called someone. I could have taken a Xanax. But I went to your apartment instead.

All I have now are my therapists and my husband, who, while still here—he just won the last two rounds of Uno, and my sister is pissed—is no longer the appropriate audience because of what I'm entertaining: what life might be like if I left him.

—Me

PS: I've been searching for Whitney Houston online, and I found old clips of her reality TV series: an undisciplined crew follows her and her husband around. High and unfiltered—Houston and Brown, not the crew—the couple is particularly crude and angry. But Houston was also something else: in love. I spotted genuine affection and attraction between her and Bobby. Also noteworthy was her tremendous dissatisfaction with the public and its constant invasion of her privacy, sanctioned camera crew notwithstanding. Whitney was unhappy in the public eye. The half dozen clips I've watched make me doubt whether her disillusionment was only an outgrowth of her being closeted and trading one love for another, or whether it was the logical consequence of unwanted fame, of the racism she faced behind the scenes, of the highs and lows of drug use, of her faltering singing voice.

Dear Ben,

I've been getting up earlier than usual. In a full house, dawn quiet is a unique and productive quiet that allows an industrious person, or even an ambitious one, to get work done. I'm behind on a grant application, on submitting my spring semester syllabi, on writing a chapter for a forthcoming biostatistics textbook. I can't even seem to commit to pleasure reading; I'm thirty pages into *Catch-22* and fifteen into *The Count of Monte Cristo*—the bookcase in my childhood bedroom has remained mostly unchanged since I left home twenty-five years ago.

Instead of accomplishing anything, I've been daydreaming about a future in which you are a part of my family. Funnily enough, I've run into a logistical issue. You wouldn't really fit. My parents' home is a modest one that can barely accommodate the return of the current members of the family. How could it accommodate you?

The barriers to polyamory are plenty.

Today is Christmas, and there are several children—my own, plus their cousins—hopping around the tree like electrons under a heat lamp. I'm in my preferred corner of the living room, doing my best to smile and type, smile and type, until my mother comes over: "What happens inside that big brain of yours? What are you thinking?" she whispers.

I say nothing, which does nothing to placate her.

"I know something is bothering you."

"I'm okay," I respond.

She insists, "You don't have to tell me, but I want you to know you're doing everything right. You're in better shape than your father and I were

· 239 ·

at your age, and you'll be in much better shape than us when you reach our age. Don't overthink everything."

She has no idea about you because I still haven't told her anything, but there's a part of me that wishes she would figure it out, save me the trouble of coming clean. I rip a Costco croissant in two.

"Those have dairy and gluten," she says.

"I brought my pills," I respond.

She eats the half of the pastry that I leave on the plate before steering the topic toward her poor health. Arthritis has damaged her spine, her mobility, her dexterity, her spirit, she explains. I say pat and unconvincing things while she sips her coffee.

"Growing old is miserable," she responds.

"What you need is a big life change to snap you out of the low-level depression you have," I say, before realizing the advice would serve us both well.

I reintroduce the idea of her and my dad moving closer to me or one of my siblings. This paradigm shift would bring us all peace of mind because the effort of caring for them is minor in comparison to the effort of worrying about them at a distance.

"Not yet," she says. "Unless it'll make you smile again."

"Mom. I'm fine."

"If you say so, then I believe it."

My mother offers to take the kids to a matinee so that I can work. In the process, she refers to Jules as *he*. I respond by referring to Jules as *they*, but she doesn't follow.

"Who else prefers the mall besides Jules?"

"No one. They're the only one who wants to go."

"Who?"

"Jules."

"Only him?"

MIDDLE SPOON

"Only them."

"*Them* who?"

"Jules and no one else, Mom."

I let it go because I've had this conversation before, and my hope is that the cumulative effect will resolve everything.

My father is also concerned with my well-being. "You're not the same person," he said yesterday on our way to Costco. "What's happening with you?"

"Nothing. Just work deadlines," I responded before casually asking if his car needed a tune-up. I knew my father wouldn't push further because he had used up all his gumption in the initial inquiry, a show of concern that had probably been precipitated by my mother.

I've been thinking about the brain and how it forms. Its development was one of the areas of study that most held my attention in grad school. I wanted in particular to understand how stressful child-rearing environments affected the brain's formation. As it happens, the degree of attention one receives when their brain is growing determines forever how they process information, emotions, conflict, strife, love, etc. Brains that develop under conditions of high stress don't form in ways that allow them to handle adverse events well. If one's experience in utero or early childhood is of precarity, isolation, insecurity, or violence, they'll likely develop more neural pathways in the parts of the brain associated with fear, anxiety, and impulsivity, while forgoing the development of sufficient connections in the areas that help them regulate their emotional responses. Not only that, the consistency and toxicity of stress in early childhood can alter one's lens as it concerns future stress; in other words, poorly developed brains interpret low stress as high stress, ipso facto, their stress response is on all the time.

I'm done for. Many of us are. Millions. Possibly billions. How do we

· 241 ·

bounce back from a hardened brain, from arrested development? What hope do we have of ever leading lives undefined by how poorly we deal with life?

I've been revisiting the literature on brain development, as well as perusing the science on the chemistry of love, because I want to intellectualize my way out of this pain trap. You didn't like it when I compared our love to a drug because you feared what would happen when the high subsided. I feared that, too, but we also can't deny that love is dopamine and oxytocin, and possibly endorphins and serotonin. These chemicals validate us, push away fears and doubts, exhilarate us. When they disappear, we experience something akin to withdrawal. It's not the withdrawal that we see on the streets and subway platforms, the kind that warps and sways, but it's a first cousin of that withdrawal. I feel as if I live at the behest of the hormones and neurotransmitters inside of me, when it should be the other way around.

It's about degrees. Everyone experiences heartbreak, but our origin stories set us apart, and I know very little about how your prefrontal cortex or your amygdala formed—that is, what your upbringing and consequent brain development was like. Did your parents work endless hours and interact with you minimally, angrily, in a distracted fashion? Or were they absent altogether? Were they constantly talking to you, validating you, making eye contact? The answers to these questions give a sense of how you handle stress as an adult. My stress response, for example, resembles a trailer park caught in a tornado.

Or perhaps every jilted lover eats less, drinks more, sleeps fitfully, cries involuntarily, spirals obsessively, fears tomorrow. Perhaps there isn't a single RV built to weather a cataclysmic meteorological event. And yet, I suspect someone reared in more favorable conditions would be experiencing the loss of you differently, better.

—Me

MIDDLE SPOON

——

PS: I just looked up the differences between tornado, hurricane, typhoon, and cyclone. I've done that before, but I can't retain that sort of information. I feel the same about the differences between socialism and communism, apple varieties, and the taxation powers between New York City and New York State—why can't the mayor tax the city's billionaires adequately without making it a referendum on farmers upstate?

A typhoon is a rotating system of clouds and thunderstorms that originates in the northwest Pacific Ocean.

A hurricane is a rotating system of clouds and thunderstorms that originates in the North Atlantic, central North Pacific, and the eastern North Pacific.

A cyclone is a rotating system of clouds and thunderstorms that originates in the Indian Ocean and the South Pacific.

A tornado is a rotating system of winds that forms over land and looks like a funnel cloud linking the ground to the sky. Hurricanes can precipitate tornadoes.

All of these phenomena are made worse and more frequent by increasing global temperatures and the rising heat and energy in the water and air.

Ben,

Fuck you. Fuck your immaturity. And your games. And your Grindr profile.

—Me

Dear Ben,

I didn't mean it. I was angry. And frustrated. I'd been sitting at the kitchen table with my family, all of us in the festive pajamas that my sister had gifted everyone, all of us devouring bagels and lox, all of us drinking coffee. I could see and hear everything, but I was merely a spectator, a phantom. Until my phone buzzed. "Everyone is staring at you. They're worried." The message was from my husband, who was sitting across the table. I got up then and hid in the bathroom, where I splashed water on my face before pulling the phone from my pocket and creating a Grindr account and searching your area.

You'd been online twenty-five minutes prior. Your profile said you were single. You are. It said you're fit. You are. It said you're an illustrator and graphic designer. You are. It also said you're looking for dates, friends, and no-strings-attached sex. I deleted my profile immediately, drafted the previous email, and made my way back to the kitchen.

I'm sorry.

—Me

Dear Ben,

Last night, we drove out east to visit the family of my college best friend, Devin, who also grew up on Long Island, on a coastal stretch where the public schools are well regarded and sidewalks don't exist. I've been to his home dozens of times over the last twenty-five years, but this occasion was unusual. Devin and his wife, Robin, live on the West Coast and were visiting for only a few days. At any other point in time, I wouldn't have hesitated to accept their invitation, but Devin's dad is terminally ill, and we'd been previously asked to keep our distance because of his fragile immune system. In July, he was diagnosed with a rare and rather virulent form of cancer, after which his health deteriorated rapidly. Their invitation suggested to me that the safeguarding parameters had changed.

This situation underscores our age gap, Ben. As it concerns my parents and the parents of my friends, death has, in a way, entered the room. In fact, later today we're going to visit one of my husband's friends, someone he's known since high school, whose live-in mother-in-law is also rapidly shuffling off this mortal coil; her ailment, dementia. I suspect the frequency of funerals in my life is about to increase significantly, along with the cumulative stress of second-degree deaths.

I don't know why I'm making such a big deal about our age gap. Perhaps because nine years means we'll seldom be in the same decade of our lives. Or maybe it's because when I was nine, you were zero. Or because when I was a horny seventeen-year-old, you were watching Nickelodeon. Or because when I became a father for the first time, you'd just had your first beer. There's something not quite right about our difference, some-

MIDDLE SPOON

thing a bit icky or lecherous. Historically, I've been drawn to peers and slightly older men because wisdom and experience turn me on; they make me feel secure. But as I've gotten older, the age bounds for attraction haven't shifted with me, and suddenly, I'm having an affair with a guy in his mid-thirties.

Affair isn't fair. Our relationship transpired primarily in the open. Nothing *affair* about it.

As I was saying, yesterday we visited my college friends—Devin and Robin and their kids—and drank whiskey on a couch in a festive anteroom far from my friend's sickly father. When we arrived, my friend's mother waited for us outside. Immediately, she began to cry. Whether it was because she has always been quick to do so and the occasion of her son's college best friend returning to their home twenty-five years after his first visit to effectively say goodbye to her husband was a sufficient enough trigger, or because her perfectly healthy oak tree of a partner who has been at her side for nearly fifty years finds himself, with as little warning as one can imagine, weak, useless, and soon to die, and she is facing the prospect of life without him, I don't know.

These parents—Donna and Mark—knew I was gay before my own parents did. When we were nineteen, Devin sought their counsel because he was worried about me and my drinking and my dark thoughts, which I'd slur into his ear as he propped me up the flight of stairs to our apartment most nights.

"You told them?" I asked on the drive home for the holidays exactly twenty-five years earlier.

"Yeah."

"And they don't care?"

"Nope."

"Not at all?"

"Not at all."

That's as simple and as complicated as it ever got with Donna and Mark, who never looked at me sideways, and instead treated me as I'd hoped my parents might if ever I came out to them—I did eventually; they did eventually. Donna and Mark's dispassionate acceptance wasn't only a relief but a watershed moment that might have salvaged an entire generation for me. At eighteen, I'd already mapped out the isolated life I would lead, which included a few anodyne and compassionate peers, a few exotic types with green hair and unbridled body piercings, and the gray-haired guys at the gay bar who offered me drinks and liberally patted my ass. Mark and Donna were their own category, the exception to an unjust rule who nevertheless dented my armor of cynicism. How many Marks and Donnas would I know in my lifetime?

Yesterday, Devin, Robin, my husband, and I sipped whiskey in a room with floral-print couches and short, dark-wood tables, a room that has always looked as if it were decorated for Christmas but was, in this case, heavily decorated for Christmas. We talked about our kids and their reading and writing abilities, about the latest *Star Wars* television show—Jon Favreau has power disproportionate to his actual filmmaking abilities, we all agreed—about the houses our mutual college friends had bought, about the incompetence of Democrats. And as the conversation coiled around these various topics, the pain I'd been carrying around for weeks transformed from something miasmic into something spear-shaped. I was acutely aware that I was in a place and with a people I had only ever equated with honesty, and that I was being dishonest. The dissonance grew more and more intolerable with each sip of whiskey. On the tip of my tongue sat the following declaration: *Devin, Robin, I need to tell you something. I met someone, fell in love, and I've been dealing with the breakup. His name is Ben, and a few days ago, he reached out, and now I'm*

MIDDLE SPOON

afraid our lives are about to change drastically. Would you guys still love and support us if suddenly I had two partners? Or would you think I was selfish and my husband stupid?

The tip of my tongue.

I didn't say any of it because there were other people—siblings and their progeny—coming in and out of the Christmas room, and also because Robin and Devin are people who've known my husband and me since the beginning, the entirety of our relationship, and while you and polyamory have become de rigueur topics in our Brooklyn context, they might be shocking to these friends in a Long Island context, and I wasn't prepared to be defensive. I wasn't prepared to see my friends and that sacred space differently because it might have meant seeing my past differently.

Robin and Devin are open-minded, empathic people. They're white and upper-middle-class, but they'd vote for reparations and Land Back policies if they were presented with the opportunity. They're not the sort of people who need to be convinced that the system is rigged or who would stand in the way of a restructuring or, even, a full leveling of society. All of this is to say, I shouldn't be so mistrustful. On the other hand, coming out as gay felt like an act of survival way back when; coming out as polyamorous feels like the indulgence of a spoiled and indecisive sybarite. I kept you a secret.

When it was time to say our goodbyes, I approached Donna cautiously and signaled toward Mark. She nodded before enveloping me with all of herself. Body and force. Her breaths were staccato and labored, and I could feel her tears through my shirt. Then I walked over to Mark. "I love you," I said.

"I love you too," he responded.

"I'm sorry you're going through this."

"That's life," he said before resuming his quiet.

· *249* ·

I leaned down to put my arms around him as best I could. If my friends are to be believed, I probably saw Mark for the last time.

The drive back to my parents was along a dark highway that cut through a densely wooded forest, so dark it beckoned imagination. I envisioned all of Long Island as a lush and pristine stretch of fish-shaped land. We were driving through the once-home of the Setalcott Nation, whose survivors, the Shinnecock, lived due south on a small reservation. Somewhere farther east was another reservation, where the Poospatuck lived. What a minor, insufficient, meaningful, and correct concession it would be to return these public lands to their original stewards. One policy that could snowball and change us all for the better. How likely was I to see this occur in my lifetime?

I thought also of Mark and Donna. I wondered if they had ever opened up their relationship. Hippies in their day, traveling the country in a motor home, circumstances ripe for experimentation. Perhaps Robin and Devin had also expanded the boundaries of their marriage. Or maybe things simply happened that no one ever talked about. That might very well have been the resistance to unorthodox relationships, the loudness of it all. Society would be accepting of my romantic permutations if I simply shut up about them. It's tempting. To be private and quiet, that is. But whatever relief I might derive from knowing that everyone knows and prefers not to know would be ephemeral because I am no good at disentangling quiet from shame, and I won't abide by shame. Even when uncomfortable, I feel obliged to live loudly, for fear of returning to the place where I spent my youth, the place that still exists just outside of my bubble. The place that Donna and Mark helped me to escape.

—Me

MIDDLE SPOON

———

PS: I want to amend something I said earlier. I fear I've left the impression that older gay men are an irredeemable mass of lechery. Or worse, that there's no cross-generational, nonsexual bonding among us gays. When I was young, I didn't have the capacity to understand queer elders and queer support. I knew only drunk men who eyed me the way one does a wall of candy. I saw gayness only as sex, never as camaraderie or community. I blame Reagan for this too.

To the Editor of *The New York Times*:

Yesterday in your pages there was an article about a philanthropist who endowed a medical school to ensure free tuition indefinitely. It was heartening to learn the donor hadn't required the school to name anything after her. She simply wanted to make it simpler for doctors to pursue family medicine, a less lucrative specialty that has been shunned in recent years for the more remunerative fields of anesthesiology and plastic surgery.

If only every billionaire took it upon themselves to fund the essential services and programs that make for a functioning society without asking for anything in return. Alas, we live in capitalism, a system that allows our basest instincts, namely competition, greed, and fear, to dictate our actions, as well as to celebrate them.

A friend of mine recently waited eight days in the ER for a hospital bed. It was a rather harrowing experience, not least of all because she wasn't able to get one restorative night of sleep in that chaotic warren of calamities, but shortly after being installed in her own room, the antibiotics took effect, and she went home in time to join her family for Christmas. A tremendous relief because I was scared for her. Her condition was dire, but not nearly as dire as the condition of the hospital and this country.

Every day that my friend waited, I worried about malpractice, specifically of her being ignored or given the wrong treatment. A few of us, her friends, made sure she was seldom alone, taking turns visiting and sending each other updates on her condition and treatment, so that we could advocate on her behalf to the carousel of ER clinicians that visited her daily.

MIDDLE SPOON

The biostatistician who recently transferred to my department studies the phenomenon of medical harm, and he's found that people are more likely to die or be mistreated if they come to the hospital alone, injustices that go double (or triple) for people of color, especially Black people. We cannot underestimate bias; its many forms are quite virulent, and possibly deadlier than the illness itself.

I'm grateful for one decent, nonagenarian soul who decided to gift a surplus billion from her coffers to the future doctors of one medical school, but relying on the whims of the 1 percent to fund our society is a fool's errand. Not only do we have a shortage of family medicine doctors, we have a shortage of hospital beds and hospitals and patient navigators and preventive care and jobs and social workers and affordable housing. The list is endless, but donations are few and far between.

Sincerely,
A Public Health Researcher
Brooklyn, NY

"How's family life?" I sent.

"It's nice to be home. You?" you responded.

"Also nice. Looking forward to seeing you," I sent in return.

Dear Ben,

That stilted conversation took place two days ago. You weren't required to say anything more, but my autonomic nervous system remained ready just the same. *Me too* or *Ditto* would have been welcome, even sufficient. I'd have settled for an emoji. Instead, two nights and two mornings passed before you sent, "Want to get together and talk after I get back?" as if the idea had just occurred to you, as if we were remaking *Groundhog Day.*

I put my phone away and pretended I hadn't seen your response—very mature of me. I waited until after I'd packed up the car and said goodbye to my parents.

"Do you want to take some fruit for the road? Or cookies?" asked my dad.

"No, thanks. We have plenty of leftovers."

"Did you call Simone back?" asked my mom as she zipped up Jules's coat.

"I'll message her later."

Simone is a friend from high school, my only one, and it's become customary for me to visit her and her mother when I'm in town. This time, I didn't. Simone has a conservative streak to her, and a polyamory conversation wouldn't have gone over well. She also has an intuitive streak, and I wouldn't have been able to dodge her *What's wrong?* inquiries. It was

· 254 ·

MIDDLE SPOON

easier to send her a GIF of Will Ferrell dressed as an elf ("Merry Christmas!") and, later, one of Arnold Schwarzenegger holding an assault rifle ("I'll be back").

Once I'd returned to Brooklyn, I texted you. "Yeah," I said. "This week or next?"

I was serving nonchalance, Ben.

We agreed to meet on the night of your return.

My plan is to wait for you with an order of noodles from the Taiwanese place that's become our spot, where we've eaten half a dozen times, each occasion leaving you more delighted than the previous. I realize now that watching you relish a meal—your eyes, your eyebrows, your miming of *Wow!* and exclamations of *Delish!*—was one of my favorite pastimes, despite how much I look down upon the word *delish*. Initially, I thought your exuberance was forced, as if you were putting on a show for my benefit, as if you were saying, *I'm having such a great time* or *Thank you for picking up the tab*. But your commitment to an aesthetic of unfiltered expression, or sincerity, is simply who you are, and although I typically disdain that sort of unrestrained earnestness, never mind performance, probably because I am incapable of it, probably because it's hard out here for a child of guests, I loved to witness you do it.

Ben, after the noodles and the reconciliation, I'm not leaving. Not only will I be standing outside your apartment with dinner; I'll have my laptop and my mouthguard. And I won't be rushing out early. Forget five thirty a.m.! My plan is to stay for the entire morning, and possibly into the afternoon. I've already received a dispensation from my husband, who plans to take the kids ice skating. You and I will be free to laze about in the morning, maybe even go out for breakfast or grab coffee at that small place in Bushwick that you claim has the best drip but coincidentally happens to have a gorgeous barista who resembles me, albeit a much brawnier version—do you wish I were a bigger guy? We are free to do all

· 255 ·

the things two people do when they don't have anything to do but be with each other. Something we have longed for. Unless . . .

Unless your plan is to tell me face-to-face that we have no future, again. I fear it, and yet, I'm more prepared now than I was when you lobbed the bomb nearly a month ago—a month! Nearly! You see, the nature of being dumped makes two people uneven. An air of cruelty encircles you now, preventing me from loving you as freely as I once did.

I'm dreading our reunion. And I can't wait for it.

Ben, hit me with your best shot.

—Me

Dear Ben,

The strangest thing happened today. David and I were supposed to grab dinner tonight in the neighborhood. It would have been the first time we'd seen each other since our stoop run-in weeks ago, when he swatted away my heartbreak. But when I woke up this morning, he'd sent me the following email:

Hey, Man,

I can't meet up after all today because I have a lot of work stuff going on, and I'm sleep-deprived because the baby has a cold and isn't sleeping well. But I didn't want to let more time pass before addressing our last conversation.

I'm sorry if I handled your breakup poorly. Actually, I know I was an asshole. I've wanted to apologize and to explain why I reacted that way, but I kept chickening out. Also, the aforementioned baby sleeping woes— this kid is a shit sleeper—and Megan has been depressed a little too. Besides, I think I texted you a couple of times, and you didn't respond. What's up with that!?

I don't know if you've moved on from this or if you specifically don't want to talk to me about it, so I'll explain here what I've been meaning to explain over a beer or whatever gluten-free shit you drink.

When you first told me about Ben last summer, you were bummed about him breaking up with you, but I was so busy being shocked that you had an open marriage, I didn't really have time to process what I was feeling. I think I was nice about it . . . ?

I only talked to him a few times, but Ben seemed like a cool enough guy. Maybe a little young, but he was funny. I didn't have any problems

· 257 ·

with him. I was mostly just surprised. We all were. You had a perfect marriage, and we love you guys, and it's weird to see you different. It's uncomfortable to see you walking down the street with someone else. Even when it was all of us together, it was weird. It felt like you were fucking up your marriage, like watching a friend throw himself off a cliff.

Don't get a complex. It's not like all your friends get together to talk about this, but I'd be lying if I said it didn't come up from time to time.

Anyway, your business is your business. And even if I was a little uncomfortable with a big change in your life, that wasn't the reason I acted so shitty to you last month when you told me you and Ben had broken up again.

Here's the truth: A few years ago, Megan and I also opened things up. We tried. We didn't really act on it much. She hooked up with a guy at her job. I hooked up with an old college friend. We went to a few swingers' clubs. We had a couple of threesomes. But then I met someone on the apps. At first it was just sex. But then it got to be something else. It wasn't a big deal until it was.

Megan asked me to stop seeing her, and I did. And then a few months went by and I reconnected with her again. I didn't tell Megan, but I left my phone out one time, and she read everything. We did the couples counseling thing. We took a couple vacations together, just so I could clear the new person from my mind.

I didn't tell you or anyone about this because I was embarrassed. I felt like I'd fucked up my relationship. I thought everyone would turn on me. How original: a guy having a midlife crisis leaves his wife just as they're planning to start a family! Anyway, Megan got pregnant, and we agreed to stop seeing other people. But then the "other woman" called me out of the blue, said she was nearby. Could we just get coffee, that sort of thing.

MIDDLE SPOON

It was stupid because I knew I was hooked on her, but I still met up with her. We started seeing each other again, and again, I didn't tell Megan anything.

Who needs to be honest when they leave their phone out in plain sight? Megan looked through my messages, and she got so upset, we had to go to the hospital because she started to feel cramps. The doctors told her she needed to reduce her stress levels or risk miscarriage.

That was the wake-up call I needed. I didn't want to fuck up the last fifteen years because of a fun time, and I didn't want to kill my kid before I even met them, so I stopped. And it was so hard, I started going to AA meetings and lying about having an addiction to booze because I didn't want to admit that I was addicted to a person.

When you told me about Ben the first time, I felt relieved in a way. Both of us had made the same mistake. And both of us had walked away from our wreckages. But then you got back together, and I saw how it was all working. Your husband, your kids, everyone seemed to be okay with it. It blew my mind. And instead of being happy for you, I guess I got jealous.

When you told me last month that it was over again, I felt like we were in the same boat. I'm not proud to say this, but I was happy. You couldn't have something that I couldn't have, and I felt good about that.

It took me three therapy sessions to be able to write that sentence. Give me some credit!

I'm sorry about what you're feeling. I know it's rough. And I'm sorry I wasn't more supportive.

Let's catch up soon.

Actually, one more thing, which also comes from years of therapy, which I couldn't apply to my life's circumstances, but I think you should apply to yours: stop caring so much what people think about you.

· 259 ·

Whenever we talked about Ben, you seemed happy but also conflicted. You said once that you felt guilty about having it all. You also worried about what people were going to say and think. And you were freaked about your parents finding out. I say fuck it. You only live once. Enjoy yourself, and let everyone else deal with it. They will eventually.

—David

Dear Ben,

I was pedaling my way through Brooklyn earlier, but instead of feeling light and free and climate-change conscious, I was unnerved by a suffocating impatience. It coursed through me like a nonrenewable, neurochemical fuel. A well-curated agitation can, on most occasions, shave minutes off a commute without leaving much damage in its wake. This time, however, there was something more reactive happening, a nuclear restlessness that had been catalyzed by my lateness to pick up Nico from a playdate and by the dearth of adequate bicycle options, a completely unsurprising circumstance that I nevertheless find infuriating because of how much I've come to despise the city's bike rental program—that is, the battalion of mobile advertisements for a global banking corporation that passes for a bike rental program in a grand city whose leaders have chosen to contract out a basic service to private interests, who it should be said do a terrible job of maintaining the bicycles, a failure that would be at the spear's tip of a neoconservative talking point if the bike rentals were a government-run program, a program I am currently obliged to utilize because my unwieldy ten-speed is lodged somewhere in the basement of my charming prewar building characterized by its narrow hallways and even narrower egress.

This is all to say, I mounted the bicycle in a foul mood yesterday and found myself almost immediately behind a parade of slower, more indecisive cyclists, and all of us found ourselves at the mercy of the motorcycles and motorized scooters weaving in and out of the bike lanes, another habitual occurrence I've come to abhor. I absolutely detest pedal-less vehicles in the bicycle lane. The sight of them makes me want to conjure a

· *261* ·

steel pipe for the sole purpose of jamming it into the spokes of the offending vehicle. In fact, along with dog excrement, people who vape on the subway, income inequality, and cops, the flagrant misuse of the bike lane is my least favorite thing about New York City.

This was my mindset as I zipped along the waterfront of a previously industrial part of Brooklyn, once the site of a naval shipbuilding facility and prominent gay cruising routes, now populated by refurbished and repurposed warehouse spaces, upper-middle-income condos, and car repair shops. The entire trip was just shy of three miles, but each minor inconvenience wounded me in the way major inconveniences might wound other people, in the process reducing me to a human-shaped sack of bile who scowled, weaved, and even mouthed things to his most delinquent bipedal brethren.

Some of the troublemakers—many, probably most—were workers, delivery workers who were taking the literal path of least resistance in order to do their jobs. And while I retained sympathies for their plights, I still despised them because my parents were also workers who held the jobs few folks aspired to have, and they managed to be considerate of others in the process, which isn't to say I could possibly know which, if any, rules my parents may or may not have bent or broken along the way, but generally speaking, they contorted themselves rather unceremoniously and often to an unflattering degree to abide by rules, laws, and expectations, so you'll excuse me if I've become less sympathetic to people who don't. Not very sympathetic at all, mostly contemptuous.

Actually . . .

The tirade above hews dangerously close to an aesthetical bootstrap capitalism. After all, suffering shouldn't be a legacy, right? And neither should it be neat. The business of barely surviving in a context where the politics of scarcity are employed to obfuscate surplus *should* be messy and confrontational; we might otherwise pretend it isn't happening in our

MIDDLE SPOON

very midst and, consequently, rob ourselves of the opportunity and impulse for remedy and, one day, restitution.

Perhaps.

But yesterday, I had to struggle to put myself back on this collective liberation track because I was pissed off—get on the damn road, you fucking coward motorcyclists!—and the tension coursing through me operated with the precision of fog or lava, which is to say, by the time I noticed it, it was inescapable. I found myself aggressively claiming the road, snaking my way around workers and tourists and the creative class, blowing red lights, racing against the winter's early darkness, doing the sorts of things that could catapult me into the vastness of trouble or the singularity of an emergency room. Ben, I wasn't even wearing a helmet.

In retrospect, allowing a bit of tardiness and some inconsiderate behavior to jeopardize my own safety and well-being strikes me as a terrible way to live, a short-fuse-y existence that probably originated in early childhood or at inception and possibly generations earlier in the ovum of my maternal grandmother—there's plenty of research on these phenomena, so you're just going to have to believe me. And this is exactly what I meant to elucidate in an earlier email about trains and train stations: my susceptibility to and possible propensity for internal turmoil, a sort of proximate tumult, a tumult at bay, if you will, which I have managed, for most of adulthood, to process and/or pacify and at times preempt. But I won't lie: it does sneak up on me, the fog, the lava. And this turbulence, with its inconsistent performance schedule, was there throughout our relationship, and it is this very turbulence that has felled me since our breakup.

It's even worse than I've let on. On a few occasions, I've succumbed to my nature—or nurture, or nature by way of early nurturing, or lack thereof; all right, all right, you get it. Somewhat curiously, the occasions in question have all transpired on playgrounds, they've involved other

· 263 ·

parents, and they've been in defense of my children. Sandy once noted that I do for my children what I won't do for myself—namely, stake my ground—which, seen another way, makes me a good parent, no?

I recall a run-in a few years ago with the mother of one of Jules's classmates. I recall watching her walk over to Jules with a sternness of face and a severity of gait typical of a person who expects the worst. I recall her—a tall and sinuous human—curved faucet-like and gesticulating toward a small group of children, but her attention and limb-flailing was primarily directed at my child. I also recall feeling mildly embarrassed that my kid might have been responsible for something I would have to apologize for. And so, I approached and asked if everything was all right, prepared to commiserate with her about the foibles of parenting and childhood development, but instead, she rolled her eyes and said, "Someone had to tell that boy not to be so aggressive and to play well with the other children."

The sentence was obnoxious on its own, but her decision to look anywhere but at me as she made her declaration, as well as her choice to leave my child unnamed, a child she'd known for a couple of years, achieved a superlative degree of insolence. It confirmed beyond a shadow of a doubt the reputation this parent had earned in the communal murmuring, the sort of person who thinks her child sits at the center of the universe, incapable of wrongdoing, and who takes teachers and school staff to task if said child isn't made to feel Ptolemaic. But her obsequiousness was made worse—through no fault of her own, I must admit—because it was delivered with a French accent. She is, after all, from France. And although I hate xenophobia in all its forms—she, a white mother singling out a nonwhite child, my child, as aggressive in a mostly white space is the template for a PSA on race-related bias—I loathe in particular the French variety of xenophobia because of their liberty-equality-fraternity nonsense, which looks quite nice etched in the stone of building facades or on the metal alloys of coins but is an otherwise unpracticed fantasy, which isn't to say

· 264 ·

MIDDLE SPOON

every French person is racist or terrible—I know at least four or five people from France who are quite lovely, and I care deeply for Juliette Binoche and consequently do everything in my power never to read her interviews carefully for fear she will reveal herself as outdated or hypocritical, in other words, French—but most white French people are in fact racist and terrible, despite the rather lovely month I spent in their midst twenty years ago, where I witnessed a not insignificant number of mixed-race couples of all ages, the prevalence of which made me believe, even if only briefly, that the French were neither racist nor terrible, the entirety of their domestic and international policies notwithstanding.

In any case, this tall parent called my rather sweet five-year-old aggressive, even though it was her daughter who had been chasing Jules around, and even though it was her daughter who had been bothering my baby for days, and even though I had tried several times to tell Jules not to exclude other children because they don't like it when they're excluded, and even though they had responded each time, by way of an explanation, "Daddy, she's mean and won't leave me alone," the evidence of which I'd witnessed whenever she ran up to Jules and other children while pretending to be versed in some sort of martial art that consisted of ineffective air slices and air chops. Despite all this, la mère en colère still had the audacity to label my baby *agressif*. I wasn't, as you might have surmised from this lengthy prelude, able to handle that moment gracefully. Instead, I looked her directly in the eyes and said, "I see. So you're the type of parent who likes to call out other people's children for behaviors your own child exhibits quite freely."

Et voilà.

My observation didn't go over well. Quite poorly indeed. Worse than anyone could have imagined. The parent instantly started shouting at me, called me a *motherfucker*, told me I didn't belong there, told me I was only half a man, told me she wasn't surprised at my child's behavior because of how aggressive I had just been. She went on like that for six uninterrupted minutes, most of which I spent expressionless, looking out at the swarm of children racing through the park, pretending all the nearby parents weren't staring at our spectacle, regretting my tactics, hoping the fire would put itself out. At some point, however, I tired of pretending and took advantage of her deep breath in order to respond, in my most evenhanded tone, "You are living up to your reputation."

This, of course, did nothing to quell the brouhaha. It was the opposite of quelling, as if I'd taken the contents of an active volcano and dumped them onto a small grease fire. The mother grew louder and nastier. She became the worst fear I have for myself, and I knew as she was yelling that she had been raised in an environment similar to my own. I knew she, too, had been reared by underfed wolves in a field where other underfed wolves sauntered about, looking for the barely surviving, and somehow, she'd survived, and her fashionable eyeglasses, her layered haircut, her high heels, and her pencil skirt were the proof of how far she'd come. Honestly, as I stood there silent, recording the incident—as soon as she started yelling, I turned my phone's camera on and slid it into my breast pocket—I felt like a dickhead because I knew what I'd done. I should have just walked away. Or I should have been kind and productive: *Hi, other parent. Remember me? We met a couple of years ago when our children were in day care together. You met my husband too. Our children play together all the time. I know your child's name, and you know mine. I'm sorry you felt your daughter was being mistreated, but I believe our children have a love-hate bond, and they're going through a bit of friction right now. Maybe we can find a time when they can play together in a more controlled setting.* That would have been wise, but this way of being, always ready to clap back, always prepared to pierce and wound with words, always expecting the worst, is an extension of everything I've been trying to communicate to you about how I function. It takes a secure and generous person to

MIDDLE SPOON

handle someone like me. I wondered all along whether you could be that person.

—Me

PS: It was after this incident a couple of years ago that I started seeing Sandy because, at the time, Fred's schedule had no openings.

Ben and the married man and the husband and the children move into a duplex apartment where life can be modular. There's life downstairs, and there's life upstairs. But often it's a shared life, which proves to be the difficult part for all: maintaining a preexisting family while commencing another. The married man's primary concern, or maybe it's a primordial fear, is not meeting his children's needs, followed closely by the wants and desires of his husband and Ben. They are all living out a graduate-level math problem, but it's not unsolvable. Everyone manages quite well.

The model changes over time.

One night, shortly after the return of Ben, the married man and his husband go out to dinner. There's a new French restaurant, and the frenzy has made that corner of their neighborhood unbearable, so they go to the restaurant next door, also French, and during the main course—two steak frites, both medium rare—they come to the realization that the defining characteristic of a long-term relationship is its elasticity. One can, with a bit of care, take a long-term relationship for granted, they surmise. The married man and his husband no longer have the insatiable thirst they once had for each other, only a moderate thirst with moments of desperation. They are, for better or worse, in the comfort and security portion of their shared life, where consistency has become the mode, the mean, and the median, which, they agree, is a wonderful place to be. Permanence and safety are better and more valuable than sustained thrills. But that's the thing about this situation: they don't have to choose.

Ben and the married man are in the throes of passion; consequently, the married man sleeps with Ben more often, and they go out on more dates. The husband, who is confident and easily satisfied with one French or Ethiopian or (non-French) Mediterranean or Japanese dinner out per

MIDDLE SPOON

week, isn't put off by the courtship taking place under his roof. When he feels lonely or underappreciated, he voices it at their quarterly check-in. The married couple agrees to keep their date night, in addition to the one or two times of sex per week, which fits nicely with the three or four times per week of sex that Ben requires, leaving the married man with one and sometimes three nights of repose.

Taking a separate-but-equal approach to this arrangement would have been a mistake. Their lives have to achieve a functional degree of integration, they decide. Cooperative, or communal, living. Weekly family dinners, family vacations, family fights, as well as their own time together, their own dinners, their own vacations, their own fights, their own couch cuddling (downstairs), plus dinners with the husband alone, trips with him alone, and couch cuddling with him (upstairs).

And let us not forget the children. Ben isn't immediately a co-parent, but there is a nonnegligible amount of childcare required of him. He is something like a stepdad or half dad or uncle to the kids, in addition to the kids he wants to have with the married man in the future, who will certainly be part of the blended brood and, as a result, will have two older siblings and two primary dads, plus a tertiary dad or stepdad or half dad or uncle: the husband.

Everyone is mindful of polyamory's costs. To have the time they need together and apart requires resources: money, space, time, and patience. (The bourgeoisie nature of polyamory in the US context is inescapable.) On the other hand, they're good at being frugal. They take advantage of each other's complementary and conflicting schedules. They eat most of their meals together. Four times per year, the three adults reassess. *How is this going? Are we happy? Content? Worried? How can we make this better for everyone?*

The children eventually leave—to camp, to college, to communes in Bolivia or Vermont—freeing up time and space. But by then, the care of

· *269* ·

elderly relatives rises on the list of life's concerns. And now it's no fewer than six parents to consider, plus close aunts and maybe a wayward cousin or two, which isn't to say they'll all live with them, but they'll require care in some manner.

This appears burdensome, unwieldy, and daunting, but it's also a grand adventure. More people means more love. And love does go quite far as it concerns absolutely everything.

As does habit. They grow used to one another. Everyone does.

There are problems too. This world—individualistic, litigious, patriarchal, capitalist—makes the sharing of finances across three people unnecessarily perplexing, borderline impossible. Since Ben is not legally married to anyone, they struggle to decipher if he'd inherit part of what was meant to go to the children and the husband, and vice versa. Sharing the costs for the big-ticket items, like a car or two weeks in Colombia or a pullout couch, requires thought and dialogue. They divvy up these expenses three ways according to means. The married man pays two-thirds more than Ben because he has more money. And the husband pays twice as much as the married man because he makes the most. They recalculate as life changes.

Ben pays rent, albeit a below-market price that matches, more or less, his previous below-market rent, but he keeps his previous rental, sublets it to a recently divorced friend. Venturing into something unorthodox warrants reassurances, something in the wings. Besides, everyone knows to never relinquish an affordable rental. After a year, he relinquishes the affordable rental.

The married man wakes at 6:25 a.m., kisses Ben, goes upstairs, kisses the husband, prepares breakfast for the kids, gets them ready for school, makes Ben coffee, brings it downstairs on the way to the bus stop with the older child, comes home, eats a quick breakfast with Ben and the husband, helps prep the younger kid while Ben gets ready for work, says

MIDDLE SPOON

goodbye to the husband and child, goes back downstairs, spends time with Ben until he leaves for work, or co-works with Ben if it's a day he works from home, has sex with Ben at some point before or after lunch, continues to co-work, preps dinner, picks up one child from school, comes home and either finishes making dinner (a) for all, when they eat as one large, extended postmodern family, (b) for the husband and the kids, when he and Ben have plans, (c) for Ben, himself, and the kids, when the husband happens to have plans, (d) for Ben and/or the kids, when he and the husband have plans, (e) for the kids and the sitter so that he and the husband can have date night without having to burden Ben, or when Ben has his own plans, although pizza is typically on the menu when a sitter comes, or (f) for the husband, himself, and the kids, when Ben has his own plans. Sometimes, the married man doesn't make dinner at all.

There are grocery runs, colonoscopies, evening constitutionals, New Year's Eve parties, births, deaths—in brief, life. Just like every other family, but with some additional planning. Internally, they have issues, but most of their problems come from the outside world: neighbors, friends, family, coworkers, accountants, civil servants. The keys to success are, to put it quite blandly, boundaries and flexibility. They make a life together that makes room for their various arrangements. It all works.

It all works.

It works.

It has to work.

It works, Ben. We make it so.

I want to believe this to be true, but even as I sketch the plan, I have doubts. I might very well be a fool to believe that the full, recalcitrant, and oppositional weight of society won't hasten our demise.

I have fears too. I'm afraid of not being able to make all of you happy. I'm afraid of being rejected by one or all of you. I'm afraid of a life with two white partners. You're both good people, but whiteness is an entire category of misgivings and unearned privileges, and I didn't know if I had it in me to walk this path with you. At times, I sensed you were less amenable to growing and to revolution and to criticizing (never mind destroying) the interlocking systems of oppression—it takes a lot of work to grapple with invisible things. I'm afraid of being with someone younger who has much to learn when I've already curated a life filled with like-minded people who buffer me from most of the slings and arrows. I'm afraid of the new energy wearing off and discovering there's nothing worth saving. I'm afraid of how your promiscuity and my fear of abandonment will match up. I'm afraid of being a conduit for sexually transmissible infections. I'm afraid of falling out of love with you and hurting you. I'm petrified of you falling out of love with me and hurting me again.

I'm afraid, too, of being left out.

I've broached this before, but the possibility becomes more feasible when I think of putting the polyamory plan into action. You and my husband might end up together. A scenario in which you two develop an attraction to each other is feasible. A scenario in which I'm left unfazed by that attraction—wow, talk about growth!—is less feasible but not impossible. I don't want you two to end up together, but I'd be a twit to think the possibility wasn't sitting in the corner of the room with its elephant-sized legs crossed, and I'd be an ingrate if I denied the two of you something you've both allowed me to have. Besides, if the remaining side of this triangle were suddenly drawn in, it could be beautiful. I'd propose such an arrangement if it were the only way of keeping you both.

It's strange to proclaim something so altruistic and revolting and not truly mean it. I mean the words, but I don't mean the feelings.

I've been in some form of therapy or another for the better part of the last twenty years, and I've yet to achieve the selflessness I aspire to.

MIDDLE SPOON

The time has come for me to admit I'm a person who wants equity for the world but all the spoils for himself. I still fall prey to the scarcity model; I still behave as if happiness lies in the accumulation of goods and the hoarding of resources. Love is a good. Love is a resource. So is attention. Maybe I'm the one who lacks imagination.

I must also admit I would be afraid to have these sorts of conversations with you. I think you'd find them and, consequently, me, odd and unbearable. But maybe I don't need to have these conversations with you. Perhaps you're not that kind of person or partner. Our interactions, while meaningful to us, won't lead to revolution of the self or of society. Maybe that's not what partners are for. We're meant merely to keep one another safe, healthy, and happy so that each of us can continue along our distinct paths but with more confidence and gusto. Maybe I've been wrong all along about what partnership means. I'm often wrong.

But I remain a man with a plan. And isn't that appealing?

—Me

PS: Please don't get me started on the housing market in NYC, in particular its lack of renter protections, despite our city being one of the most renter-friendly in the United States, which, I must admit, is something I've been saying for years without a clear recollection of the original source. And let's face it, "most renter-friendly" is such an empty superlative in the United States of America.

I just read the most heartening article about the public housing model in Vienna. In brief, everyone is better off when housing is public, extremely affordable, and built in a way that encourages cooperative living, vis-à-vis communal spaces and social amenities.

To be clear, I'm not drawing any correlations between Vienna and polyamory, much less Vienna and us. I take all of Europe with a grain of salt because for every egalitarian and community-oriented advancement, there are two racist, imperialist skeletons in their closet and often in their parliaments.

PPS: I think my plan might be lacking a preamble:

We, the components of this polyamorous triad, must remember our place in the larger family. Our success cannot be disentangled from the success of the children. Their defense and welfare are secondary to no other prestated goal or desire. We must therefore be forthcoming with them about the circumstances at hand. Furthermore, we must present a united front, so that they won't draw any false conclusions about the structural integrity of their family. Continued and periodic reassessments are essential. As is a clear imparting of confidence, including the requisite vocabulary to understand and talk about their atypical lives.

Dear Ben,

Forty-eight hours is what separates us.

"Do you think this is the best way forward?" Sandy asked this afternoon, after I'd emailed to let her know what had been happening since our last session. She didn't tell me she disapproved, but the formulations of her questions said as much. Fred, whom I also emailed, was less equivocal: "Your recovery time will more or less equal half the length of your relationship. The clock resets whenever you have contact with him." In other words, I'll need about five and a half months of uninterrupted abstinence from you, but no one, including my therapists, has been able to confirm whether this means absolute amnesia or just-vague-enough memories to allow me to be a functional human.

Fred also repeated what he's been saying for months and possibly years: "Your doubts and insecurities are rooted in a fear of abandonment."

"Isn't everyone afraid of being abandoned?" I've asked many times.

And he's always replied, "Not necessarily."

I took this observation to Sandy during my first breakup with Ben, and somewhat ghoulishly, I presented it as my own. In response, she said, "Let's try something: close your eyes."

"Are you going to get up and leave the room?" I asked.

"No. Now, think back to a previous time in your life when you've felt fears and anxieties similar to the ones you've felt about Ben, not only the emotional fallout of this moment, but the ever-present angst you experienced throughout your relationship. Can you?"

"Yes."

"Open your eyes and tell me about it."

I dredged up something from middle school, namely Jeremy, my best friend, with whom I was probably in love, something I didn't realize at the time. And since we were adolescents without the language or nuance to meet the moment, I spent those years feeling rejected and ultimately abandoned by someone who had no idea he was rejecting or abandoning me—the attraction wasn't mutual. In effect, he was a perfectly okay friend who didn't know he was a lousy boyfriend. Whenever he hung out with other friends over me, whenever he picked on me, whenever he didn't return a call, whenever he confided in me about the crushes he had—girls, of course—I was crushed.

"I suspect these fears of abandonment began even earlier in your life," Sandy said.

"Maybe it was when my brother chose another kid as his playmate instead of me. I've seen this between my own kids. They're inseparable mates at home, but Nico, as the older sibling, will ditch Jules whenever his peers enter the arena, which wounds Jules deeply; it's nothing short of heartbreak. Maybe something similar happened to me in my youth."

Sandy nodded and then nudged me to go back further.

"Or maybe there were moments in my early days when I needed more attention and warmth than my parents were able to muster, and I have been after these reassurances ever since."

I might be a person who wants more even when he's had enough. In ophthalmological circles, I'd be a minus eater. My eye doctor explained the phenomenon to me a few years ago, while I sat at one of those machines that measures the strength and accuracy of our vision. The one that flips through lenses while the doctor scrolls through slides and calls out, *A or B? B or C? D or A?* Well, apparently, I'll keep going. Even when I've achieved the correct prescription for my eyes, I'll insist the stronger prescription is crisper, bolder, better. A minus eater, he called it. It's like gluttony through a looking glass. I wonder if I do the same with valida-

MIDDLE SPOON

tion via human connection. I need to keep hearing that people love and appreciate me, and even when they've said and done plenty to make me feel loved and appreciated, I manage to find a reason to believe they don't or that their earlier efforts were disingenuous. I'm so afraid of being left, I convince myself I've already been left.

Jesus Christ.

But I'm not a lost cause. If we give this another try, I'm going to work hard at not assuming the worst. I'm going to tell myself whatever I need to be happy. I'm going to become a walking mantra machine. *I have value. I am worth the love I seek. I have plenty to give. You'd be lucky to have me. You'd be better off with me. I will not fret over the future. I will not be mired in the past. I will live in the moment. This might also be Reagan's fault.*

I'm going to do this whether we reconcile or not.

—Me

Dear Ben,

Sixth grade is the absolute pits, not least of all because middle school children are cruel and moronic, sometimes both at the same time. I was reminded of this last Thursday, when I picked up Nico. I noticed he was a bit sullen, but after a few blocks, all I'd extracted were a series of *ehs* and *uh-huh*s. As we waited for the G train—the B62 bus decided to stop running—he finally opened up. It seems some bully-like child had walked over to him at the end of his lunch period and knocked the tray out of his hands.

Yes, the tray out of his hands.

What is this human instinct to be so incredibly unoriginal and repetitive? We deregulate after the slightest improvement of an economy that was toppled by deregulation; we scapegoat minorities when shit isn't going well for us under the pretext of humanitarianism, we invade countries that don't bend to our will and install puppet leaders who later stand up to us, whom we immediately label dictators and proceed to dethrone because of ensuing and purported humanitarian crises; and we cut taxes on the rich for no damn good reason. Humans are truly stupid. And one of those stupid humans, who was undoubtedly raised to be cruel because of the cycle of cruelty, picked on Nico in the most unoriginal manner possible. And as Nico was on his knees picking up the scraps of food—luckily this happened after he'd eaten his lunch—he became overwhelmed with a desire to strike the little heathen who'd picked on him, but, "Dad, I knew I wasn't supposed to hit, so I just got really frustrated and started to cry. And then the kid and his friends started to make fun of me for crying," Nico explained.

MIDDLE SPOON

At that point in his story, I wanted to build a time machine in order to be in that cafeteria with him and drag those little bastards by their ears and noses to the principal's office. But since I lack the engineering skills required to build things, all I could think to say as we waited, our backs pressed against the white tile, our breath somehow still visible, was "I'm sorry, honey."

"It's okay," Nico responded, his head low, but not as low as it had been a few minutes prior.

"And," I added, "you don't have to be embarrassed about crying."

Nico then looked up at me with wide eyes and an open mouth that signaled either pity, dumbfounded surprise, or *What did you say?* At that moment, not only was the guitarist with the amplifier standing next to us singing "Baby Can I Hold You," but the Queens-bound G train was pulling into the station on the track opposite us.

"Why would I be embarrassed?" Nico said after the station had settled down again.

"I don't know," I responded, somewhat embarrassed for myself and society at large.

"Dad, when those kids asked me if I was crying about the tray, I said yes. I told them I was an emotional person, and it was okay to cry because it's true and because that's what you always say to us."

Ben.

I nearly cried too.

There I was thinking the crying part had likely compounded his predicament, that he'd been humiliated by his involuntary emotions, but his currency had been indignation, without a scintilla of shame to accompany it. That realization did something to me. I think it was pride, but it might have been hope too. I felt, in that space of swirling chaotic humanity and just-adequate engineering, that my kid was better than me. In a way, he presented the possibility of a future more improved than my past, a

· *279* ·

version of this world in which we might feel freely, without fear of stigma or repercussions of any kind. An emotional awakening was taking place everywhere, all at once. Perhaps we were living through a revolution.

As a parent, I've come to understand how essential my role is in stewarding my children toward confidence. I now have a sense of how much patience and how many resources are required to instill a sense of security in another human being, which explains why it's in short supply, certainly for me, and probably as it concerns those brats who bullied Nico.

Confidence and security are what allowed me to pursue my relationship with you. Hear me out: It took me nearly twenty years to be with a man who wasn't my husband because I feared the consequences. This isn't to say I've been trying for twenty years to find you, but you certainly wouldn't have been possible if I hadn't first had the foundation of my marriage. Put another way, my husband is both the reason why I will not give myself fully to you and the reason why I can give myself to you at all. A conundrum.

As I see it, I have options:

(a) Find someone else to meet my needs who's more amenable to my circumstances.

(b) Go back to who I was before and rediscover the joy of the last two decades.

(c) Find other ways to meet the needs you elucidated.

(d) Wait patiently for you to discover how much you need me.

"What if I'm the person you're meant to spend the rest of your life with?" you asked me once. We were in your bed, awake because of your horrible neighbors whose habit of sitting on the stoop next door at all hours with an entire speaker system blaring and pulsating as if it were a midday Sunday in July made peaceful slumber unattainable. It was a weekday in October.

MIDDLE SPOON

"It's possible," I responded before rolling onto your back and taking the scruff of your neck between my teeth.

Perhaps I was going to realize you were the only person I wanted to spend the rest of my life with, but I didn't want to build a life with you on that premise. I wanted to build it on the foundation that already existed.

—Me

Therapy prep—for Fred, who is more interested in interpreting dreams than Sandy is:

The other night, I dreamed I was in the dining room of a restaurant full of familiar strangers dressed for a special occasion. The chairs were braided wood. The lighting was somehow bright and also quite dim. I wore a bespoke three-piece blue suit, and I carried a bag of clothes (more fine attire) that I may or may not have stolen—I had a familiar sinking feeling, the one where I am about to be accused of stealing despite having a perfectly legal explanation for why I possess the things I possess. As is the nature of dreams, I suddenly found myself in a long line for the bathroom, which I could barely tolerate because of my intense urge to urinate, so I walked to another bathroom at the other end of the restaurant, where I encountered another line of people, more people than could have possibly fit in the entire restaurant, but there they were, chatting and waiting, in my mind. Just then, I looked up, and my husband was standing beside me. He had a vacancy in his eyes, not the look of someone with an urgent desire to pee, and instead of greeting me, he matter-of-factly announced he was dating several men and then proceeded to rattle off a list of acquaintances, coworkers, and a mutual friend. Before rage took a complete hold of me, I managed to ask him if he was on PrEP. When he said nothing in response, I began to punch him, rather decisive strikes that transformed his face into something claylike and droopy. There was no trace or smell of blood, but I knew I was doing something terribly violent and gruesome. And then, the scene changed again, and I was back to searching for an elusive bathroom, but not before a man in a wheelchair emerged from the back of the restaurant with a machine gun and began shooting indiscriminately into our crowd. I woke up, as frightened as I was angry,

MIDDLE SPOON

frightened by the bullets and angry at the imagined dalliances of a man whose only crime was lying soundlessly beside me.

The dream, which was certainly fueled by heartburn and a full bladder, revealed me to be a selfish and hypocritical man-child who wants his husband to be completely devoted despite not being fully devoted to him. I don't know how to explain this sort of egomania. I continue to believe it has something to do with my brain development and upbringing.

But maybe not.

My husband isn't interested in the complications of dating other people. Periodically, I suggest he try to meet someone, but I don't mean it. I'm just trying to be fair, despite my aversion to being fair as it concerns the men in my life. My husband doesn't agree: "You need this more than I do. Being equal doesn't make this equitable."

The nerve! That's the sort of social justice speak I've introduced into our lives, and he's turned the tables on me. And quite astutely, I don't mind saying.

I tried once to explain my needs to Ben using terms of equality and equity. We were mildly inebriated and walking in the East Village; we'd been at his actor friend's postshow drinks. *She was amazing, but the show was terrible* had been our quiet consensus. As we made our way toward the L, he argued my marriage was all the reason he needed to be nonmonogamous with me. If I weren't married, he said, he'd be all mine. He didn't buy my equality-equity pablum. To be fair, I wasn't trying to *sell* him anything. I sincerely believed what I said. He needed me in order to be happy. My husband needed me in order to be happy. And I needed both of them in order to achieve the same degree of happiness.

Strange that I should become the poster boy for polyamory when, until only recently, I equated it with polygamy, nothing more than a relic of religions and cults, a tool for keeping women subjugated.

I didn't set out to be a pioneer. Historically, I hate most self-proclaimed

· 283 ·

pioneers. I also detest spotlights and unnecessary attention. Give me a background, and I'll endeavor to fade into it. And yet, here I am desiring attention from multiple people while advocating for a family structure that will no doubt draw unwanted scrutiny. This is, in a way, the story of my life. Nearly everything immutable, as well as by choice, in my life has raised eyebrows. Maybe I'm addicted to unwanted scrutiny.

Or maybe this is simply the middle child in me subconsciously seeking attention.

Dear First Love,

"Hon? Are you awake?" you asked me an hour ago, about an hour after I'd fallen asleep.

"Not really."

"Sorry."

"It's okay. Something wrong?"

"Not really."

"Sounds ominous."

"I've been thinking."

"Sounds dangerous."

"Can I finish?" you said.

"Sorry."

"I've been thinking about you and Ben."

"Sexually?"

"No! Stop interrupting. I've been thinking about your impending meeting."

"Do you not want me to go?"

"No. Well, no. But maybe. It's just that you're getting better. I know you're still going through the rough part. And I can see you're not yourself. But you're better than you were a week ago. And much better than three weeks ago. Seeing Ben last week seeded hope, for better or worse. I'm afraid seeing him again will only set you back if he doesn't want to restart things with you."

"I thought you wanted me to resolve this."

"No. I never said that. I want you to be healthy and happy. I don't actively want you to pursue another relationship."

· 285 ·

"What are you saying?"

"I'm saying I want you to take care of yourself. And I'm not sure if being with Ben or restarting things with Ben is the same as taking care of yourself."

"Meeting with him might lead to closure."

"You can get your own closure by keeping your distance. It's the more painful route, maybe, but since you're already halfway there . . ."

"If I believed I was halfway . . ."

"Consider it."

"I will."

"No matter what you decide, I'm here," you said.

"I love you," I responded, and then I searched for your hand under the covers and did my best to get back to sleep. But I couldn't: "Hon?"

"Yeah?"

"Is this just about me being happy? Or are you having second thoughts about me and Ben, about disrupting our lives?"

"I don't know."

"What exactly?" I asked.

"I truly don't know. Maybe I've been wrong about all this. I know you think I'm a robot. Everybody thinks that. And I am a little. I don't care as much about things as you do. Then again, it could just be the difference between having OCD and not having it. All I know is I feel secure about our relationship. If something or someone makes you happy, I'm happy for you. As long as you still give me what I need, as long as you're here for the kids, I don't care. So far, you have. I don't have any complaints."

"So what's the problem?"

"I guess I'm wondering if I'm wrong not to care more. People keep asking me if I'm okay. And when I tell them I am, they look at me like they don't believe me."

"Who?"

MIDDLE SPOON

"Doesn't matter. But it's annoying. I know what I feel, and still, when people look at me like I'm crazy for allowing you to have another partner, I start to wonder if I am a little—"

"Crazy?"

"No, but maybe broken."

I wrapped my arms around your back and chest and kissed the nape of your neck until I felt your breathing slow and a light snore hum in tandem with the white-noise machine. For me, there was no slumber after that, so I wandered into the living room and attempted the crossword, Thursday edition, on my phone, until the college sports and opera clues stumped me. After that, I simply lay on the couch thinking.

You met Ben several times, and you got along about as well as the situation and the circumstances permitted. The conversations—*The Lord of the Rings*, Trump, gay fiction—were robust but forced. One time, fearing I was the off-kilter fulcrum, I suggested you two go out for a drink on your own, but neither of you was interested. I admit I was relieved.

You've done everything right. I don't care about the judgmental folks who project their own insecurities or the conservative folks who lack imagination. Why would we want these people to have a say in our lives?

Remember me at twenty-one: inexperienced, afraid, apprehensive, cocky the way only young people can be? The reactive nagging, the purity tests, the self-sabotaging martyrdom. Another person would have run for a nearby exit, but you remained steadfast and unfazed. I'd always assumed your impassivity was the natural outcome of well-heeled nurturing, but I've come to a different conclusion. Your demeanor isn't only the limbic buffers of a privileged upbringing; your sister and your brother, after all, are both insufferably scattered and on the tail end of four failed marriages—two each. No, I think there's something in your nature, maybe genetics, but probably epigenetics (predisposition + conditions = constitution). A preternatural unflappability that has, for more than two

· 287 ·

decades, served me well. Me, a poorly constructed schooner; you, a tremendous body of placid water.

Remember the traumatized shih tzu my parents adopted years ago, the one who'd convulse and bark at the slightest noise or movement? I was convinced they'd erred in taking it into their home, but after only a few months, everything was different. The little terror had transformed into a pleasant, four-legged marshmallow. I asked my mother what had changed, and she said, "He just needed to find the right home." But when I asked my father, he said, "Your mother hugged that dog every day, todo el santo día, and when he barked or scratched, she hugged him tighter. She never stopped talking to him."

Honey, no matter how much you tell me it isn't, I cannot rid myself of the notion that my love for Ben is disrespectful to you. Of course, I want to believe you're correct, and I want to live in a world in which nothing is atypical or untraditional. But I live in this world, and worse still, this world lives in me. Until I fully believe that being with Ben isn't an attack on you, I am in effect taking advantage of your grace, and I will continue doing so while hoping that I, too, learn to believe as you do. In this moment, however, I wish I could wipe him from my memory, so that I might go back to loving you as completely as you deserve. I promise that if Ben and I reconcile, I won't stop loving or needing you. I will find a way to make this all work.

—Me

Dear Ben,

I took everyone's advice, and I fucked someone else.

It began this morning, after my husband had taken our kids to another kid's birthday party. I was alone and jittery about seeing you tonight, and instead of using the time to read or work or catch up on any number of television series, I settled into my default setting: the downward spiral, the slick funnel of likely, improbable, and impossible scenarios that run the gamut from reconciliation, to never seeing each other again, to death. At some point during my descent into this contained and rather manageable madness, I heard the words I'd been hearing for nearly a year: *Go fuck someone.* Previously fraught and unappealing, the now pithy and unassuming suggestion became the epitome of practical. Before seeing you again, I told myself it was wise—nay, necessary!—I do something to test the integrity of my feelings for you.

I texted the recently divorced epidemiologist with wall-to-wall books and the penchant for Amaro Montenegro, "Thanks again for inviting me to your class. I hope the students enjoyed it."

"They certainly did. As did I. I've been meaning to invite you out for a coffee or any other token of appreciation you might deem worthy."

"Not necessary, but I'd be happy to meet up sometime. Maybe in the new year."

"How about in an hour?"

And that's how it went. At eleven thirty this morning, I met him at a tinsel-covered college bar on the Upper West Side. I had a martini that was four dollars more expensive than it should have been; he had a Manhattan; we split a bag of salt-and-vinegar chips. We raced through our drinks, and on the walk up to his third-floor apartment, I surreptitiously fished out half of a Viagra from my coat pocket and confirmed the condom in my wallet.

I'll spare you the details—the second drink, the hit of pot, the playlist that included both Luther Vandross and the Smiths, the kissing and oral sex on the couch, the condom fumbling, the main event in front of his bathroom mirror. But I must divulge I fucked this man the way you liked to be fucked, with a heightened degree of disregard. He moaned for nineteen uninterrupted minutes before we both got off, which was a relief because in order to evaluate the success of this intervention, it couldn't be confounded by its quality. If it had been mediocre sex or a bad vibe, I wouldn't know if its ineffectiveness in helping to forget you was because I am incapable of forgetting you or because the experience had been suboptimal.

I can now say with some certainty that having great sex with a very attractive epidemiologist who keeps a neat apartment only makes things worse. On the long cab ride home, the guilt and self-hate, perched as they were on my shoulders, their crow-like talons digging into my flesh, were almost too much to bear. I wasn't only left missing you more than I had before; I was afraid you'd hate me and that I'd again taken advantage of my husband.

I don't understand how people do this, have sex with people they barely know and whom they may never truly know. The intimacy of sex triggers emotions I can't easily set aside. However temporary, I bonded with the epidemiologist, a near-perfect stranger who, at best, is now an imperfect stranger. I know some part of me remained with him because the entirety of me didn't get into the cab back to Brooklyn.

This is probably why everyone has recommended I have sex with several people. With each encounter, the degree of caring will diminish, until the men I fuck in beds and on couches and in bathrooms that aren't

· *290* ·

MIDDLE SPOON

mine don't matter to me at all, until you become nothing more than a silhouette of infatuation. I believe you figured this out a long time ago.

—Me

PS: I'm not going to tell you about the epidemiologist.

PPS: The cab cost seventy-five dollars—before tip!

Dear Ben,

I messaged Sandy on the way home because I wanted counsel before meeting you. She responded, "I don't want this to become a habit, but since we didn't meet last week, I'm making an exception. I have a twenty-five-minute slot, but please note that the insurance company will bill you as if this were a full session."

I said nothing of my dalliance with the epidemiologist because of the abbreviated session time and because my shame was still dewy. I focused instead on all the possible scenarios and outcomes of my meeting with you. All of my fears. All of my hopes. I did my best to empty the contents of my brain so that I might arrive clearheaded on your doorstep.

It was while I rambled on that Sandy interrupted me: "The words you're saying make sense, but the sentiment is irrational. You cannot spend your life trying to plan for every contingency. Let life happen to you. What are you afraid of?"

"Everything."

"Can you narrow it down? What are you afraid of today?"

"Getting hurt."

"No one wants to be hurt."

"I know, but—"

"You can't avoid pain, and your efforts to do so are labor-intensive."

"Am I supposed to walk unprepared into these situations?"

"In a way, yes. Ben might hurt you. He might not. He might love you. He might not. He might cheat on you. He might not. There are no guarantees in this life. Every time you step foot outside, you risk encountering all manner of dangers, but you still leave your house, no?"

MIDDLE SPOON

"Yes, and—"

"Treat love the same. Treat your health the same. Treat your work the same. Embrace the uncertainty. The obsessive ruminations and reassurance-seeking are not fixes. They are shovels that keep making the hole you need to fill bigger."

"Everything you're saying makes sense, but I can't even begin to imagine how to overcome these feelings."

"Imagine your fears are a cold lake. Imagine you step one foot in. Your instinct will be to pull it out. But what if you walked farther in? What if you sat with the cold? What if you allowed your body to acclimate to the discomfort of not knowing what's next?"

"I can try—I will try. But how should I deal with it if he wants to get back together? What if I'm destroying my marriage? And if I do—"

"You don't know. We don't know. No one does. And I find not knowing a more interesting way to live than trying to calculate everything ahead of time."

Sandy removed her dark-rimmed glasses and pinched the bridge of her nose, which made me think she was frustrated with me. I was frustrated with myself. I was going to ask her if she was upset, but it seemed like a self-serving bit of information gathering, of the kind she'd just told me to forgo.

"Please forgive me, but I've been on video calls with clients all day. I have a minor headache," she explained. "If you don't mind, I'd like to end the call here."

"That's completely understandable," I replied. "I'll see you at our regular time next week."

"Best of luck tonight. You're capable of surviving this and more. Much more. Remember that."

—Me

Dear Ben,

I waited for you outside of your apartment. For fifteen minutes, I waited, all the while rubbing my ungloved hands together and bouncing subtly on the balls of my feet. I'd intended to bring us the wavy noodles with lamb from our favorite place, but just as I walked into the restaurant, I got cold feet. I feared you'd receive the meal as smothering or inappropriate, so I left and arrived at your place empty-handed, despite knowing you'd be hungry. Second-guessing kindness was a crap way to begin our reunion, possibly a portent. To make matters worse, second-guessing appears to be a hallmark of OCD, so I felt doubly defeated as I waited for you.

When the black sedan pulled up to the hydrant and you opened your door, I approached and reached for one of your bloated duffel bags. I wanted to kiss you, but your face narrowed and you pulled away from me rather forcefully. It wasn't only your demeanor that was cold; the temperature, too, had dropped. And to top things off, you seemed to have a cold. Your eyes were moist, your nose red. And still, you invited me upstairs. I followed your breath, now certain you were about to end things once and for all. My pressing concern quickly became whether it'd be a kind or brutal encounter.

As I removed my shoes, and you your coat, you walked past me. I stood up and grabbed your arm. I was trembling. You looked straight into my eyes, and before either one of us could cry, I pulled you toward me and wrapped you in my arms, ignoring the effort you made to break free. I felt as if I were hugging the trunk of the last tree in the forest. It was then I heard you sniffle, and your arms appeared around me. We re-

MIDDLE SPOON

mained that way for an eternity, probably a minute, an interval that was, depending on the assessor and the moment in which it was assessed, either endless or fleeting. I knew then this would be amicable, which put me at ease but also made me desperate; that brief time with you was all the time I had to make you see I was worth the inconveniences that accompanied life with me. In one conversation, I had to prove that an upside-down world was right side up.

It's three a.m., officially the day after, and I'm experiencing the exhaustion of three a.m., of heartache, and of closure. I will finish this email another day, but for posterity's sake, it was essential I transcribe the early moments of our meeting. I want to remember them clearly for a long time.

Goodbye,
Me

Dear Ben,

Larry, the psychiatric nurse practitioner, required only fifteen minutes of my time before arriving at his assessment: "Yes, I feel confident in saying that you are afflicted with obsessive-compulsive disorder." The bald, mustached man with a gap between his front teeth then offered to send a Zoloft prescription to my pharmacy. It happened so quickly all I could think to ask was whether the drugs would help me deal with the heartache. "In fact, they might because they will bring down your level of anxiety, allowing you to process the situation with more clarity," he explained. In the millisecond it had taken for him to respond, I'd wished for him to say no. I didn't want a pill to make me better. I wanted to grit my way through this emotional quagmire; I wanted to intellectualize my way to sanity. Alas, I lost my battle against science, Big Pharma, and time. An hour after our call, I had a voicemail telling me my prescription was ready. Around the same time, Larry emailed me the name of an OCD specialist.

Despite my efforts to think less, I've been spending plenty of time thinking back over the events of the last year, in particular the surprise birthday party I organized for you at the bar in Bushwick, the one you love for its martinis, a martini that is perfectly fine but not one I would travel for. Why would I? For an overdone cocktail by an overzealous bartender? Why does anyone add floral liqueurs or infuse additional floral scents into gin? Gin is effectively a fermented bouquet of flowers and fruits. There is no dearth of accents. But you liked the bar and the martini they served, so we went.

We hadn't known each other for very long before your birthday, just a

MIDDLE SPOON

few months, but we were already both quite smitten. We were seeing each other often, texting each other obsessively, exhibiting an exaggerated degree of kindness. The week prior you'd gifted me a pair of simple but stylish jogging pants, the kind with tapered legs reminiscent of the pants worn by MC Hammer but much subtler in their flare. It was a sweet gesture that meant more to me than it should have; I'm wearing the pants now.

The bar was crowded, and I'd been stalling to get us there because I wasn't sure if your friends had arrived, and because I wanted to delay the moment. I found myself suddenly embarrassed at having planned you a surprise party so early in our relationship; I didn't know your friends well enough to have been coordinating with them by way of clandestine text messages over the previous weeks, and I was worried they were judging me, but I fell prey to my gallant nature. I think I pulled it off—the surprise, that is. Your mouth was an O, but your eyes widened into bewilderment and possibly discomfort.

The very idea of a party came after you'd told me you never make a big deal for yourself, which I took to mean you don't like planning your own birthday events. I convinced myself that you had placed emphasis on *myself*, "I don't usually make a big deal for *myself*." As if to say you like making big deals for others, and you'd like someone to do it for you, but you would never do it for yourself. But on the night of your birthday, at some point after you'd spotted your friends in the booths tucked behind the decorative plants, your demeanor shifted to nervous. Had I misinterpreted your emphasis or, worse, misplaced it? Maybe all those months earlier you'd said, "I don't usually make a *big* deal for myself," meaning you don't like to make a fuss for your birthday.

Why did I have to be so exuberant? Why couldn't I have contented myself with our wonderful dinner at the understated Vietnamese place with the spicy red curry dish that left both of our palates on fire? Why did I have to add florals to the gin?

· *297* ·

ALEJANDRO VARELA

That night had already included a delicate moment, when we ran into my friend Kyung-Ji—KJ for short. She'd been at the restaurant having a minor reunion with two of her college friends, and as luck would have it, she'd been seated at the table behind ours. The drama was of a minor key. I hadn't seen her in many months, and so she wasn't aware of your existence, or even that my husband and I had opened up our relationship. It all unraveled quickly: KJ and I ceased our embrace; she turned toward her friends to introduce me; you walked into the restaurant.

"This is my friend, Ben," I whispered while nodding in your direction.

Before the words had left my mouth, I regretted them. I regretted not only the act of speaking them but the very existence of that phrase in my psyche. You've never been my friend.

I was ashamed, but you were unaware because you hadn't yet reached us when I'd downgraded your status. I had just enough time to correct the record, which I did. "My boyfriend! This is Ben, my boyfriend," I said with too much excitement. If KJ had feelings on the matter, she didn't voice them. If she was deducing or deciphering anything, she was doing so at the subtlest of levels, and you wouldn't have picked up on the anomalies in her demeanor because you didn't know KJ. But they were there. In the sliver of a moment that followed my revelation, her eyes briefly went blank, and her smile contracted just long enough to indicate surprise and possibly curiosity and maybe even dislocation. I wish you hadn't been there; better yet, I wish none of us had been there, in that restaurant, that is, or any restaurant really, because I would have otherwise explained the intricacies of our situation, instead of leaving KJ with the impression that my marriage had fallen apart or that I was having an illicit affair.

This was the very sort of misunderstanding that often worried my husband. He joked once that I should wear a T-shirt emblazoned with "My husband knows I'm cheating on him." An example of practical wit-

• 298 •

MIDDLE SPOON

tiness that underscored how uncomfortable he was with our relationship being misrepresented.

Anyway, you eventually settled into the after-dinner birthday drinks at the bar with the gilded martinis, and we had a great time, until the boyfriend (Ramón) of one of your friends showed up. He's not a particularly gregarious guy, but he's always been cordial to me. You, however, disdain Ramón. You'd previously labeled him smarmy, unfriendly, and a misogynist, so I felt bad when he walked in and sat across from you at that long oblong table near the front of the bar that had given us ample warning of Ramón's arrival. As usual, he didn't participate much after a brief round of curt hellos. He ordered an IPA and kept the hood of his hoodie on, revealing only the bottom of his scowl. The rest of the table was wide-eyed, hair-conscious, and sipping one of the bar's signature cocktails. I didn't pay him much mind—after all, I'd enjoyed IPAs in my gluten days—but at one point, his foot touched mine under the table, an odd occurrence considering the width of the table and the effort required of one to make physical contact with the person across from them. I didn't think much of it, until I noticed him glancing at you. They were furtive glances, but unmistakable. And still, I chalked it up to his weirdness, until . . . I saw you glance back. Not once, not twice, but three times you looked over at him, even though he wasn't the person you were talking to. That's when it dawned on me: Ramón was stretching his legs to make contact with yours, but he'd mistakenly touched mine.

After that, I began to spiral, which consisted of my immediate matriculation into the surreptitious glancer club with you both, where I did my best to decode whether I was seeing what I thought I was seeing or whether I was merely drawing conclusions from my own insecurities. Strategically and obsessively, I watched you both, all the while spiraling further, but never drawing a definitive conclusion. I continued that way

· 299 ·

until I couldn't withstand the self-induced vertigo, so I pretended to go to the bathroom and called Traci.

"I hate that feeling," she said. "Been there many times."

"What's wrong with me?"

"Don't do that. There's nothing wrong with you. We both have strong intuitions. You might well be right. But you could also be mistaken. The evidence doesn't add up, honey. All you can do now is live in the moment. For Pete's sake, don't ruin the guy's birthday. Tomorrow, you can ask him about it or gather some more info. Not tonight," Traci said with a sniffle.

"Are you okay?" I asked, knowing I didn't have time for a full update.

"Yeah."

"What is it?"

"Same old marriage shit. Same old job shit."

"I'm sorry."

"Don't worry about me tonight. We'll talk tomorrow."

I went back inside the bar and stopped looking at your eyes and his eyes and told myself you were too genuine and you liked me too much to be sleeping with your friend's boyfriend while telling me I was the only person you were sleeping with. I ignored the Iago-like voice in my head: *Ben is the kind of person who relishes the thrill of dangerous liaisons. Ben likes brown guys like me, and Ramón is a brown guy like me.* I focused instead on the fact that you placed your hand on mine and periodically caressed my thigh while asking if I was okay. *Ben is the kind of guy who performs affection with me to make Ramón jealous, a game they've probably been playing for years.* I did my best to drown out that voice with gin, until I was inebriated enough not to care if you were screwing Ramón. Then we went back to your place, and when you asked me for the nth time if everything was all right, I lied and told you my stomach was bothering me. "There must have been gluten in one of the dishes," I said. We went to bed, and when I had trouble getting off, I envisioned you atop Ramón, and I came instantly.

MIDDLE SPOON

What sort of masochistic nonsense is that? All my life I've been like this, mining pleasure from the caves of insecurity. In fact, in the weeks after your birthday, whenever you'd be too busy to hang out or didn't respond immediately to my messages or calls, I'd assume you were meeting up with Ramón, rendering me sick, sick to the point of arousal, which made me want to get off, which I would, all the while thinking of you hurting me. At least I controlled the encounters that took place in my mind. At least I was the arbiter of when, where, and how Ramón fucked you, and as a result, I felt powerful.

Eventually, I stopped caring about Ramón. Your affections for me grew reciprocally and rather exponentially alongside mine, and with the aid of my therapists and friends, I came to believe I had fabricated the evidence of an affair. I focused on the good instead, like that time you abbreviated your vacation plans to be back to me a day earlier or, generally speaking, how you changed your life around to fit into mine—husband, kids, career, and all.

And now I wonder if these sorts of incidents were merely the manifestations of an undiagnosed mental illness, where I was the perpetual private investigator who'd been contracted to prove that I was destined to be unhappy.

—Me

PS: There was another thing I never told you. A week or so before you ended things again, I noticed that the lube I bought you—bought because you were using a cheap and ineffectual silicone-based blend that I detested not only for its sticky properties but also because it required a tremendous amount in order to be effective, and I argued in the early days of our relationship, when you were still seeing other guys, that if you were going to continue to bareback with other men, you should at the very least use good lube, which would reduce the risk of microtears in the anal cavity and rectum and, consequently, the transmission of infections, a warning you didn't care much for because you're on PrEP and feel like a superhero, the kind of caped, unsheathed crusader who came of age in the new century and therefore fucks as if he came of age in the middle of the previous century, with little fear of consequences, as if nothing had happened between 1975 and 2001. Anyway, I noticed that the lube in your nightstand had decreased in level since the previous time we'd had sex at your place, which was uncommon in the final months because you were spending more time at my place in an effort to acclimate to the blended family model we'd been sketching out.

"Would we eat all our meals together?" you asked once.

"Probably just dinners."

"And what would the kids call me?"

"Ben."

We'd usually have these conversations after we'd rolled around, both of us warm and sweaty from our exertions but also from the exaggerated heating systems in NYC, as well as weary from the broken sleep attributable to the terroristic clanging from those same heating systems. In any case, unlike at the outset, when we mostly had sex at your place, we almost never had cause at the close of our relationship to use the lube in your bedside drawer, which is why I was surprised at its change in volume. It was nearly imperceptible, but I'm fairly certain it had dipped. Why, Ben? Why would there be less lube in the bottle? You don't use lube to masturbate. You only use it to get fucked.

I told no one about this, not even Traci. I was embarrassed by the degree to which my insecurities were controlling me, so I pretended I hadn't noticed. I vanquished the fear and moved on. I was, after all, having sex with someone else besides you. It would have been hypocritical for me to deny you the right to do the same. At least you used the good lube, no?

MIDDLE SPOON

No, Ben, it's not just the sex; it's the lying. We agreed we'd tell each other if we had sex with other people. You know how unnerved I am by dishonesty, by the thought of something happening behind my back. It's worse than the act itself. If you couldn't be straightforward about that, you probably lied about other matters as well, and you'd likely have continued lying for the rest of our lives. In that regard, I'm better off without you.

Just now, as I was typing the previous paragraph, I briefly believed you had never lied and that you were madly in love with me, which was almost certainly the case. It felt wonderful to sincerely believe that narrative. I felt relieved and, well, good. But then the fear of being wrong about being wrong gave way to another layer of fear and embarrassment at the very thought of my having been right all along and the prospect of being made a fool by you. That feeling has more grip; it's more pervasive than the one characterized by trust and happiness. And yet, having felt good, even if only ephemerally, inspires me to work toward feeling good again. I'll use that charge, that incentive, to move this along. I'll email the OCD specialist.

PPS: The KJ incident on the night of your birthday illustrates one of the most difficult parts of this polyamory business: the constant coming out. I loathe it. Twenty-five years ago, I began a four-year process of telling everyone in my life I was gay, and that was plenty of coming out for one lifetime, and as far as I'm concerned, it should have banked me an endless supply of coming-out credits. I should have the right to live my life out loud and proud, without having to ever explain myself again. The entirety of society should have to glean. The Gleaners, Ben. The explanation portion of my being is over.

· *303* ·

Dear Me,

It didn't work out. It was never going to work out. Sometimes, you think you're the only one who didn't see that. Or maybe you knew it all along, but you're more of an optimist than you want to be.

It's been two weeks since you and Ben saw each other. You've been doing your best to forget everything, but today you became afraid of forgetting everything.

The two of you had as emotional and respectful a conversation as anyone in your situation could have. If you weren't still crestfallen, you'd be proud. Actually, you are proud.

You agreed to never see each other again. To be fair, the demand was yours, and Ben acquiesced. He thought it was an extreme request, but he hadn't accepted an earlier proposal for the two of you to wean yourselves off each other.

"We could set a breakup date on the calendar and see each other with less and less frequency until we reach the final day," you explained.

"That's a crazy idea and sounds like something Gwyneth Paltrow would propose," he said.

"Actually, it's a harm-reduction approach more aligned with my public health training," you responded.

Ben laughed, but he was too committed to his intermittent crying for the laughter to take root.

"In a couple of months, we could try talking," he said after he'd composed himself. "That's probably enough time."

"Remember our last breakup?" you responded. "How long did it take for us to get back together after we saw each other?"

MIDDLE SPOON

He wiped his nose with the cuff of a cutoff sweatshirt, for a moment revealing the hoariest and sexiest portion of his abdomen, leaving you wondering if he'd meant it as an invitation. "So we never see each other again?" he asked.

You suggested you'd probably cross paths at some point. After all, Brooklyn wasn't so big, you argued, despite being as big, population-wise, as Chicago, the third-largest city in the US. You'd surely end up in the same train car or gay bar or elevator one day. You said all this knowing well you'd both lived in New York for years without ever running into each other, and you might live the rest of your life without ever seeing him again. You were tempted to say this, too, so that you might elicit more emotion from him and possibly trigger a sea change, but you couldn't bear to watch him cry any longer without the freedom to put your hand on his back, so you kept the pessimism to a minimum. Instead, you sat on the bench in the kitchen where one sits to take off (and put on) their shoes, with your boots half off, your coat on, and your gloves in your pocket, the perfect metaphor for your purgatory: Stay an eternity or leave imminently?

You and Ben talked for nearly two hours—eventually, you removed your coat, emptied your pockets, and sat on the couch—where you agreed on the following:

1. You were in love.

2. Being apart would be miserable.

3. The only thing preventing you from being together was your marriage.

4. If you were to leave your husband you should come back to Ben immediately.

5. You should be nice to each other if you crossed paths, particularly within the next six months.

6. You should block each other on the various social media platforms.

· 305 ·

You also agreed that if there were something urgent to communicate, like a sexually transmitted infection, you had the right to track each other down, an addendum to your cold-turkey policy, which effectively served as an admission that he'd been having sex with other guys since before your breakup. You knew it to be true, and still, it hurt to have it confirmed; a small drop of pain in a bucket on the verge of overflow.

You told Ben you would avoid any places where he might be. You would return to your life as a married father couch potato hermit.

When you'd finished listing these agreements, Ben said, "I get to keep the restaurants in my neighborhood, and you retain the rights over the ones in yours; everything else is fair game."

You didn't push back on this stipulation, but in retrospect, you're a New Yorker, and you won't cede any ground in this regard. Ben remains, as far as you're concerned, a transplant who does not yet deserve to claim sole ownership over any parcel of the city that made you who you are today.

Okay, okay, that wasn't a very nice thing to say. In fact, it bordered on xenophobic—not against Ben, per se, but against the idea of foreigners—because you believe the bar for participation in society should be incredibly low, almost nonexistent. One arrives in a place, they plan to live there, they buy coffee, they ride the subway, they should have the right to live there, to vote, to work, etc.

"I can't fathom a life where we never see each other again," Ben said.

"Traci told me recently that after six months, even the love of your life might just be a guy with a great ass that you vaguely recall."

"I'm going to take that as a compliment," Ben responded.

"Anything is possible."

"I'm sorry I never got to meet Traci."

"Me too."

• *306* •

MIDDLE SPOON

"Maybe we'll be better by summer. We might run into each other at Jacob Riis."

"They're tearing down the old sanitarium. Riis will barely last longer than us."

Ben's crying became more sobbing and less sniffling when you said that. You didn't bother to ask if that was about Riis or you.

You'd quickly rekindle what you had if you saw each other too soon. Your unique connection could only be severed by amnesia or death. To move on, you'll have to stop existing, or you'll need to forget Ben altogether. Ben's complete disappearance from this place—Earth, that is—might offer fleeting consolation, but if there's something worse than not being with him, it's knowing he's not in this world. Nothing worse.

When it seemed your conversation had ended, he said what he'd been alluding to but had never before said: "Leave him. Stay with me."

"I can't," you responded. *Can't* connoted an involuntary hardship. Saying that word somehow stripped you of your agency. It was inaccurate, so you immediately corrected yourself: "I won't."

You were tempted to explain that if your relationship with him was on the ascendant, and if you could care for him as much as you already did, who knows where you two might be with more time. There was a chance you'd leave your husband. There's a universe in which that very thing happens, but you weren't sure if it was in this universe, and so, you didn't suggest it. You simply trailed off and put your elbows on your knees and your head down.

"I love you. A lot," you said to the floor.

How could something so pure and magical have come out of your mouth so inarticulately? you wondered.

Ben wept heavily as he walked toward you and the door. You rose and stuffed your hands into your pockets, somewhat uncertain of what he'd do next. His eyes lacked the keenness and intensity to which you'd grown accustomed, but in a burst of emotion, he threw his arms around you. You couldn't reciprocate because he'd pinned your limbs to your sides, but you found a way to hold on to his waist, making sure to press your face to his. You stood there uninterrupted, your lips tracing his cheek and ear on their way to his neck. He moaned because his neck is one of the most alive places on his body. You both kissed, first lips only, then with all of your mouths. To keep him, you had only to say one thing, but you couldn't. Instead, you said, "Please. Don't do this." The look on his face was clear: you hadn't said enough. You opened the door and left.

It was the first time you'd left Ben's place without doubling back to kiss him again or without stopping on the creaky, imperfectly painted maroon stairs to see if he was still standing in the yawn of his door, which he always was. Every time. You didn't do any of that because you were suddenly overcome with the desire to end the pain. The quicker you left the scene, the sooner you'd be moving in the direction of better, or at least different. This is what you believed.

On the walk to the train, you regretted not having stayed longer, not having promised him the world. You put in your earbuds and listened to fast-paced music. You didn't feel like dancing, but you needed to hear something that might move you more quickly into the next phase. You settled on "Frankly, Mr. Shankly" because it had been on your mind since you'd heard it at the epidemiologist's apartment.

On the ride home, you tried to read a Natalia Ginzburg book on your phone, but you couldn't read more than a few lines at a time without recalling what you were trying to forget.

You attempted flirting. Your eyes cruised the car and spotted no fewer than six attractive gays—it was the L train after all—but no one returned your interest; in fact, one man rolled his eyes and moved away from you, which was perfectly fine since you didn't have the requisite urges or gumption to commit.

How did Ben do it? you wondered. Did he think of you while he was having sex with other men? Or was it all compartmentalized for him?

Who cares? You were done trying to figure out why people were different from one another. It didn't work out. *Move on*, you thought.

This time around has been marginally easier than the previous breakups. There are bootprints in this snow. No surprises. Less shock. You've spent less time crafting scenarios because you'd previously crafted them all. And because the OCD counselor—Erica—implores you to interrupt the cycle of obsession, anxiety, and rumination. Erica is simultaneously stoic and kind, and you meet with her online on Tuesdays and Thursdays. You no longer meet with Fred or Sandy.

Your husband continues to check in and offer advice, but you're focused on being someone enjoyable and interesting, like you used to be. Not talking about Ben is helping. It reduces the frequency of dopamine hits. Apart from therapy and a few meandering thoughts, the emails are the primary source of him. To that end, you've decided to stop writing them. They helped you get through the worst, but now, they're merely keeping the pain alive.

On the other hand, you need another outlet. Biweekly therapy isn't quite enough, and your health insurance says you've met your quota for any more sessions per week. You might do something bold and revolutionary—on a personal level, that is. Something to snap you out of this.

You're going to tell your mom about Ben. Neither an email nor a face-to-face conversation, but a phone call. The remedy for a broken relationship is the evolution of another, you've determined. You've tried to not care what other people think about you, to live your life freely, boldly, but you're not that person. You are part of a fabric of people, a community, and it's important that you have their support and understanding, even if that means asserting your self-determination with a bit of deference. Tomorrow morning, when your mother calls, you're going to say *no* when she asks if you're okay. And *yes* when she asks if you have something on your mind. You're going to tell her everything. She'll be upset, but not as upset as she would have been if you were still with him. Then again, she might surprise you. She might be more open-minded than you've imagined all along. She might even have her own stories to tell. Unlikely. And even if she takes this poorly, at least you'll have another of life's travails to consume you, which will undoubtedly hasten the end of Ben.

—Me

PS: You chatted with KJ this morning. You hadn't talked to her since the night of Ben's surprise birthday, when you told her he was your friend before telling her he was your boyfriend. You often go months without talking to KJ, but you feared she'd been put off by the poly revelation. Nothing of the sort. She texted to ask if you'd lead a public health workshop for people who'd been formerly incarcerated—she does prison abolition work. You're going to grab coffee with her this week to discuss the logistics of the project.

After you thought you'd finished your exchange with KJ, after you'd walked a few blocks listening to the Michael Nyman and David McAlmont collaboration from a few years prior, she texted again: "I'm all about living liberation now. And that means we explore, experiment, and expand our realms of experience. We have been building our village by turning into this ethos every step of the way. That is how we grow new muscles, ways, hearts, and paradigms! Not easy, but so worth it and needed. New

MIDDLE SPOON

concepts or frameworks remain empty without the journey to speak to the application. Keeps it all so much more honest and human. Love you guys."

You're going to carry that with you into the next adventure this life offers.

Dear Ben,

Two weeks ago, the buzzer rang, and I went down to open the door without asking who it was because I'd been expecting a delivery, a new bathing suit. Since our breakup three months earlier, I'd been doing all I could to regulate my levels of oxytocin and dopamine, including an SSRI medication, counseling, and going to the gym four times per week. The workouts quickly became my religion, a source of purpose and distraction and therefore sanity. And while it might be difficult to fathom, I'd committed to these new regimens because I wanted to be a better version of myself irrespective of you or your lasting effect on me.

The new yellow-and-blue-striped Speedo began as the centerpiece of an elaborate fantasy that could be summarized easily: We run into each other on the beach this summer. I'm aloof and ripped; you're regretful and single. But you were no longer a part of that fantasy.

It wasn't, however, my bathing suit waiting for me downstairs; it was you. You were standing behind our large front doors, most of which were beveled glass panels that refracted your image and produced an altered version that both doubled and halved you, as well as the bouquet of supermarket flowers, the bag of grapes, and the tears in your eyes.

"I know I'm not supposed to be here" were your first words. "And I won't be mad if you ask me to leave, but I haven't been able to stop thinking about you. I tried moving on and seeing other guys—I know, I know, insert slut-shaming here, I don't care," you said. Then you paused for a moment to drag your sleeve across your dripping nose. You pulled your phone from your pocket—"Give me a second," you said as you scrolled

· 312 ·

MIDDLE SPOON

through it. Then you began reading, "I'm not the same without you. I've decided I want to try. Not just try; I want to make this work. It's not the life I saw for myself, but it's the life I want. I've had time to think and decide I would rather have a convoluted life with you than the one I have without you. Take all the time you need, but I want you to know I'll be here waiting. Not, like, here at your front door, but you know what I mean."

I'd never seen you so jittery or prepared or transparent, although I had many times before seen you cry. I didn't know what to say because my inclination was to say something funny, but the moment called for sincerity. Before I could decide, you spoke again: "Are you going to say anything?"

"No," I said. Then I grabbed the grapes and your hand and led you up several flights of stairs and into my apartment, where we proceeded to have the sort of sex people never forget. It was noon and warm, and I didn't have class or office hours, and I didn't have to pick up the kids from school for several more hours. We lay in bed afterward, without any pressure to speak. Apart from the subtle noises produced by our glances, our smiles, the rustling of sheets, and your periodic declarations ("I guess we're doing this"), we were silent. I must admit I let my mind wander. In the quiet, I concluded polyamory and even afternoon sex were indulgences primarily for the unemployed, freelancers, or the leisure class. I also began to regret that I hadn't asked you if you were still an assiduous taker of PrEP, but I stopped myself and followed the protocol for interrupting obsessive thinking: I sat quietly with the discomfort of not knowing while it filled my chest cavity and buzzed in my hands and feet, while it poked at my intestines, while it dissipated slowly, and while I returned to stasis. To myself, I repeated, "Maybe, maybe not. Live with the uncertainty."

· *313* ·

We've been together ever since.

You feel mine, Ben. Not like property, but like particles reunited.

Our conversations have been gentler and more honest. We're no longer responding to each other's doubts with sarcasm. We're listening; we're comforting each other too. The irony of us being willing to discuss our fears and suddenly not having any fears to discuss is not lost on me.

It's also not true. I have doubts and concerns, all rooted in fears, but their collective grip is weaker than it was before.

It's the fate of Nico and Jules that most concerns me. Before becoming a parent, I believed children were resilient; they'd adapt to anything because they're younger, more pliable versions of adults who also adapt to most things. I wasn't wrong, but I hadn't quite understood how much their health and safety are rooted in routines and how much my husband and I represent the ultimate routine for them. My presence is a routine. My couch potato–ness was a routine for them. Disrupting these rituals is destabilizing for them and for me. Doing so for the sake of our relationship feels, at times, selfish.

"That's society," Fred said—I returned to Fred last week because the treatments for OCD and anxiety are different. "That's Catholicism and being an 'other' who concerns himself more with how he's perceived than with living."

You've been spending the night more often, usually Tuesdays, Thursdays, Fridays, and Sundays. Last Sunday, I slept at your place, and I woke up with a severe case of heartburn, the kind that travels up into your throat, leaving caustic distension in its wake. We'd eaten at a Mexican restaurant with terrible drinks but delicious bistec encebollado and menudo and a server with sprawling forearm tattoos and a substantial mustache who I found very attractive and who you pretended not to notice,

MIDDLE SPOON

possibly out of respect for me, although I argued there was no need to obfuscate our attractions for other people because I've found these things are better left said. In any case, it was three a.m. when I woke, and the heartburn had become insomnia had become fear had become regret had become an impending, albeit familiar, sense of doom. I'd led you on, this was never going to work, and I'd abandoned my family (even if just for one sanctioned night), who were asleep across town, which isn't that far in terms of distance, but I couldn't rid myself of the notion that if my husband were to have a medical emergency, like a heart attack or a stroke—we're rather young and healthy for that to happen, but I was spiraling a bit, and that degree of common sense holds little water in the wee hours—I wouldn't be there to help him, and isn't that exactly what marriage and partnership are, thick and thin, sickness and health? There's no doubt I would be there for him, but I'd have to be there literally in order to be there figuratively, and I wasn't. I was with you. And although I loved being next to you and your light snores and your smooth skin and your warm feet, I felt an aching, beyond the acidic porcupine in my chest and throat, and a hopelessness because I would never, despite my best efforts, be in two places at the same time.

"I just don't want to feel less than," you said after the server had set the menudo and bistec on the table. "I don't want to move in and sleep alone every night."

Instead of responding, *I'm not yet sure how that will work*, I said, "Of course you won't."

You seemed content with my response, but I felt as if I'd just made an untenable promise and inadvertently laid a faulty foundation for us, so I backtracked.

"Actually," I said after the server had brought us more tortilla chips, "I would need to be upstairs for most dinners and nighttime routines and sometimes for general TV- and movie-viewing, which doesn't mean you

· 315 ·

couldn't join or that we wouldn't continue going out on dates or establish our own habit of curling up on the couch. I want to be up front about this."

In response, your face became that angsty knot I've come to find endearing. I wasn't sure if I'd asked for too much or if I'd fallen short of your expectations. "Of course," you responded. "I know I'm joining a family. I just want to make sure we get enough time together."

"Me too," I said.

That seemed to be the end of that conversation, but it left me thinking about the arrangements and configurations in our immediate future, and how I might have inadvertently left the impression that my husband was a duty or a necessary evil, when in fact he's nothing of the sort. I want us three to be equal, and while I realize you and I have an explosive type of chemistry that will require more care at the outset, I can't imagine a scenario where it's just you and me, even after the kids grow up and leave home. And although I believe I've made this point in the past, I didn't have the heart to underscore it during dinner, and instead I sipped on that terrible pinot noir that tasted like balsamic vinegar but without any of balsamic vinegar's virtues.

I waited a few beats before framing it another way: "I mean, you would probably go out more often than I would, no?"

"Sure, sometimes. But I hope you'll want to go out too."

"Of course I will. And the times when I don't, I will take advantage of our time apart to be with the kids—"

"And your husband."

"Right. And then you come home, and I will spend time with you."

"And you'd sleep with me?"

"Yes. But sometimes, when you're asleep, I could have some quality time—"

"With your husband."

"Yes."

MIDDLE SPOON

I didn't explain what *quality* meant, but I believe sex was implied. I think so because you took that moment to take a big swig of your margarita. I hope, too, that cuddling and laughing and snacking and general life-planning were implied. I think they were.

The next morning, a couple hours after the heartburn, I raced across Brooklyn's pothole obstacle course back to my place, set Nico and Jules on their respective tracks toward publicly funded enlightenment, and then knocked on the bathroom door. "Come in," my husband shouted from the shower. I took off my clothes and stepped into the small space behind him. "I'm late for work," he said. "I don't have time for sex. Sorry." I wasn't trying to seduce him. I wanted to share with him all my predawn fears, which I did, while he lathered and scrubbed and while I lathered and scrubbed.

After we'd dried off, he told me I shouldn't live my life preparing for the worst, like a heart attack or a stroke, which is effectively the crux of every therapy session I've ever had.

"I love you, but I'm not going to deny that I sleep better when I sleep alone," my husband added. "If you can use that to your advantage with Ben, by all means. It's just practical. Besides, you're home when I most need you."

While I was swabbing my ears clean, my husband patted my ass softly. He then pulled the towel off me and took a handful of the flesh with force before pressing the tips of at least two fingers inside of me. "I have time before my first meeting, if you want to have a quickie," he said.

Our romp was passionate and efficient: my husband spent one minute on his knees behind me, we spent two in front of the bedroom mirror, and then five on our bed, before both of us came at the same moment. Because we could. Because we always have.

I don't know if anyone can be *the one* during the actual living of life. These sorts of proclamations are better made retroactively, at the close.

· 317 ·

I spent days reassured by the conversation and encounter with my husband. But then the doubts returned, briefly, albeit with potency. I was tempted to contact Larry, the psychiatric nurse practitioner, to ask for an increase in my dosage, but I resisted. I did my best to imagine the cold lake and my body acclimating to the temperature. But one evening, the fears overtook me, and I began wishing for irrational things. During my nighttime oral care routine, I spotted a white plaque on my right tonsil, and I hoped for it to be a sexually transmitted infection so I might have the pretext to end things with you—not because I would ever leave you for passing along gonorrhea but because it would mean you weren't being truthful. When the plaque turned out to be a partially masticated oat, I concocted a worse scenario. I imagined you saying something racist or classist at a dinner party of all my dearest friends, something so vile I could never forgive. That seemed unlikely, so I prayed for a simpler exit. I envisioned you calling me to say you'd made a mistake, again. That you wanted more than I could ever give. That we'd never be able to take a two-week vacation. Or that we'd never truly live equitably. And that you didn't want to share me at all, not with my husband or with my kids.

If society supported us . . . If we knew more unorthodox relationships and families . . . If there were more mainstream examples of what we're trying to do . . . As it stands, everything is working against us. The trip is an absolute joy; the path, however, is less than desirable.

But don't panic. I'm not giving up. I'm going to sprinkle some pixie dust (therapy, SSRIs, Xanax, honesty, yoga) over the situation and make everyone happy. It's not as if we're building a colony on Mars or trying to secure an Oscar nomination for Alfre Woodard or establishing a national health service or passing a thirty-six-dollar minimum wage pegged to inflation. We're simply redistributing love, affection, and commitment be-

MIDDLE SPOON

tween three adults. And two children. And our communities. We can do it. There doesn't have to be an end to us. Nothing's preordained.

Right?

Love,
Me

Acknowledgments

My gratitude, as always, to Robert Guinsler and the folks at Sterling Lord. Thank you to Ibrahim Ahmad for his dedication, intelligence, and empathy. Thank you to Ruth Liebmann, Lara Phan, Beth Koehler, Logan Hill, Colin Webber, Elizabeth Pham Janowski, Sara DeLozier, Molly Fessenden, Patrick Nolan, Rebecca Marsh, Kate Stark, Andrea Schulz, Brian Tart, and everyone at Viking and PRH for their care and enthusiasm.

Thank you to Lisa Chen, Rosalie Ryan, and Brett Goldberg for their early notes on this book. Thank you to Catherine Lacey for her later notes. Thank you to everyone who reads and supports my work.

My love and appreciation to the people who make life more than just a series of days, in particular to Matias, León, and Camilo. To my (three) parents, my siblings, and all the cousins. As well as to everyone who sits at our dinner table.

And to Jeffrey.

100 YEARS of PUBLISHING

Harold K. Guinzburg and George S. Oppenheimer founded Viking in 1925 with the intention of publishing books "with some claim to permanent importance rather than ephemeral popular interest." After merging with B. W. Huebsch, a small publisher with a distinguished catalog, Viking enjoyed almost fifty years of literary and commercial success before merging with Penguin Books in 1975.

Now an imprint of Penguin Random House, Viking specializes in bringing extraordinary works of fiction and nonfiction to a vast readership. In 2025, we celebrate one hundred years of excellence in publishing. Our centennial colophon features the original logo for Viking, created by the renowned American illustrator Rockwell Kent: a Viking ship that evokes enterprise, adventure, and exploration, ideas that inspired the imprint's name at its founding and continue to inspire us.

For more information on Viking's history, authors, and books, please visit penguin.com/viking.